THE HAMMER'S EYE

DONALD I. FINE, INC.   New York

THE HAMMER'S EYE

by R.A.

SCOTTI

For my brother Frank

"So 'ere's to you, Fuzzy-Wuzzy . . .
You're . . . a first-class fightin' man"

—by Rudyard Kipling

"... Sir, 'twas not
Her husband's presence only, called that spot
Of joy into the Duchess' cheek ..."

—Robert Browning

CHAPTER
ONE

1924   No whistle shrieked. No loudspeaker blared. No notice was scrawled on the slate board announcing the one o'clock train from Gorky as it slid into Paveletsky Station, vapors of steam dissipating in the icy air. A question had preoccupied the station master: Should the train, empty except for the body of Vladimir Ilyich Ulianof, be listed under arrival or departure?

The train doors opened and a phalanx of men dressed in black suits and ties stepped forward, the first contingent forming two parallel lines to raise the coffin to their shoulders... to bear the weight of their Bolshevik world.

Vladimir Ilyich Ulianof, five foot three inches, a.k.a. Lenin, was returning to Moscow for the last time. He had been their leader, their inspiration, their messiah. When a stroke two Christmases before left him semi-paralyzed, they were as weak as he to resist his transfer to a villa in Gorky. He needed to rest and recuperate, it was said publicly. And Gorky became his Elba.

Outside Paveletsky Station an artillery gun carriage drawn by six matching horses as black as infamy waited to make the five-and-a-half-mile journey to Red Square. The loyal few, the band of brothers, waved it aside and carried the coffin on their shoulders through the street, changing bearers every half mile. It was a long way from 14 Spiegelstrasse.

August Merriman watched, indistinguishable in his great coat and astrakhan from the thousands of silent mourners who lined the route to the Nobles Club, now headquarters of the Proletarian Labor Federation. The coffin bearers suffered the cold and their burden, pride a thousand times fiercer than weariness as they walked the final mile to the columned hall where Tsar Nicholas's courtiers had gambled, blind to the fact that they were risking an empire.

Lenin lay in state for seventy-two hours, the question of arrival or departure never answered. Mourners streamed by like moving water, a human river of sorrow three-quarter million strong. They'd walked in minus-thirty-degree temperatures, some from villages forty and fifty miles away, the men wearing home-sewn black ties. Merriman stood with the rest through the bone-chilling afternoon and into the night, his foreignness unnoticed in his shared grief. The line inched forward through the snow. Wood fires burned along the length of it every hundred yards or so, the soot like a shadow darkening the snow. Factory whistles whined. Peddlers hawked hot pies. Cannons boomed. Except for the sounds of weeping, the crowd was silent.

It took five hours to reach the hall. Five hours to gain a moment beside the red coffin, to look on the yellow face, like a wax museum figure, the reddish beard freshly trimmed, the mask of death severe. The Order of the Red Banner was pinned to his green military jacket. Moscow in January, 1924 —more than a new year, a new era in the Bolshevik revolution. August Merriman had never known such cold.

1988   From a tiled piazza suspended over the Gulf of Naples, he stood watch again, his eyes on the present, his mind preoccupied with the past. After so many years the time had finally come to sever his ties with Mother Russia. It was his eighty-eighth birthday. His imprint was stamped on history, and the new man in the Kremlin was changing the rules.

While the Great Communicator was, it seemed, losing his touch in America, the Greater Communicator buffed his global image as a man of action tempered with reason—a new phenomenon in the Soviet Union. Not a party bureaucrat nor a KGB strongarm with a paranoid view of world history. A man of the eighties who would be as daring as Deng in Peking... a *Time* magazine man-of-the-year, no less. Thus are the myths of history made, Merriman thought.

Through U.S. Navy-issued binoculars he focused on a myth of a different sort. Angelica Merriman, age twenty-six, as golden as the sandy cove where she lay stretched like an offering to the sun god. Five foot nine inches of subtle strength and sure temptation. Blonde, blue-eyed, silken-skinned, Angelica lay on her stomach. Her back and buttocks, which swelled around the stingy V of blue bikini pants, were browned like a native's. Raising herself on an elbow, she stretched and turned over, each motion liquid and deliberate. Her breasts were bare.

Merriman tensed at her movements. Angelica was his granddaughter, illegitimate, an accident of history. He had known a girl for a week in wartime Berlin—Lynneth Carrington. A daughter was born from that affair, and twenty-some years later this exquisite granddaughter. He took Angelica into his home, gave her his name, lavished her with his love. None of that stopped him from being excited by her beauty.

Had her grandmother Lynneth been so perfect? Had his wife Prudence? After so many years of marriage it was difficult to remember. One went to bed in summer with a girl— slender, green-eyed, passionate about her beliefs and her beloved—and woke up one winter morning to a woman, trim if no longer ephemeral, still passionate in her beliefs but no longer trusting. Prudence had never forgiven him for Lynneth, although she had married him anyway.... "Mr. and Mrs. Alfred Peter Schaeffer request the honor of your presence at the marriage of their daughter, Prudence Agatha..." Very proper, very formal. Prudence always paid close attention to appearances.

For their forty-sixth wedding anniversary, after flying to Germany and telling Merriman that she was satisfied that the girl's claim was true, she had presented him with Angelica. It was a gesture he could not entirely fathom—was Angelica an apology for failing to give him the child and heir he had always wanted? Or was she intended to be a constant reminder of the betrayal his wife still nursed?

Merriman suspected the latter, but he could never be sure with Prudence. Even now she remained a surprise to him, and he had stopped trying to understand her motives. The joy Angelica brought into his life reduced the answer to a personal footnote of only passing interest, a point of curiosity not of consequence. At least that was what he had come to believe.

In Sorrento in May it was easy to believe in myths and to imagine Paradise. The weather was warm without the intensity of summer. Apricot and orange blossoms wreathed the classic pink stucco villa, and anchored in the harbor down the Amalfi Drive, which wound with treacherous curves and breathtaking views, a yacht to rival the QE2 rocked on the turquoise sea. *The Prudent Angel,* complete with its own silver-bladed chopper. Visible signs of August Merriman's wealth and power. He had many more: a baronial castle in a preserve above the Hudson, a townhouse in Georgetown, a fleet of private jets, an art collection that could fill the best museum... And he was not shy about them, having found that impressive accoutrements made mundane ideas profound and mediocre proposals arresting.

Training his binoculars down the cliff again to the spit of sand where his granddaughter lay, Merriman thought that Angelica was the perfect girl and May in Sorrento the perfect time and place to be alive. He wouldn't stay, though. He never stayed in one place more than a few days, a few hours. In spite of his age, he moved from country to country, continent to continent, the way other men moved from room to room. In the cove below, Angelica sat up and reached for her bikini bra. Instead of putting it on, she turned toward her grandfather, presenting a flawless profile. Merriman adjusted the binoculars a hair. Even her nipples were tanned.

"How's the view from the terrace this morning? Naked and nubile enough for you?" Prudence's intrusive voice had the tart bite of a Macintosh apple.

Wetting his lips, Merriman turned to counter his wife. "There's a lovely little sloop anchored just off . . ."

Although she claimed the binoculars, she didn't bother looking through them. "Angelica is baking again, I suppose."

Merriman smiled. A businessman, he'd learned to win by cutting his losses early, and he'd seen enough to fill an old man's dreams, even if he could no longer act on them. "I'm a connoisseur, Prudence."

"I call it a dirty old man," she said.

"You don't appreciate beauty, that's your trouble. You don't have time for it. You're too wrapped up in grand ideas. They've sapped all your passion. I can remember—"

"A grand idea is the purest beauty—not bouncing tits or bare ass. What can they do to save the world?"

"I don't know about saving the world, my dear, but they can do a hell of a lot for mankind. You used to, too."

"So I've been told, August." She turned away with a shrug of disinterest, as if challenging him to ask by whom.

She was an asset, probably the most valuable he had acquired through the years—and the worst of it was, she knew it. Countless times her instincts proved correct, especially playing East against West. They were perfect counterparts— Prudence philosophic and analytic where he was a man of action. They fed each other's needs, nurtured each other's vanities. Without her his ambitions would not have spanned the globe. He would not have become ambassador to all nations, citizen of none.

Prudence Schaeffer Merriman, twelve years his junior, born to old money and privilege, bred to be a lady—the schools she went to all began with "Miss"—a Lady Bountiful. Nobility came easily to her because the ordinary things that rake illusions raw—the worry over where the next dollar is coming from and the next meal, and how far each will stretch—had never touched her.

Prudence had moved flawlessly from the cocoon her parents encased her in to the rarified world of private academies and Ivy League college to the unique position of Mrs. August Merriman, an intellectual virgin, her youthful ideals intact. She'd come of age during the Spanish Civil War when democratic passions were frenzied and had seen her only brother, George Aloyisius Schaeffer, killed, a casualty of the Abraham Lincoln Battalion in the Battle of Jarama.

Merriman had met her in 1937 on the steps of the U.S. Embassy in London when she was trying to get her brother's body back. Three years later they were married. And now there were two women in his life—Prudence and Angelica...

Prudence had stopped at the threshold and was considering her husband over her shoulder.

"Joseph just put the call through to Livermore. Pointer will have lunch with us on Saturday. You'll have to talk with Angelica today... unless you've changed your mind about sharing her."

Merriman did not answer immediately. He was a shrewd user of men, and he had made a thorough study of David Pointer. The Lawrence Livermore National Laboratory was the Los Alamos of the eighties, the center of research on the Strategic Defense Initiative. Like Oppenheimer before him, Pointer was a pure scientist, challenged by the task he faced, though troubled by the destructive power he might unleash. On the personal side, he was very much alone, no immediate family and still brooding over the break-up of a long-term affair.

Merriman did not doubt his own ability to manipulate this young scientist. Combining his persuasive powers and Angelica's charms, he planned to milk Pointer, use him as a private pipeline to the most highly classified information on S.D.I. August Merriman did not see himself as any kind of traitor. Not at all. He was a businessman, a global broker, a patriot—not of one country but of the world—proud of his achievements and not above asserting that everything he did was for global stability as well as his own agrandizement. He was an old man, though, and time was catching up with him. In Moscow the new General Secretary was sweeping the Kremlin clean, rooting out the old wood—the men with whom Merriman had collaborated for years, using them as they used him. The time, it seemed, had come to bow out— but on *his* terms, with one final master stroke of global brokerage. For international stability . . . and for August Merriman. A good slogan, he thought. It was a matter of pride even more than power. And no one understood that better than Prudence.

"I haven't changed my mind," he answered finally, "about anything."

"Good." Prudence's tone was brisk but her smile was warm and satisfied, like the weather, the place, the view from the terrace. "I'll tell Joseph there'll be four for lunch Saturday . . . and believe me, you'll have no trouble convincing Angelica to use her persuasive powers on David Pointer."

Merriman turned away, content to leave the details to his wife and secretary, and took up his binoculars again, moving them along the length of his granddaughter's fluid body. Admiring its symmetry and grace, he considered again his wife's generosity. Their marriage was childless. It was Prudence's only failure—and just as well, he thought. A child tended to be a burden and, more often than not, a disappointment. But a grandchild was a joy unalloyed. Especially this one.

CHAPTER
· TWO

"Octogenarian . . . Humanitarian . . . The man whose personal warmth and courage thawed the cold war . . ."

The words rolled off the Russian's tongue like insults as he scanned the pages of the KGB dossier, as thick as a World Book and almost as ambitious. The more he read, the more grudging admiration he felt for his predecessor who had compiled it. Under Yuri Andropov's iron rule the KGB had done its job thoroughly. He had chosen agents, training and planting them so that their covers were impenetrable. A gardener of genius. It was his subtlest skill. August Merriman was a friend of the Kremlin, but the old spymaster had understood that even friends need to be watched.

The General Secretary shifted uncomfortably. He'd been reading so long, his foot had fallen asleep. Except for the pins and needles that were tingling along the sole into his toes he was a satisfied man. His power was hardening each day. In a few months he'd unseated the old guard, kicked Gromyko and Drobynin upstairs, cleaned out the army brass, stalled the arms talks while simultaneously making the Americans appear intransigent, postured before the world press and orchestrated a summit meeting with the U.S. President, underscoring the issues to be put on the table. And that was just the beginning.

He smiled to himself. Since the war, superpower history

had been a geopolitical high-wire stunt. But he had a new strategy for disarmament that would send the West on an historic free-fall. Everything seemed in place, waiting for implementation.

Flexing his toes in black hand-stitched Italian loafers, the Secretary got up and limped the length of his office, rolling his weight from his heel to the ball of his foot to work out the cramp. The office was a high-ceilinged corner room on the fourth floor with long arched windows that looked across the Kremlin, citadel of the Romanov empire, fortress of the Soviet republic, stronghold against invasion—Mongol, Tatar, Napoleonic, Nazi.

Within the red-brick battlement walls, twenty-feet thick and more than sixty-feet high, was a repository of Russian history: the apartments of the imperial family, marble walls covered with silk tapestries; subterranean prison cells; the Ivan the Great Bell Tower, traditionally the tallest building in Moscow; the golden room where the Tsarina received official visitors; Lenin's study, occasionally opened for public viewing; Napoleon's cannons . . .

The Secretary looked down at the Square of Cathedrals, the Kremlin's ancient center—the heart of the Soviet state, framed by three majestic houses of God, and in the shadow of the Praesidium of the Supreme Soviet religious services were still offered almost a century after the revolution. He preferred not to dwell on the irony of it, though being an intelligent man the irony was not lost on him. Beyond the gilt domes of the cathedral, gleaming like the eye of the Almighty, and the onion-topped watchtower, he could see Red Square and a patch of the Moskva River in one corner. So much history. He had become a part of it and an architect, and the next pages, he believed, would be written in his hand.

Returning to his desk, the Secretary stirred a spoonful of jelly into the tall glass of black tea that was always kept filled. Although the glass, contained in a metal holder, was cold to the touch he drank the tea anyway and turned back to the file.

Once before in superpower history, when the West was developing the atomic bomb, the Soviets had been at a disadvantage, until they were able to secure America's secrets. Fuchs and others had been instrumental, but they weren't alone. August Merriman had been privy to vital, highly classified information. In an adroit move that served both their interests, he had brought the scales of power into balance.

The Secretary drummed his stubby fingers on the desk. An executive's desk, tubular steel, sleek and black. The rest of the furnishings matched it—a corporate man's complete office decor, out of place in the old world grandeur of the room itself. He wasn't bothered by the incongruity because it was, after all, like Russia itself.

As for Merriman, he was a dinosaur now, like Gromyko. He knew too much and had too many Committee members in his pocket. But if he could be useful one more time, the inevitable could at least be postponed... The General Secretary studied the file, not skipping a detail about Merriman— or the agent who had been assigned to him. Merriman was almost as cautious as Andropov had been. But he had made one mistake... a romantic attachment, Berlin, 1939, that resulted in a child and eventually a grandchild. And now Anatol Dostankov, the enterprising young counter-intelligence chief, had devised a way to use the information to the Kremlin's advantage.

Dostankov was waiting in an anteroom with the KGB Chairman to make his special report. The General Secretary pressed a button on his desk, opening the door, and motioned them in— a magnanimous leader, always receptive to the proposals of his comrades. He tapped the dossier.

"August Merriman and this Operation Counterpoint... an intriguing idea, ingenious even. I want a full briefing."

KGB Chairman Viktor Chebrikov placed himself in the chair in front of the Secretary's desk, as immovable as one of

Napoleon's cannons and just as outdated, Anatol Dostankov
thought, and with a thrust of his chin ordered his assistant to
answer. Dostankov shifted, paced, approached the desk,
clasping clammy hands. He had never been face-to-face with
a successor of Lenin in a private meeting.

"Comrade Secretary," he began, "put your mind back, if
you will, forty years to Europe in the grip of the Nazi terror.
The greatest scientific minds of the century fled west. Einstein, Fermi, Teller, Szilard, Wigner, von Neumann,
Bohrs... I could go on. That brain drain gave the West the
atomic bomb and NASA."

"Now," the Secretary said, "the most brilliant young scientists are Americans, working on the Strategic Defense Initiative—so dangerous to us. Our nuclear power is set up for a
preemptive strike because so many of our warheads are on
land-based missiles. If Star Wars succeeds, our preemptive
advantage is lost... worthless." The Secretary threw up his
hands. "We'll be racing to catch up as we did in the forties
and fifties."

"But if we can create a *new* brain drain" Dostankov moved
closer, flowing east, from the U.S. to the U.S.S.R... using
August Merriman as a conduit..."

He had the enthusiasm of a new father, the Secretary
thought. Chebrikov had come because he was the chairman,
but the operation was clearly the younger man's brainchild.
The Secretary scribbled a note to himself on his memo pad as
he spoke. Anatol Dostankov would bear watching.

"Merriman funds the American Science Foundation, and
the ASF funds David Pointer. He is—"

"I know who he is."

Dostankov's nervousness eased. The Secretary was ignoring Chebrikov and concentrating on him. He grew confident,
almost cocky.

"Operation Counterpoint is already in place. I have taken
a beautiful agent, given her an impeccable cover as the
granddaughter of the powerful entrepreneur Merriman and

introduced her to the *wunderkind* of the U.S. Star Wars effort. Once he's compromised, the scientist will be given a choice: defect to Moscow and continue his research for the benefit of the world instead of the parochial, clearly aggressive interests of the U.S.—or be exposed. If the latter, the agent's identity will be leaked, the scientist discredited and his security clearance rescinded, setting back the entire SDI project. In either case, we can't lose. August Merriman believes he is performing a service for world peace by supplying us with invaluable information. If his reputation is damaged in the process . . ."

The General Secretary gave a dismissive shrug. "A minor casualty. His usefulness is over anyway."

Dostankov smiled at the Secretary's interruption. It was a compliment to his own cleverness.

"In Moscow we'll supply Pointer with all the customary trappings Americans in particular live for—cars, money, dachas. And most important of all, I believe, we will give him his own laboratory." Dostankov had no concrete knowledge of the scientific resources that would be available, but he had heard reliable talk of a futuristic anti-missile lab somewhere near the Afghan border, and he understood the Soviet apparatus well enough to assume that the Kremlin had its own Star Wars—cloaked in the tightest secrecy.

"Dushanbe." The word formed on the Secretary's lips but he did not say it. Dushanbe could be Pointer's, every scientist's dream—his own laboratory, a scientific Shangri-la on a mountain peak near the Afghan border and the town of Dushanbe—a complex more modern than the Lawrence Livermore National Laboratory and joined by heavy power cables to the hydroelectric plant at Nurek.

While the U.S. was working on a defensive shield using X-ray lasers to knock out Soviet missiles in space before they reached their targets, the Soviets were concentrating on lasers that would penetrate deep into space to blind the enemy's early-warning missiles and strike incoming ones. It was like a two-way mirror. It would make the U.S. vulnerable to attack and leave the U.S.S.R. safe from retaliation.

But his scientists lagged well behind the Americans in laser and particle beam technology. They had no single physicist, no group of scientists, who could match wits with David Pointer on directed-energy weapons, and they needed to develop supercomputers and space-based sensors to direct the projected anti-missile system. For the laser beams from Dushanbe to be flashing into space by the end of the decade, Soviet science would need to make giant strides. Impossible, unless . . .

"If Operation Counterpoint succeeds," Dostankov was saying, "it should not be difficult for the American to convince his friends to follow him." He smiled. "How would you say it in English . . . a sabbatical in the U.S.S.R."

The Secretary was smiling too as the KGB men left. The agent and her control were being monitored closely. If anything went wrong, she was expendable. Locking the dossier in his desk, he checked his watch. Six minutes before he was due to meet the press. He took a comb from the inside pocket of his jacket, carefully combed the few remaining hairs across his crown, wishing Chernenko had lasted long enough for him to go through with his planned hair-transplant; flicked the shoulders of his jacket for dandruff; adjusted the pictures on his desk—three photographs in matching gold-tooled leather frames: his daughter, granddaughter, and his wife, chic and smiling. He pushed her forward, building her up as the Soviet Jackie Kennedy, and by contrast with the other First Ladies of the Kremlin, she was. The western press never failed to mention the photographs in every story—a family man, open, personable, so different from his predecessors, who never imagined the mileage to be gained by a few pictures conspicuously placed. The First Secretary had not studied the lives of the American Presidents since Roosevelt for nothing. He remembered the adulatory reports: "There is a gust of fresh air in the

Kremlin . . . " He buzzed for his aide to remove the empty tea glass. He was prepared to meet the western press, to talk about the success of *glasnost* and his hopes for an arms control agreement that would be a first step to a ban on all nuclear weapons, including the American Star Wars project.

He enjoyed performing for the West. Such an appreciative audience, so touchingly eager to believe the best of him . . .

"Mr. Secretary, have you any plans to tear down the Berlin Wall?"

"Tear down the wall." He repeated it with an inflection that made it impossible to tell whether he was echoing the *Der Spiegel* correspondent's question or making an historic statement. "It is not our wall, gentleman. It is the German Democratic Republic's. If it were, I could answer your question. Since it is not . . . " He shrugged.

"With the new pipeline to Iran and other proposed steps to improve relations between the two countries, is it your ambition to increase your influence and presence in the Persian Gulf and replace the U.S. there?" The question was asked by the *Le Monde* reporter.

"Iran is our neighbor, so what we propose is a Good Neighbor policy. Why be enemies when we can be friends? If we can help to bring peace to the Persian Gulf, so much the better. For now, though, it is strictly good neighbors."

He recognized the correspondent from *Newsweek*: "You said the new arms control treaty is a first step. What do you propose for the next step? And do you have a timetable for nuclear disarmament?"

"Not a timetable, a dream. It is more powerful, don't you think? What is a timetable?" He shrugged and turned up his hands. "It is an arbitrary schedule. But a dream is what drives men to greatness, what fires every revolutionary idea. Look at Gandhi, Mother Theresa . . . Like your own Martin Luther King, I have a dream."

The questions went on for forty minutes. Never in memory had a Soviet leader allowed himself to be openly questioned by the foreign press. *Glasnost*. He was a man of his word. By the act of making himself available, he had scored a coup. He could not lose, or so he felt.

CHAPTER
THREE

David Pointer thought of Lawrence of Arabia, but instead of vast sands, manicured lawns stretched as far as the eye could see, interrupted with rectangles of flowerbeds. A blue and white striped tent, as large as a Cape Cod cottage with net sides that zipped shut, was placed on the lawn. A straw rug carpeted the grass, and in the center of the rug a glass-top table was set for four. Against one flap of the tent was a serving table. The colors of the tent were carried through in the place setting—the placemats and napkins were blue linen, the dishes white bone china, a basket of delphiniums and freesia formed the centerpiece. A picnic lunch—cold lobster, avocado slices with vichyssoise to begin, champagne to drink, and an assortment of fresh berries with *creme fraiche* for dessert—without the usual incursion of insects . . . one of the prerogatives of spectacular wealth that Pointer had never considered before.

Behind the tent, and standing guard over a broad sweep of Hudson Valley, was August Merriman's home sweet home, a baronial castle complete with everything except moat and drawbridge—impressive, fanciful even, huge stone squares chiseled into canopies and arches, towers, turrets. A far cry from the Spartan office that Pointer called home in the Lawrence Livermore National Laboratory, a one-square-acre weapon-research center sunk in a dry California valley. He felt as if he should pinch himself to make sure it was all real.

When the long-distance call came from Italy the week before, he had been sitting at his computer terminal, mourning Louise Rosen who had walked out on him after four intense years. The call had surprised him, but it was neither the greatest nor the smallest surprise he had received. As a graduate student on a fellowship grant at Livermore, Pointer had been elevated to the heady air of space science celebrity—the superstar warrior of Livermore—because of his theories on X-ray-powered lasers. Still, he was ambivalent about his work. He had been an anti-nuke activist when he had arrived in California, in favor of a nuclear freeze, not a new class of weapons that would bring the arms race to space. His dream was to win a Nobel Prize for applying space-age technology to biological and medical diagnostic tools...

Pointer had lowered the volume of the Verdi *Requiem* that was playing on his tape deck so that he could hear his caller better. Although August Merriman's money had sent him through MIT and brought him to Livermore, he had never recieved a personal message from the man, let alone an invitation to lunch at Durandana, Merriman's Hudson River estate.

And now here he was listening to the great man himself, confiding, expansive. The lunch was superb, but Merriman was too busy pontificating to notice...

"I've been talking to the Kremlin for sixty years, keeping the door open through decades of hot and cold war. I've known them all, from Lenin right down the line—Stalin, Khrushchev, Brezhnev, Andropov...*there* was a Machiavelli. I thought I'd be dealing with him for a decade, at least. Even I had no idea how sick he was. After Chernenko the old order changed. Don't get me wrong, this new Secretary General is as single-minded as any of them, but he's a master of the media. Rock stars play Leningrad now. Can you believe it? And the Kremlin has its own PR spokesman..." He was shaking his head.

August Merriman should have been a big man, Pointer thought—large in stature to match his achievements. Instead the first impression was one of smallness. Napoleon, Lord Nelson, Lenin—history was riddled with them. Conquerors, actors, entrepreneurs—small men driven to achieve big things, to play a role on the stage of history, any stage. There must be a whole library shelf of books on the subject, and Merriman was probably a textbook case.

His face was as lined as a grid, the nose small, the lips meaty, eyes like slits, gray lights glinting out through wrinkles, catching every nuance, flashing with pride, arrogance, conceit. Even with the wrinkles he looked closer to sixty than eighty. There was no hesitation in his step, no frailness in his voice, no weakness in his handshake. Too active to worry about gaining weight, he seemed vital and eager with a zest for making yet another dollar, another deal. For Merriman, he suspected, it was the thrill of the game that really counted, the excitement of making things happen, moving and shaking.

"You're fortunate, David. If I may say so, you've had things handed to you—scholarships, opportunity... What I have, I earned myself. By give and take. That's what all business comes down to—history, too. Take my first trip to Moscow... the country was in the grip of famine, millions were starving. So Lenin had to *give* a little, step back from pure Communism and make concessions to foreign capitalists. Which meant to *take* from them. Which is where I came in. And the rest, as they say, is history."

Merriman told a good story, Pointer thought. Still, for all his wealth and power, the polish was thin. What he had was no doubt thanks to his wife, Prudence Merriman. David had been told this before he came to Durandana...

Invitations to her Washington parties were coveted. Thinkers and politicians of east and west met in the Merrimans' Georgetown drawing room, confident that no thought they uttered would come back to embarrass them. So much ice thawed. Although she was a committed champion of social justice, she kept her own views low-key, provided a clubby, informal forum for others.

They made a striking couple, August and Prudence Merriman—he roughhewn, she the epitome of elegance. A husky voice tinged with in-bred condescension, hair swept up, long neck, the skin still smooth if fragile now and pulled a little too tight across the bones—good jutting bones, cheekbones, jaw bone, hip bones. Tall and slender, a lady to the manner born, as Pointer's mother would have said. She wore white and a hat even in the tent, a natural straw with a single white flower, the brim turned up on one side, and sunglasses, which she never removed, although Pointer did not doubt that behind them she was watching his every move, fixing him in her mind, deciding his character, intelligence, background, upbringing, future, potential, assets and liabilities.

She could probably be as warm as a summer's day or as biting as March rain if it suited her. But tender, sympathetic, the womanly virtues—he suspected not. All in all, though, a stunning woman if not one he especially cared to know better. He'd take an earth mother any day, overweight, encompassing, fresh-baked bread and goosedown comforters, or his own mother, Irish with a sharp wit and big heart who would do anything for you and no please or thank you needed.

The conversation swirled, occasionally making eddies in Prudence's direction, though she added little to it. Merriman was garrulous, a showman. Prudence listened, reticent, absorbing.

And then there was Angelica Merriman. Through most of the lunch she was almost as quiet as Prudence, leaving the conversation to the men. But her presence was a statement more eloquent than any made during the meal. Sitting opposite her, Pointer was surprised he could even find his voice. Her sundress was a floral pattern, with spaghetti straps and a full skirt. Girls in their summer dresses. When she leaned forward he could see the white skin below the tan where her breasts began.

There was another person in the tent, like a fifth column, standing sentinel by the serving table. "Joseph," Merriman called him. Height, size, hair color, eyes, features—all average. Yet there was something about the man, an unctuousness that had the same effect on Pointer as running a nail along a blackboard...

"I'm grateful that I'm in a position to help a promising young American like yourself," Merriman was saying.

"I want you to know that I appreciate all you've done."

Merriman waved away the sentiment.

"I'm not looking for thanks. That's not why I invited you here. I wanted to meet a goddamn natural resource in the flesh. That's what you're being called, you know. There hasn't been a scientist since the Manhattan Project who's come up with an idea that has the revolutionary potential of your nuclear-powered X-ray lasers."

So much of his research was classified that Pointer had gotten out of the habit of talking easily to civilians. It was as though anyone outside the clique of engineers and scientists at Livermore was not an enemy, exactly, but certainly an alien. He stole a glance across the table. Angelica caught him looking and winked. When the color rose in his cheeks, she smiled and he felt a bare foot slide under his trouser leg, the smooth toes working their way up. Merriman was waiting for him to say something. Pointer heard his own voice, which sounded normal enough, but he had no idea what he was saying, or if he was making any sense. He tried to concentrate on the conversation.

"I like to think that I've learned a lesson from the Manhattan Project scientists. I don't want to wake up one morning appalled by what I've created... I try to look at my work positively—developing a force for life." God, that sounded

pompous. "I mean, a world armed to the teeth with the most
devastating weapons ever invented." He smiled, foolishly he
thought. Well, the hell with it, press on, "I'd like to help
develop a sort of space-age Excalibur... the Lone Ranger's
silver bullet that can shoot across the heavens at the speed of
light and zap missiles out of our enemy's hands. Maybe I've
seen too many movies—or maybe I'm rationalizing and a
little drunk—but that's what I believe..."

Prudence Merriman's sunglasses made it impossible to
judge her reaction, although Pointer couldn't shake the feeling that he was on trial. August Merriman, on the other
hand, seemed to accept every word.

"That's what I like to hear, decisiveness, backbone. I
wouldn't give a penny for a pipe dream. It it's a *good* idea,
it's possible. But don't just think about it, go out and do it.
Make it happen because no one else is going to do it for you.
that's always been my way, and I must say it's paid off. You
know, back in 1921 I said I had a business proposal for Lenin,
and everybody said I was crazy. To presume that Lenin
would even agree to meet me, an American capitalist and a
twenty-one-year-old kid, was absurd enough. To seriously
believe that he'd buy my plan to improve Soviet trade was
preposterous. I was in Riga on the Baltic Sea at the time with
Herbert Hoover who was trying to work out American relief
aid for the famine victims—two young whippersnappers
with high hopes for the world and what we could do to
change it. Looking back, I'd say we each made a difference,
each in his own immodest way."

A captive audience, Pointer thought, and there was no
stopping the old man.

"As soon as I got word that the meeting was scheduled I
high-tailed it back to Moscow. When I got to the Troitski
Gate and the guard took my passport I considered calling the
whole thing off. I won't deny that I was nervous as I walked
through that gate for the first time. I crossed a bridge and

found myself inside the Kremlin in a square courtyard. There was nothing in it except me and Napoleon's cannons."

Angelica's bare feet were now in Pointer's lap. He was sure everyone knew, but Mrs. Merriman was eating her lunch calmly, Joseph was passing warm rolls, and Merriman was still holding forth.

"Lenin's office was on the second floor of what was the High Court of Moscow in tsarist days. I was shown into a large anteroom where his secretary, Glasser, sat behind an enormous rolltop desk. She was a hunchback, even smaller than Lenin, and fiercely protective of her boss. Double doors led to Lenin's office."

Pointer helped himself to a bun and tried to listen to his host. He was sure Joseph knew the exact location of Angelica's toes, but he didn't know what to do about it.

"He had the most brilliant, penetrating mind I've ever met up with—and believe me, I've known just about all of them —a dreamer but a doer too, as I like to think I am. I was an American capitalist but my idea was good, good for Russia and good for me. It didn't take us long to form a friendship, and the rest, as I like to say, is history."

Merriman leaned back. He had told the story many times before, but he never seemed to tire of hearing it again.

"Pointer, I'm not telling you all this just because I like to hear myself talk, though I admit I'm not your shrinking violet. I'm telling you so that you'll go back to Livermore and give 'em hell, as Harry Truman used to say. You're too young to remember him, a great American, and don't let anyone tell you otherwise. You can be a dreamer, as long as you don't leave it at that. You've got to be both— a dreamer *and* a doer. That's what makes for greatness."

At the moment Pointer was dreaming about what he'd like to do with Angelica. Prudence's sharp voice cut in.

"You haven't touched your berries, August. Why don't you concentrate on your dessert now and let Angelica show Mr. Pointer the gardens. You've been talking his ear off."

"Fine idea." Merriman stretched across the table to clap Pointer on the shoulder. "Keep up the good work, boy. We'll talk again. There's so much I want to learn from you."

It was the most serious thing he had said all evening, but he kept smiling the same happy, disarming smile.

CHAPTER
FOUR

"What is Livermore like?"

Linking his hands behind his head, Pointer leaned back against the trunk of a red oak and tried to think how he could explain a made-up atomic metropolis of eight thousand to this overpowering incarnation of every man's fantasies. How could he explain *anything* when her eyes were fixed on him and her closeness was an invitation waiting only for his acceptance.

"Livermore was invented by Dr. Edward Teller in an empty and flat California valley in the 1950's... Actually, it has the characteristics of a carcinoma—rapid growth, unnatural proliferation. Whether or not it's malignant is a question that can only be answered with time."

Pointer began giving it the old college try, but perverseness had become a habit with him, and it was difficult to break even under the most desirable circumstances. "I'm sorry, Angelica." He shut his eyes and shook his head. "I can't help myself sometimes... most of the time."

She was stretched out on the grass beside him on her side so that she could see him, her head propped on her hand, long hair flowing artfully into a cluster of buttercups... the same color as the buttercups. When he opened his eyes again, she was standing over him, smiling.

"I'll help you then. All you have to do is obey. It won't be

34

painful, I promise." She held out her hands to pull him up and into her arms.

What the hell. He took them, allowing himself to be led. He had always had a problem with blind obedience, even as a kid, refusing to answer to anyone who hadn't earned the right to tell him what to do. But Angelica's directive was different. He could make an exception this once—and she was German, after all. She didn't know any better.... Holding both his hands, she wrapped them around her waist and leaned into him and he stopped the rationalization.

The view over her shoulder was a sweep of water, the Hudson snaking south carrying a few sailing boats, like ship models from such a height, and a nation's history—Mad Anthony Wayne's midnight raid to retake the fort at Stony Point, General Benedict Arnold's heroic action at Saratoga to defeat Gentleman John Burgoyne and turn the revolution around for the colonists, and his infamy at West Point when he surrendered his loyalty and honor to Major Andre... The history of a place is what gives it character, he thought. Otherwise it's just like fooling around with Mother Nature. Without perspective, interest wanes.

Pointer felt a certain pride at the notion of making a small part of history, not, for God's sake, that he put himself in a class with Jefferson and Franklin (two of his heroes) but for sure Star Wars was going to change the future, one way or another. It was the scientific breakthrough of the century, and he was in its vanguard. Like it or not, he couldn't separate himself from the project now. The challenge was too great to walk away from. He sympathized with the dilemma of Oppenheimer, the scientist and the man—committed, ambivalent, driven—because he felt it himself. Louise never could understand why he didn't simply denounce the whole effort and quit, although he'd tried, God, how he'd tried, to explain it to her.

She left him, she said, because their wavelengths were short-circuiting each other. Well, in Angelica's arms now he was in the grip of an electrical storm. He could feel the currents entering his body, making him forget commitment and sharing and altered consciousness, Daniel Ortega, equal rights, banning the bomb, famine . . .

He laughed out loud, thinking if Louise could see him now with such a feast, the ultimate woman as sex object! Angelica kissed his open, laughing mouth—an experience perhaps the most liberating of his life. He was possessed by an urge to rip off their clothes and take every advantage that any man had ever taken of any woman.

"David, you surprise me," she murmured. Her breath was quick and warm against his cheek.

"I was only following orders," he said, disengaging himself. He'd never imagined being caught on the rebound could be so . . . so healing.

Louise had been pretty much like the other girls he'd been able to attract, except more so: hair long enough to sit on, straight and brown; pendulant breasts, wide rumps, thick in the legs, pretty enough faces but rather too intense. They took themselves, their relationships, and life in general, with high seriousness. Louise was like a vociferous Mother Nature in jeans or kaftan, and he had expected to spend his life at her side. They shared so much—Bach, Zen philosophy, Szechuan orange-flavored chicken, William Carlos Williams' poetry, disarmament . . . Pointer was going to invent a new kind of X-ray that would revolutionize medicine. Louise was going to change the world too, an anti-nuke crusader. Their operational words were sharing, relationship, commitment. And then Pointer went to Livermore. Although Louise followed, it was only on a trial basis—she believed she could save him from himself.

Pointer listened to the *Dies Irae* for weeks after she cleared her peasant blouses, cotton underpants, diaphragm and Rolodex from his apartment. The walkout had come after heated, repetitive arguments. Their relationship dissolved on the grounds of irreconcilable differences, Louise seeing an intrinsic contradiction in a nuclear system that was supposedly purely defensive. When the rhetoric and recriminations were cleared away, the issue was simple. She insisted he quit his job and Pointer refused.

Looking at Angelica now, he realized that what Louise lacked was the grace that came with a certain lightness, an ease about herself and him. "I guess I should be going," he said reluctantly. "I don't want to outstay my welcome with the Merrimans."

"You're not." Her voice was assured, her body pliant, fitting itself against his. She looked at him from under lowered lids. "Anyway they've gone and left you to me."

A whirring, wind-beating sound drowned out her words, and Pointer saw the silver blades of a helicopter rise over the river. "There?" He pointed with his eyebrows.

Angelica nodded. "You can stay as long as you like now, because there's only you and me."

"And the servants."

"They won't bother us."

For a moment Pointer got the discomforting feeling that he'd been set up—very neatly, irresistibly—but it was quickly overwhelmed because Angelica's tongue was doing things to his ear and her whispered promise was pushing his imagination into overdrive: "You can have anything you want from me, David."

Flat out, how to resist such an invitation? But he didn't want to seem over-eager. Not with a fantasy. He wanted first to admire her, discover her, like a work of art—hell, a masterpiece. But hardly made of marble. This masterwork of nature was very much flesh and blood. Especially flesh.

"Do you want to go back?" she asked, mistaking his hesitation.

Pointer shook his head. This couldn't be happening to him. Not David Pointer, he wasn't the type—he was too short, too skinny, his ears were too big and he was too "brainy," so they said.

In Angelica's arms he felt like a nocturnal animal coming into the sunlight for the first time—dazzled, confused. Until then science had been a consuming passion and everything else was a foil to it, even Louise. A star warrior, a knight of SDI, as consumed with his research as Galahad had been with finding the grail. And Angelica was Elaine, the fair Elaine, the lily-maid of Astolat... and the treacherously beautiful Guinevere... His imagination leapfrogged, hurdling stumbling blocks, plodders. It was, some said, what had made him the most valued scientist at Livermore.

"Come on." Angelica broke away and began to run through the gardens in an easy, long-legged lope.

The sun had begun to drop, her shadow lengthening in the softer light. The gardens spread around them like a park, white wrought-iron Victorian benches along the brick paths, beds of snapdragon and phlox bordered with petunias, day lilies, irises, African daisies and nasturtiums in a hundred shades of yellow, orange, red, pink. Beyond the gardens were a lake, swimming pool, tennis courts and around it all stretched acres of woodland. A private reserve, almost a country within a country, the kingdom of August Merriman, and Angelica was waiting for him at the castle door.

"Incredible." He shook his head.

"I know. It's hard to believe that this is New York—all this and Times Square and the World Trade Towers and the Statue of Liberty." Her smile deepened the color in her cheeks.

Pointer shook his head. "That's where you're wrong. We're not in New York at all. We've left that far behind and we're in a world known only to you and me, waiting to be explored."

Her laughter bubbled like a natural spring. "So inside your pure scientific mind lurks a true romantic. I suspected as much."

He bowed from the waist. "Lord Byron is alive and well and working at Livermore."

Angelica's room was decorated in lavenders and pinks. Light flooded in from three windows hung with curtains of the same floral design as the dust ruffle and canopy on the double bed. A bed of violets. He thought of his own unmade bed and of Louise's futon. There seemed to be throw pillows everywhere, solid pinks and lavender stripes. The rug was white and thick underfoot. The tables bare except for a vase of pink snapdragons and a travel clock. The dressing table with fluted pink skirt was bare too except for a brush and comb, perfume bottle, cosmetics.

Pointer went to the windows and stared out, unable to believe his outrageous fortune. A red hawk banked over the river. Otherwise the sky was empty, and he was alone in a sumptuous castle with an eminently available princess. Uncomfortable though he was with the role of prince, he wasn't about to relinquish it. Certainly not to an intruder. He stood absolutely still, listening, straining to hear.

"Is the view more appealing than I am?" Angelica's voice shattered his concentration.

"No, I thought I heard something just outside, as if someone was listening at the door."

"It's just Joseph wondering whether to knock with the champagne. You worry too much, David. Or you're too suspicious. It must be your work."

Once again he got the momentary feeling that he'd been set up for all this. The champagne was chilled in readiness. All was in order . . . He turned away from the view.

"What do you usually do when you're alone in your aerie?"

Angelica stood in the middle of the room, contemplating him serenely. She moved a step closer.

"Don't you find it lonely?"

"Never." She shook her head taking a second step.

He frowned, a man in grave thought. "Don't tell me that Angelica Merriman is a closet drunk."

A third step brought her close enough to be touched.

"I'm really a very shy fellow—"

"You talk too damn much." Taking his hands, Angelica turned them over and kissed the open palms. Her body leaned into his as she reached up for his lips.

"This is your customary—?"

"Shut up." She breathed the words against his lips.

His arms tightened around her, pressing her against him as he answered her kiss.

She felt him hard against her thigh and his tongue thick inside her. She drew back. "Joseph will bring the champagne, if you like."

Pointer thought of Joseph lurking in the stoney shadows, the perfect servant, always in waiting, and discreet. "Champagne can wait," he said, unzipping her dress.

She wore no bra. Her skin held the scent and texture of roses. Remarkable. The curve of her waist made her breasts seem extravagant. Cupping them, he circled the dark nipples, marking his territory. She had already kicked off her shoes, and she slid down her dress and panties in one motion.

He stared. Even in her nakedness, Pointer couldn't believe Angelica Merriman was happening to him. Beautiful women didn't fall into his life. He was more accustomed to fertile brains and flabby bodies.

"Did you really plan to seduce me when your grandparents left?" It sounded petulant and silly when he said it, as if he was complaining that she was luring him into her bed against his will, when it was clearly evident that his will and other more obvious parts of him were enthusiastic partners in the seduction, planned or spontaneous.

"I couldn't wait for lunch to be over."

"But why me?" He was embarrassed to take his clothes off

in front of her. He had a good ass, round and muscular, but the rest of him . . .

Angelica moved in his arms. "I want to see if you're as brilliant a lover as you are a scientist."

"If that's all, I can tell you—"

"And I like the way you listen. So few men do. You seem to know that all this—" She lifted her breasts and turned slowly in front of him so that he could appreciate the full extent of her problem, "all this can be a trap."

"Not bad as traps go," he said, trying not to think how much he'd like to be caught in it with no chance of release.

"I told you, you can have everything you want."

"And you, Angelica, do you ever get more than you want?" It was a try at sounding worldly, cool, but it all dissolved as she began unbuckling his belt.

"Let's see, David." She laughed, a rich, intimate sound. And when she knelt in front of him, her long hair brushing him, he felt like Clark Kent and Captain Midnight and He-Man, the Masters of the Universe and all forty Knights of the Round Table.

CHAPTER
FIVE

On a nautical map Little Compton looks like a *rara avis*, its long beak thrust into the mouth of the Sakonnet River.

The rest defies charting, the preserve of Yankee wealth and class, the idyllic meld of country and seashore (about equidistant from Boston and Providence) with none of the commercialism of Newport or the tourist traps of Cape Cod. And every advantage: herds of prize Guernseys grazing behind low stone walls in meadows that slope down to the water, antique silos still in working order, small private beaches, lovely summer houses perfectly appointed without being ostentatious, a roadside stand with the best homemade ice cream in New England, an exclusive country club and, when you've had too much of a good thing, a single rude saloon out at the tip of Sakonnet Point. At the heart of all this is the village green, exactly as it has been since colonial times—the white steepled church, straight and true, the graveyard beside it, a general store, a package store.

Everything a man needs, Matthias Conrad thought. Spiritual and liquid sustenance, not necessarily in that order. And when they're no longer enough, a final resting place. Straightening up from the vegetable row he'd been digging, he shaded his eyes with a dirty hand and squinted across the rutted drive and open field to the distant road, Field and road were divided by a stone wall built by some distant

Conrad who'd gathered rocks from the uncleared land and piled them up in a loose fit that withstood time and hurricanes.

Although he tried to pretend otherwise, Conrad was itching to find out why Nora Hewitt was driving all the way from Langley, Maryland, to Little Compton, Rhode Island, and to his front door. It wasn't a social call. He knew Nora too well for that. But it could be nostalgia, affection, a heightened us-against-them feeling. Or something more interesting?

Since his retirement Conrad had passed into CIA legend as "the Dean" of intrigue, spoken of in awed, almost reverential tones. There had been other names, more or less flattering, but the Dean was the most fitting. In appearance and inclination he resembled an Ivy League professor—rumpled with owlish glasses and balding head, Harvard College, '31, Phi Beta Kappa. His passion was the thirteenth century —the age of discoveries, of Gothic splendor and noble hearts, when architecture, faith and love soared, women were ladies and men were armoured. In fact, Conrad was a university doctor and a medievalist, sidetracked into Wild Bill Donovan's OSS during the war. He had never made it back to academia.

Now he had a surfeit of time and little inclination for it, having discovered that nobility is too costly and love is never pure but comes with its own *quid pro quo*. There would be no ivory towers for the Dean. None could contain his iconoclasm. Instead he pursued the purity of lettuce rows, tomato plants, squash of four different varieties, peas, beans, and eggplant for its lovely lavender flowers.

Conrad had returned to the red leaf heads when Nora Hewitt drove in. Her dusty Honda Accord bumped along the worn path through the empty field. Wiping his hands on his stained khaki pants, (Brooks Brothers vintage 1955), Conrad shuffled over to greet her. Nora Hewitt was immutable, he thought, like truth, if slightly disheveled, slightly overweight, slightly eccentric. It was easy to misjudge her, a mistake she rarely made about others. They went back a long way together, so many years they could both qualify for protection on the endangered species list.

Though one-of-a-kind, Nora constituted an entire species herself. She had never had a husband, lover, boyfriend, girlfriend, or sexual urge of any kind—at least none she'd admit to—yet she was anything but a prude. Loyalty and humor were the virtues she prized in others and prided herself for. A diehard of her class, upper-middle, WASP, she lived by the Golden Rule with a twist: do unto others as you expect others will do unto you . . . and do it first.

"Dear Matthias." She didn't get out of the car so much as extricated herself from it and started toward him, both hands outstretched. "Dear, dear Matthias. It's like old times seeing you again . . ." Unfazed by the state of his hands, she grasped them and stood on her toes to peck his cheek. Forty-eight hours without a shave, her mind clicked automatically, and stinking. " . . . though I didn't expect to find you so *au naturel*, if you'll pardon my French."

"Admirable tact, my sweet, when you mean to say I smell. How was your trip?" The familiar wry smile and the cigarette stub, clinging to his lip and moving as he spoke, made her heart warm to the task ahead.

"Interminable."

"You knew it would be."

"I did, but I had to see you, Matthias."

"I didn't know I meant so much to you."

"Of course you knew," she muttered reproachfully, "but even if I were pining away I wouldn't inflict myself on you without an invitation. Good heavens, I'd be mad as the Hatter to drive this far for something merely personal. The truth is I'm afraid to trust it to anyone but you. The Agency has changed and the people in it . . . well, they're a new breed, terribly bright but not very clever."

Conrad turned and started toward the house, an old man's shuffle, but Nora could never remember him walking any

other way. "A good story deserves a good Scotch. What do
you say, old girl?"

"I'll use the facilities while you mix the drinks." She followed him into the house and up the stairs.

Except for the master bedroom and bath, the second floor
was open. From the kitchen Conrad watched Nora disappear
into the bathroom and come out a few minutes later, her hair
freshly combed, her wide face softened with a new layer of
powder. She sat on the couch, her short legs just reaching
the floor, bounced once or twice to settle herself, then
opened her valise and waited. When he was seated opposite
her, Scotch in hand, she leaned forward, ready to take him
into her confidence.

"I've been digging around for want of anything better to
do," she began in the unexcitable, matter-of-fact tone that
she had always reserved for stunning secrets. "It amuses me
. . . and the young Turks around me. I suspect they think
ancient history is where I belong." She gave a short, self-de-
precating laugh. "At least it keeps them out of my hair and
leaves me free to do pretty much as I please."

"And what has it pleased you to do?" Conrad asked. Without a kick in the pants Nora might meander on for an hour
setting the stage for whatever she had to tell. She liked to
take things step-by-step, to construct painstaking detail by
apparently insignificant detail. It worked for her but it drove
him crazy. Always had, still did. And, of course, she knew it.

"I've been rummaging, picking through old files—some
that go back forty years—taking a little from this and a bit
from that and trying to fit it all together. Sort of like con-
structing stained-glass windows. You remember how I love
stained glass, Matthias?"

He nodded. "I also remember that the rose window took a
few decades to make."

"Touché, but I am flattered that you remember so well the
way I like to operate, and you must admit it has payed off
rather well. Remember Hamburg, '58, the—"

"The apple torte."

"No, it was cherry, I believe."

"Each to his own, my sweet."

She cleared her throat. "Memories can be tricky, but they're not why I'm here." She reached for her drink, thought better of it and sat back. "The fact is that when I finished raking through the past, and cutting and fitting and gluing the slivers of my colored glass, so to speak, they made for a single quite dazzling rainbow effect."

"And at the end of the rainbow was the proverbial pot of gold?"

"Yes, but this one is very, very tarnished. It belongs to one of the most powerful entrepreneurs in the country, a man on personal terms with every world leader, who has made billions trading with the eastern bloc." Her voice dropped by force of habit even though they were alone. "I am convinced that he was instrumental in giving the atomic secret to the Soviets. The Rosenbergs were dupes. And I hate to think what else he has bartered . . . is *still* bartering."

Conrad felt his blood surge, as it had in the old days before Congressional watch-dog committees and blue-ribbon presidential commissions had made the Agency anemic. Nora didn't have to spell out the name. It could only be one man —and he was still operating on a grand scale. He licked his lips in anticipation. "At long last, lovely . . . August Merriman . . ."

Nora nodded, surprised, though she knew she shouldn't be. Matthias had the kind of mind that possessed by a less intelligent, less clever man would jump to dangerous conclusions. "Eighty-eight-years-young, born in Napa, Washington, June 19, 1900. Father: James Merriman, killed in World War I on the Somme . . ."

She had the vital statistics at her fingertips, and she recited them with dead seriousness, the way she made the Way of the Cross once a year on Good Friday. She was Episcopalian on a level with the Queen of England and the Arch-

bishop of Canterbury, still it was her only concession to an
authority higher than her own eminently sensible brain. Or
maybe it was an annual act of mortification, performed with
the sure knowledge that intellectual arrogance could be the
deadliest of sins. Although he had few mundane scruples,
Conrad was too smart ever to be guilty of that offense, which
she appreciated.

"Mother: Marguerite Brodsky Merriman, also deceased.
Russian born. She took over the family business and ran it
herself until August was old enough to operate it..." Nora
went on ticking off the facts, reliable as a computer."

Conrad, Nora knew, resented mechanical brains and the
mechanized men and women who programmed them. Before
the computer takeover at Langley his mind had been the
repository for virtually all of the most sensitive intelligence
data. And he had shared or withheld it judiciously, insuring
that he—not the Director, the Congress or the President—
would be the single most powerful intelligence force. That,
of course, was before the post-Watergate purge of the
Agency when the nation beat its collective breast and hung
out its soiled laundry for the world to see in a futile effort to
regain the illusion of innocence. He had taken the humiliat-
ing purge personally, as he had taken everything that af-
fected his beloved Agency.

"The family business was minerals, and Merriman still
dabbles in them, especially platinum from the Urals. Now
you well know, Matthias, I'm no psychoanalyst, but I'll wager
Merriman does it out of nostalgia or sentimentality—or
some motive too foreign for a logician like me to understand."

"It that's true, it's the only sentimental bone in the old
coot's body." Conrad's myopic eyes twinkled at her over the
owlish tortoise-shell glasses. "Merriman likes to play the
humble grandfather to the press but don't be fooled for a
moment. His ego, enormous though it is, doesn't come close
to his wealth. August Merriman has never done anything out

of sentiment, unless there was a profit to be made. His heart is solid gold bullion."

Conrad slumped in the wing chair and brought his mouth down to meet the glass of Scotch he held. The fingers, curled around the tumbler, still bore traces of the earth he'd been turning when Nora arrived. She noted it as she noted every detail, cataloguing the changes since his forced early retirement. Her own highball stood untouched on the coffee table between them; her handbag, valise and files spilled over on the couch beside her. A huge picture window dominated the wall to her left, presenting a dramatic view of the sea beyond. For a moment Nora stared out at the distant line of blue formed by the meeting of sea and sky. The couch and chairs were blue, too, upholstered in a linen blend a shade or two deeper than either sea or sky.

The house and vegetable garden behind it were Conrad's extracurricular passions. He had actually built the place himself, board-by-board, over years because so much of his time had been consumed by the Agency. "Physical work," he had once told her, "frees the brain to soar or wallow, to be outrageous." Nora was sure that every nail hammered, every stud fitted had brought forth a fresh plan from the Dean's devilish mind.

The house surprised her. Not the Danish Modern furniture, which like all of that style lacked character. It was safe, neither tasteful nor tasteless, chosen by someone afraid to be accused of being too gauche or too bland, too pretentious or too dull. Matthias' wife was the guilty party, Nora realized the instant she noted it, and for the first time felt sympathy for Charlotte Conrad. Unlike Matthias, Nora knew what it felt like to mistrust oneself, to lack confidence in one's decisions. Which was why she was sitting on the blue Danish Modern sofa with an enviable view of Narragansett Bay instead of in the CIA director's functional office presenting her case against August Merriman.

No, once she realized it was Charlotte's choice, the furniture didn't surprise her. But the house itself did—a spacious two-story rectangle with a pitched roof that sat on a rise in the middle of an open field facing the sea beyond. It was designed to take advantage of the view, with the living quarters—living room, dining room, kitchen, master bedroom and bath—upstairs. The first floor seemed almost like a mistake, or a necessary adjunct—work space, spare bedrooms, a place to drop fishing tackle and waders or store empty vegetable flats. Nora loved the sea, loved to sail, yet she could never be content with that alone. Appearances notwithstanding, she found it difficult to believe Matthias was. She'd expected to find him itching to be back in harness, starved for the delicate details that had always been his stock in trade. To be on the outside, unable to even peek in, must be the most excruciating punishment, she thought. And yet he appeared as benign as Mr. Chips.

"Jesus, Matthias." she blurted, "what do you *do* here all day, every day?"

He peered over his glasses, which had found a permanent settlement midway along the bridge of his nose. "Putter, my sweet. Putter and putter. I recommend it when your number comes up. It is eminently satisfying. Nothing like a ripe tomato on the vine to restore the psyche, renew the faith."

"I can't believe you've turned your back on all that juicy double-dealing without a regret. You thrived on it, Matthias."

"You're digressing, old girl," he said and sucked in the Scotch. Nora's back straightened perceptibly and her expression tightened, automatic reactions to the slurping sounds he made. "You were telling me about the mighty August Merriman. I didn't mean to lead you off the straight and narrow."

She smiled, not in amusement but to let him know that she was no man's fool, particularly his—the Dean, she knew, never did or said anything unintentionally—and resumed her catalogue.

"Married for the first time in 1920, Meredith Marie Jenkins, his highschool sweetheart. The next year he made his first trip to Russia to fulfill his mother's last request that some small part of her be brought home and buried in her village cemetary in Satka. Her wedding ring was in his breast pocket when he finally reached Moscow. Meredith had started out with him, but she only got as far as Zurich. Didn't travel well, I guess.

"Merriman wrote about his arrival in Moscow in the old *Saturday Evening Post*. I think it's worth reading a few lines." Nora put on a pair of Ben Franklin glasses and selected a Xeroxed sheet. "'My first impression of the Soviet Union was the poverty. It seemed ground into the streets, etched on the stolid, enduring faces.'"

Conrad grunted. "From the tyranny of the tsars to the tyranny of ideas. The Russians changed masters in 1917 but the old enslavement goes on. But let's not leave young Mr. Merriman on the road to Satka, wherever the hell that is."

Nora put down the paper and took off her glasses, holding them by the bow. "It's in the mineral-rich foothills of the Urals. Remember that Merriman's father had left him a mining concern, so several strands of his life seem to come together here. The plight of the starving Russians must have touched him deeply, and he came up with a plan—quite basic, really. What the Soviets needed—and nothing has changed in this regard—was hard currency. He proposed to sell minerals from the Urals to the West and use the cash to buy farm equipment, tractors and grain, for all of which he would pay himself a generous commission. Russia needed all the humanitarian help he could provide, and if it made him wealthy and powerful in the bargain, so be it."

"A touching story," Conrad interjected.

"Apocryphal perhaps, but consistent with all the rest, and true or not, it gives the feel of the man. I think we're dealing with a missionary here—something of a zealot even."

"A Mother Theresa with a numbered Swiss bank account?"

Conrad shook his head. "I'm not so sure Merriman is anything more than a man blinded by his own ego."

"Mother Theresa with a Swiss account and a sublime ego," Nora said so matter-of-factly that Conrad choked on his Scotch.

"Don't the latter two negate the first, old girl? But let's get on with it."

Nora tried not to show her annoyance.

"Lenin bought the arrangement, and August Merriman's unique relationship with the Soviet high command began. The Allied blockade had been lifted in 1920, so there was nothing stopping him. Gradually he added lumber, caviar and, of course, furs to his list of exports, and along the way he began collecting ikons, buying them cheap because no one wanted religious art then. Today his collection is truly breathtaking, the envy of every major museum."

"Ikons," Conrad muttered. "That's probably what Merriman thinks he is."

"By the time Stalin came to power," Nora went on, ignoring the aside, "his company was a pipeline for every Western firm doing business with the Soviets. His export-import business ballooned, with offices in Berlin and New York as well as London. As Stalin became increasingly repressive, though, Merriman saw the writing on the wall. He moved out of Russia . . . but he always kept one foot in the door, and when Hitler began making noises in Germany, Merriman seemed just the man to coax Uncle Joe into the Allies' corner.

"It was around this time, too—1940, to be precise—that Merriman married for the second time, Prudence Schaeffer Merriman. There are also indications that he had a liaison with an aristocratic English woman during this period. It's not significant, really. I only mention it because Merriman seems to have adopted the woman's granddaughter, evidently convinced that the girl is his grandchild as well." Nora clicked ahead in the clipped accent of privilege and educa-

tion. Bryn Mawr was years behind her but she still had the
voice. "The peculiar thing about the arrangement is that
Merriman's wife Prudence seems to have found the girl and
brought her right into the bosom of the family. And believe
me, Matthias, she's nobody's Little Orphan Annie..."

Conrad stared out the window. Prudence... Prudence
Schaeffer. He had to comb far back to his most sensitive file,
but she was still there in all her passion and glory—his rich-
est memory.

Matthias shook his head. He was still fooling himself. Prudence was the "fun-while-it-lasted," "all-good-things-have-to-
end" girl who'd walked away without a tear. She was better
than clichés, but she'd certainly used them to dispose of him
in favor of August Merriman. Or maybe she'd taken up with
Merriman later. Although he'd never been sure of the chro-
nology, Matthias had always secretly hoped to see Merriman
fall on his face one day...

"Whatever his sins, the man is a remarkable business creature, a salesman without peer. When the Cold War was at its
chilliest Merriman evidently decided he could thaw it himself by exporting the entire Bolshoi Ballet—probably the
first cultural exchange since the Revolution, and an annual
event ever since. An extraordinary success story, when you
look at it on the surface. A sort of international Horatio
Alger."

Nora took her first sip of Scotch. "That's pretty much the
picture of how Merriman got solidly entrenched on both
sides of the curtain—or wall, if you prefer."

"You tell a hell of a story, old girl, but when are you going
to get to the juicy stuff—the meat and potatoes?"

Nora stiffened. She didn't like to be rushed, believing
wholeheartedly that it was so important to see the full picture. "Well, it's not absolutely clear when Merriman began
giving more than economic assistance to the Soviets. On our
side, Harry Hopkins was the first to allow him a free hand

with the Russians in exchange for keeping the White House informed. It was probably a gradual process, though, to cut through the redtape—no pun intended—which they say is even thicker in Moscow than in Washington. But one self-deception leads to another. I mean *our* self-deception.

"By '43 he'd already committed himself. He was a member of the Top Policy Group at the time, which supervised the atomic development program, so he was privy to exactly what Stalin wanted—information basic for making a uranium bomb. Of course, the Soviets were our allies then, and to be fair to Merriman he and a lot of others believed that by withholding information on the Manhattan Project we were prolonging the war, or at the least delaying victory.

"Whatever his motive, it's ancient history now, but from what I dredge up, Merriman passed along specimens of an isotope critical to developing the bomb. After that a lot of other people got into the act, as you well know, Fuchs, Greenglass and the rest. But at the outset Merriman's information must have been vital. Then there was the U-2 incident. There's no doubt now that Merriman tipped off Khrushchev, then turned around and arranged the prisoner exchange. Each side's buddy. . ."

Nora went on with her dossier of betrayals, large and small, but Conrad decided he had heard enough. It wasn't the past that interested him. It was the future—the next move for the benefit of August Merriman and the U.S.S.R. He leaned forward, closing the distance between them. "Who else have you confided in?"

"Why, no one, Matthias. I came to you—"

The ice in his glass clinked. "Then leave those papers with me . . . for safekeeping."

It hit her suddenly. He was her friend, her mentor. But after all the years they had worked together she now realized that Matthias Conrad was ready to take advantage of her. Worse, to him she belonged to a past that he, the Dean, had invented and controlled. She'd been *allowed* to stay around because she made no waves and could be useful. And she'd been grateful. She had nothing to retire to, not even a vegetable patch. The Agency was her home, her family. Her life.

"Where's Charlotte? You haven't even told her I'm here."

"Your dear friend Charlotte? She prefers to stay in Alexandria than be closeted here with me, a case of Dewar's and a pile of horseshit."

"You're too hard on yourself."

"I don't mean me, my sweet. The horseshit is just that, a pile of manure for my kitchen garden. There's nothing like it. Every time you sink your teeth into a lush tomato here you can be sure it sprang from earth hot and steamy with horseshit."

She should have expected that from Matthias. He hadn't changed. Only the objects of his interest had.

"But you digress, Nora. We haven't finished with August Merriman—not by a long shot."

She detected the slight rattle of phlegm in his throat... he'd been smoking a lifetime, non-menthol non-filter. If the surgeon general nailed a bull to the White House doors, he wouldn't join the reformation.

Nora's back straightened, her ankles crossed tightly, holding herself in close check. "I'm not sure how to handle such explosive information. That's where I hoped you might... direct me."

"Just give it to me."

"And you will see that it gets into the right hands...?"

"I'll take care of it in my own way. I think you can trust me to do that."

Could she, she thought. "You're retired," she said.

"I was until you showed up at my doorstep and lured me back with what I take to be a special request from the Director to handle the Merriman case personally."

"Matthias, you wouldn't—"

"I want everything you have on Merriman...all that stained glass, every shard of it." He went on slurping his liquor, his eyes brighter than they had been in years. "I want to marvel at your rainbow, sweet Nora. I've never seen a stained-glass rainbow. Surely you wouldn't deny me that small pleasure."

CHAPTER
SIX

They say spies come in three stripes. The ideologues, passionate and unreliable—the Whittiker Chambers of the business. The whores of the trade who do it for the money, nothing more—like the Walkers, father, son and uncle—they seem to have proliferated since his arrest. And then there are the professionals—some, true adventurers, others, accountants—whose abiding interest is the trade itself.

August Merriman was none of the above.

Matthias Conrad knew about spies—and even without Nora's help, he knew more than most about Merriman. He operated above governments, above the usual espionage in which small, dull men and women bartered bodies and souls for secrets. He was a pragmatist without ideology who used all sides, and allowed himself to be used when it served his purpose. Intimate of Bolsheviks, princes and presidents, but shrewdly, friend of none.

Merriman defied his times. During the post-war years when the Soviet Union and the United State raced to become superpowers, he moved easily in both spheres. When the Cold War prohibited all concourse he earned a fortune trading with the Reds. When the slightest hint of pink was enough to destroy the most exalted career, he lived in splendor in a Hudson River estate with a direct line to the White

House. In the Red hunts of the fifties he wasn't even questioned by the House Un-American Activities Committee.

Merriman was completely trusted, or mistrusted, by both camps. He'd helped arrange the release of captured U-2 pilot Gary Powers, pointed a finger at Russian agents operating in Europe, forecast the Soviet arms build-up in the Middle East... It was the price paid for the license to trade freely with the enemy. But evidently the Soviets were more expensive, and, as Nora laid it out, if Merriman were still operating on a grand scale...

Draining his whiskey, Conrad concentrated on infiltrating the brain of August Merriman, to imagine his antagonist's motives and means.

The evening was windless. The high marsh grass stood thick and motionless beside the salt pond. Daylight lingered high in the sky although the edges of the pond had darkened. Conrad liked to watch the day disappearing, it had become one of his favorite activities since his retirement. Beyond the pond the sea was an indigo smear, none of its mysteries visible except in the imagination of the hoary old spymaster, once feared, now forgotten at the Agency except as legend. At the north end of the salt pond an egret lifted over the water.

"You're always sitting in the dark, dad. It's kind of sick." Beth switched on the lamp beside his chair. In the incandescent glare her face was as complaining as her voice. He had spent a dark, clandestine life. It was too late to change his ways. An old dog... etc. Picking up his empty glass, he shuffled to the kitchen, got some bread to feed the birds and poured himself another Scotch.

"Your fly's open again, dad." Beth shook her head. In his faded flannel shirt, stained, beltless khaki pants and mud-crusted workboots, her father looked like a handyman, jackof-all-trades, which was exactly what he claimed to be. Her boyfriend hadn't even recognized him.

"A tired bird doesn't leave his nest. You and Tom don't have to worry."

Conrad had been looking forward to Beth's visit. Now that she was here, though, he wished she hadn't come. Blonde and taut... Tautonic. His brain played mindless games. Without Charlotte to distract them his daughter was an intrusion. Although he loved her, he had, more or less, felt that way about Beth ever since Charlotte had announced her pregnant state. And in his retirement he'd grown accustomed to loneliness very quickly. It was just as well that Beth had decided to stay in California after finishing Stanford, he thought, because he didn't want to fight with her, and unfortunately that was mostly what they did when they were together... bicker. She was so much like Charlotte, though smarter, and crueler. Poor Tom, Conrad thought. He was a ski bum, maybe the slopes would save him. Or he'd take up another pastime, like Scotch.

"Tom and I are going over to Newport for dinner at Cooke's. We'll be late, dad, so don't wait up for us." Beth had a small pert face, freckles across the bridge of her nose and a figure that would thicken as her mother's had unless she watched every calorie and swore off childbearing.

Conrad turned away. Going out to the pond with his crumbs and his Scotch, he cast bread upon the dark waters, not expecting to find it after many days, and allowed his mind to drift like a boat without captain or anchor. Nora Hewitt's mind never drifted. It was against her principles. She set it decisively on a course, the changing winds of tide and fortune accounting for any minor deviations. Which was how she had uncovered such damning evidence against August Merriman.

Conrad considered her strengths and limitations as clinically as he would a double agent's. She was a friend, one of the few he could claim—though most friendships were a

matter of convenience. Nora Hewitt was a good egg, the kind
of woman men liked but never considered loving. Plain,
brainy and overweight, she was born to be on a pack of Old
Maid playing cards. Except in color her hair hadn't changed
since her college days—cut just below the ears, parted on
one side and held back with a gold bobby pin. Her style was
classic Peck & Peck—MacMullen blouses, wrap-around
skirts, cable knit sweaters and flat-heeled, tasselled shoes. A
terrible cook, a disinterested shopper, a superlative snoop.
Although she seemed too solid and sensible to embark on
anything as quixotic as espionage, Nora had been one of his
best operatives. She had a librarian's forgettable appearance
and an archaeologist's persistent mind. No detail was too insignificant for her painstaking consideration. That had been
her weakest point in the field, and her strongest advantage
ever since. Conrad savored the irony of it, which had led her
to deposit her bounty at his door.

In the general housekeeping that followed his departure
from the Agency, Nora had been grounded. She was a rem-
nant of the past—the embarrassing, much maligned past
that Matthias Conrad had created. Though allowed to stay
on, she was treated like a slighly dotty maiden aunt—a daub
of local color in what was becoming an increasingly faceless,
bloodless company. Nora was shunted into a research slot on
the Soviet desk, a safe spot where she was more an archivist
than an agent. The assignment was a dismissal, but she had
an uncanny knack for turning the worst odds to her favor.

Everything that she had told him rang true, except Prudence Schaeffer Merriman's largesse...out of character on
several levels. Nora had no way of knowing that—and
Matthias no way of forgetting. He rememberred the last
night better than their first meeting, bitterness having more
staying power than pleasure...

It had been a victory weekend in New York to celebrate
his graduation from Harvard, summa cum laude, and the
first time he'd spent the night in a hotel with a woman. Pru-

dence Schaeffer, nineteen years old, and ready to break every rule. She was supposed to be staying with friends on Riverside Drive, not in a room he'd reserved at the St. Regis overlooking Fifth Avenue. He had planned every detail—a steak dinner at Toots Shor's and tickets to the Broadway hit of the season, *Sweet Adeline*.

Wending their way arm in arm down the Great White Way after the show, Pru hummed the score they had heard, still playing in her memory. Her dress was pink and her cheeks were flushed to match, and *he* had never felt more in the pink. New York was still pretty much of a horizontal town then, the occasional church steeple standing out above a skyline of brownstones and brick townhouses. The vertical city was at the threshhold. the Woolworth and Chrysler buildings, revolutionary a decade before, were being imitated, but the iron-and-marble elegance of the Belle Époque was still much more than a memory, and even the street lamps retained the nineteenth century style. He had kissed her under one of them. His heart had been louder than the roar of the iron-trestled El's hurtling north-south, keeping the avenues shadowed and dusty, or the clatter of horse-drawn wagons carrying ice and milk alongside the trolleys that came up from the Hudson Ferry terminals at Forty-Second and Courtland Streets.

An occasional apple-seller hawked on a corner, but the city was yet to feel the full effect of Black Thursday... Hoovervilles all over town, beneath the Third Avenue El, in the sheltered underside of the Brooklyn Bridge, in Central Park's Sheep Meadow... disfiguring Manhattan like barnacles on a sea rock... the breadlines and ragmen's mournful cries.

Toasting Pru with bootleg champagne, Matthias had thought the world was at his feet, all things were possible, and women were the true wonder of the world. He was one-and-twenty, and he'd given his heart away. Sunday morning came too soon. It was then she told him about all-good-things-coming-to-an-end and that it had been fun-while-it-lasted.

Conrad never went back to New York until August 15, 1945, when he stepped off a carrier ship...

Thousands of revelers spilled into the streets. Strangers danced and hugged each other, weeping and laughing. Victory V's flashed on all sides. America was having the party of her life. The war was over. We'd whipped the bastards and the GI Joes were trooping home, every boy a man, every man a hero. It was a national catharsis. Booze flowed like water on the sidewalks of New York. Pounds of ticker tape streamed from the windows. If you were wearing a uniform, the city was your oyster. Good girls, wholesome faces streaked with tears of pride and joy, would kiss you and lay you as gladly as they'd shake your hand. Strangers would ply you with drinks.

The crowd's excitement was contagious. Conrad had let himself be swept up in its gaiety. the anonymity was comforting. He accepted it all as if it was happening to somebody else—the drinks, the kissing, the hugs, the backslaps and the broad-hipped girl from Ozone Park whose name he never quite got or couldn't remember. She had screwed him in the back seat of a Checker cab at Battery Park, the eternal torch of Lady Liberty a distant beacon through the window.

"Will we ever feel as good about ourselves as we do tonight?" he had asked the glassy-eyed girl when he'd gratefully spent himself in her.

"It was good for me, too, if that's what you're asking," she said, rearranging herself.

"I meant it in a... larger sense."

"You were big enough, fella, honest."

"No... I mean the country, the nation, we, the people." Conrad felt stupid trying to explain.

"Don't go getting the wrong idea, now." She was putting

on fresh lips. "I'm not the kind of girl who does it with just anyone . . ."

Liberties freely given and freely taken, he thought now, and remembered Pru in pink at nineteen. Her picture was in the morning paper, on the front page of the *Herald Tribune* over the caption "Peacemakers; Mr. and Mrs. August Merriman. The freewheeling entrepreneur is calling for a new League of Nations—a United Nations instead of a third world war." Conrad had tossed the paper away and caught the red-eye to Rhode Island, where his mother waited for a last look at him.

When he arrived Maude Conrad was propped up in her big four-poster. A fan hummed in the corner. Her delicate hands had become boney claws and lay limp on the linen sheet. Her shoulders jutted through a powder blue satin bedjacket like the edges of a hanger. Her face was thin, the skin drawn tightly across it, making every feature seem over-sized. To Matthias she was still beautiful.

"I've come home to stay," he promised. "You'll be all right now."

Maude took his hand in her frail one and kissed it. He sat beside her on the bed and she stroked his hair the way she had done when he was a boy. They both knew it was a lie, but it was a nice lie to dream about and die with. "I couldn't have you come home to an empty house, Matt. I never did when you were in school, and I wasn't going to begin now that you were at war."

He had buried his face in her lap and cried. It had been easier to be brave in war than with his mother. "I thought I was such a hero—"

"You don't have to be a hero with me. You don't have to be anything except what you are." She had clung to his hand as if it were life itself. By midnight she was dead.

Conrad buried his mother in the colonial cemetery beside the white church, between his father and grandfather. A simple service. When it was over he had gone home alone, locked the door and gotten very drunk, until he was so violently sick he'd thought he was going to die too. As soon as he'd felt well enough to face another liquor bottle, he had started drinking all over again. He consumed everything he could get his hands on, washing it down with a bottle of creme de menthe and a fifth of Pernod.

It was then the Bill Donovan called him to Washington. Conrad sold the house, moved to D.C. and started dating Charlotte. But Prudence was the only girl who had ever reminded him of his mother.

The pond was an inkwell. The egrets were nesting for the night. Beth and Tom had gone. Conrad walked halfway around the rim, shuffling through the tall grass to the old tool shed he used for an office, the damp sand giving way to his heavy boots. He turned the combination lock without looking at the numbers and went in.

The shed was a single square room no bigger than an outhouse, windowless and bare. The roof was slanted, the walls scarred with rusted nails. The only furnishings were an oak rolltop desk and his mother's cane rocker. A tufted green chintz pillow, so faded that the floral design was all but invisible, was pushed down into the hole in the rocker seat. It was the one touch of domesticity. There were no pictures to relieve the eye from the splintering boards, and no electricity.

Conrad struck a match, lit a cigarette and the kerosene lamp on the desk, then sat down to open the package from Nora. It had arrived by UPS with a "Get Well" greeting card attached, although there was little chance of that.

Nora wouldn't have sent him everything, he thought leafing through the pages. She would hold something back to protect herself, her position—nothing obvious, but nothing trivial either.

He thumbed through the pages, pausing to look at the photostats. There was a picture of the Yalta Conference, with

Merriman and Alger Hiss talking together in the background. One with Churchill and Merriman on the steps of 10 Downing Street. Merriman at Camp David with Eisenhower. A young Nixon and an ageless Merriman in front of the Kremlin Wall—probably the famous kitchen debate. The Merrimans and the Kennedys walking along the beach at Hyannis port—he brushed over that one, barely looking at Pru... The kind of pictures that successful men hang on their office walls to impress visitors, nothing of consequence, nothing that gave a clue to more than the public side of the man.

Conrad knew as intimately as any man the bitter clandestine struggle behind the public peace-posturing—the ongoing game of nuclear brinkmanship waged by schizophrenic superpowers. Was August Merriman changing the odds...?

Conrad dragged on the Camel and coughed, loosening the cigarette from his lip. He couldn't stop hacking. His vision blurred. Opening a desk drawer, he groped for the silver hip flask he kept stashed there and took a long swallow. The whiskey burned then soothed... his own prescription for earthly salvation. He coughed and drank, coughed and drank.

Wiping his eyes and mouth, he went back to Nora's gift, not studying the pages but letting his eyes pass over them as if they operated by osmosis independent of his mind. Nora had kept herself busy. August Merriman's life and times were catalogued in her neat script as straight and round as she herself was, the kind of hand that was perfectly mated to Crane's pale blue notepaper. As usual she had been thorough, the information broken down into areas—business, political, social, personal, philanthropic, cultural.

A full life lived to the hilt, Conrad thought. He started with the personal, skimming over the pages. There was no mention of the fact that Merriman's wife had ever known another man, although there were several notes about her. "Believed to be a powerful influence on her husband"...

"Always at his side in his globe-trotting"... "Personally directs his philanthropic and cultural activities"... "Childless."
Nothing that surprised Conrad. At nineteen Pru's intelligence had been as fierce as her passions. They'd talked for hours about socialism and capitalism, God and Marx, Darwin and revolution, poverty and the Wealth of Nations, exchanging the intense, brilliant, smokey insights that never came again once one left college. They had burned with idealism and youth, the two interchangeable, believing that greed and fear were not endemic, that man was perfectible and the world well worth saving. If she had remained true to herself, Pru must have matured into a formidable woman. She always set her own rules. Independent, self-confident, arrogant even, she had believed she could do anything. She and August Merriman, he had to admit, make a singular couple. Conrad was beginning to wish that Nora had never come to Little Compton.

He turned to "Philanthropic" and went down the impressive list alphabetically. Tax lawyers dreamed about such a write-off, a foundation, nobly named, being a perfect front. Skipping over the Heart Association, National Cancer Foundation, Radcliffe, the Police Athletic League, Big Brothers and the like, he marked a small X beside others—six in all. He went back to "Personal," curious to find out more about Pru's largesse. Unless she had mellowed considerably with age, he couldn't imagine her allowing another woman's grandchild into her home.

Again Conrad was impressed by Nora's thoroughness.

"As far as I can ascertain," she wrote, "August Merriman committed one indiscretion in his life, in Berlin in 1939..."

CHAPTER
SEVEN

Her name was Lynneth Carrington. They met in the summer, the aristocratic English girl who had attached herself to Hitler's entourage and the brash young American on a secret U.S. mission to persuade the Russians not to sign a pact with Hitler. The liason was Merriman's last impetuous act. Since then he had learned to be cautious in affairs of the heart as well as state. Yet he never regretted Lynneth. Not for any illusion of love—there had been none between them—but because forty years later she left him a legacy. Angelica, his single blind spot and his greatest joy.

Nineteen thirty-nine was a heady time to be in Berlin. The Führer was riding high. Austria and Czechoslovakia had fallen without a shot, their sovereignity trampled under the storm troopers' hob-nailed boots. Soviet Foreign Minister Vyacheslav Molotov was meeting with Joachim von Ribbentrop to discuss a non-aggression pact. And Merriman was there, ostensibly persuading the Nazis to build a state-of-the-art iron refinery to fuel their war machine. He had already sold a similar plant to the Soviets, and Molotov's presence in Berlin, it was felt, would serve as a testament to his good faith and to the soundness of his proposed investment.

Even then Merriman saw himself as an emissary of world peace to convince Molotov that a pact with Hilter was ill-advised. It had the potential for bringing an end to the Western world as it was known, and inextricably drawing the United States into the mix, thereby broadening the stakes if Hitler declared war.

Lynneth Carrington, twenty-four, English-slim and porcelain-skinned, was caught up in the Nazi fervor. Wagner, it seemed, stirred her soul, and Hitler stirred her blood. Compared to the strict, sheltered life of an English boarding school, Berlin had the excitement of a carnival, the thrill of living at the dangerous edge. Handsome young heroes flocked to Hitler's side—Edward, Prince of Wales, and the American flier, Charles Lindbergh. To Lynneth the seeming invincibility of the Nazis was intoxicating. The swastika became her cross, Hitler her messiah. Irony added to the perverse fascination—bred to British understatement, she responded to the Nazis' rhetoric and ostentation.

The Carrington family was sufficiently eccentric to meet the criteria for British aristocracy. Historically, they were either pacifists or anarchists, so at first Lynneth's absorption with the goings-on in Germany was looked on with benign amusement—a family phenomenon in a class with the time Great Uncle Thornby Carrington took off with a troupe of itinerant players.

Churchill had been sounding off from the War Office about the threat of German militarism, but was at first roundly ignored. Winston's bluster, they said. But later, after the first bomb hit London, Lynneth's "flirtation," as it was called, had become a family embarrassment. Letters home were heavily censored by Lady Carrington before she read them aloud to the family at tea. Her growing infatuation with the German leader and his cause was glossed over, making the letters brief, little more than salutation and closing.

"Lynneth always did have extremely large handwriting... like a child's, really," her mother would pronounce, turning over the pages before anyone could question why so little was written on so many sheets of stationery. Privately, Lady

Carrington had begun to worry about her daughter's clearly erotic descriptions of the Nazi Schutzstaffel.

Lynneth's preoccupation with the SS was a way to come closer to her idol. Like a schoolgirl, which she remained in most ways, she fantasized about replacing Eva Braun. At a picnic in the Black Forest, the Führer actually brushed her cheek and asked her to look up his brother in England when she went home. At that moment Lynneth made up her mind never to go home. The ground was a bed of pine needles, and the faces of the uniformed children looked up at Hitler with faith and wonder. He was more than a shepherd with his flock. There was no docility in the faces—he was a hypnotist, a magus, a sorcerer with his experiments.

When August Merriman went to Berlin, Lynneth belonged to the group of hangers-on who followed after the Führer. She had the petal-like complexion of so many English women and a breathless excitement at being close to naked power.

Merriman's mission made him desirable. Although it was secret, Lynneth had her own intelligence-gathering services. Gradually, and without realizing it herself, she had become the whore of the SS, every officer she accepted was another stepping stone bringing her closer to her idol. Each swore he had direct access to the Führer. Hitler had become her obsession. Every compunction, natural or learned, was sublimated to her ultimate goal. She swallowed their lines with their semen.

At first Merriman was surprised to find a young English girl as fresh as Devonshire cream in such a group. Soon after, he was surprised and flattered by her attention. Access to Hitler's inner circle drew her to him, magnetically and pragmatically. Anyone who touched the Führer could touch her. Her excitement was palpable, irresistible. In her fashionable flat they pumped each other, one for information, the other for enjoyment. Uppercrust English women, he had found, were too passionate for their public-school men. Strip off their sturdy walking shoes and tweedy suits, and it was the old story about the book and its cover.

The walls of her flat were covered with Hitlerabilia—framed photographs, posters of the Olympic games with the Führer lighting the torch of freedom, newspaper clippings of rallies and goose-stepping troops. They went to a rally together one night, a sea of military uniforms, the faded gray tunics and spiked helmets of the Imperial Army mingling with the new army's green, the black of the Waffen SS, the sky-blue of the Luftwaffe. A gallery of spotlights illumined the stage where Hitler stood, flanked by young officers erect as statues, bearing the flags of war. An enormous swastika was painted on a curtain behind him.

The throng replied with a single voice, right arms raised in salute: "Heil Hitler!" Lynneth with the rest of them, face flushed, eyes glistening. Merriman felt himself being drawn into the pulse of the crowd, the voice of hope and pride that rang as clearly as the soprano voices of a boys' choir, the pure race, the master race, the pride of Germany . . . the steamy night, the rampant militarism, the ruthless purge of old friends and the new enemies were overlooked in the mesmerizing power of the moment, in the voice compelling them to pledge their loyalty, their blood, their lives.

Lynneth swayed against him in the grip of an excitement both sexual and something more. It was orgiastic, cathartic—the crowd's single voice strengthening with each salute, brooking no dissent, no reservations, the Führer, the Fatherland, first in the minds and hearts of the master race. They were left drained and exhilarated.

When they made love, she was gentle yet ebullient, a mountain spring. The angles of her body were cushioned, he remembered well, circles and ovals as soft and pink as her complexion. He took her with him one night to a dinner the Soviet minister gave in Hitler's honor. Later she was passionate, as if the ardor aroused by being in the sublime presence was too intense to be contained. In the morning

Merriman left Germany and Lynneth without regrets, not suspecting that he had left anything behind except the memory of their brief affair.

Lynneth was a romantic, as would be her granddaughter, a legacy of romance in the genes.... One month after Hitler went to his *Götterdämmerung,* Lynneth killed herself. Erika Heinler, Lynneth's personal maid and only servant, found the body. Merriman remembered the woman, a close-lipped peasant, lines of defense drawn deeply in her face, glints of mistrust coloring her eyes. Beside Lynneth's Dresden delicacy, Erika had looked like a stereotypical bull dyke. He had wondered about that... the mysteries of one woman, any woman. There would be no flights of romantic fancy for Erika.

A few weeks after he quit Germany, while the official Allied envoys were in Moscow presssing their case to Stalin, Ribbentrop flew in, the promise of a slice of Poland in his pocket, and the Hitler-Stalin Non-Aggression Pact became history.

By then Merriman was in Boston, formally requesting Prudence Schaeffer's hand. His first marriage had collapsed after five years. The truth was more mundane than he cared to admit. He'd married Meredith because it was the only way she'd give up her virginity, mistaking the excitement of first sex for something lasting. A divorced man at twenty-five, and why not, get out as soon as the arrangement begins to sour.

When he got home from Russia he filed the papers. Meredith didn't fight the divorce. She hadn't seen him for more than a few months of their married life—Meredith Marie Jenkins, a brunette with fly-away hair and a turned-up nose. Merriman never forgot a face, even an ex-wife's. It was a source of pride with him. Not to mention a professional asset.

CHAPTER
EIGHT

"So much of success is being at the right place at the right time," said August Merriman. The man on one level was like a perpetual bromide, Pointer thought irreverently, seemingly more of a super-salesman than the acute financial wizard, he had once imagined. Looming larger than the rest was his self-importance. Pointer chinned himself up on the parallel bars for the fifteenth time, then gave up.

"And taking advantage," Pointer added, as much to show he was listening as to make a point.

"I prefer to call it seizing the opportunity," Merriman corrected. He was riding at forty miles an hour on a stationary bike in his private gym at Durandana.

The gym had every advantage of an expensive health club —an Olympic swimming pool, sauna and steam room with a Jacuzzi and hot tub, a weight room, indoor track, squash court, and enough Nautilus machines to take care of every portion of the human anatomy that dared to bulge. So much for so few, Pointer couldn't help thinking.

Bicycling on an open road, he'd be puffing to keep up with this eighty-eight-year-old dynamo. His angst level rose steadily as Merriman went on with his pep talk. A lifetime over-achiever. Pointer's reports had always said, "Fails to live up to his potential." Then he hit graduate school and some things, at least, began coming together.

"Anyone can recognize the need of the moment," Merriman was saying. "The skill comes in figuring out a way to answer it that also benefits you, thereby making the need an opportunity. Take my first trip to Russia. All political differences have to be put aside for humanitarian reasons when millions are starving . . . you saw it again in Ethiopia. It was a fine thing to give food, but that wasn't enough. I saw a way to affect a long-term recovery.

"What does a miner, and a very young miner, know about agriculture, you might ask—and Lenin did. 'What do I know about agriculture? Not a damn thing,' I said, 'but I didn't come here to waste your time.' In a few words, because he was a busy man, I outlined my proposal. 'We have no trade agreement with your country,' he said. It was his only argument.

"'You signed with Britain last year, so I'll have a British company,' I answered in a bad imitation of a cockney accent, 'a working bloke's small business.' That was the beginning, and the rest, as they say, is history." Merriman shook his head. "What a man he was. I wish you could have known him, Davey boy."

Pointer cringed. No one except his mother had ever called him Davey, and not even she had called him Davey boy. Merriman didn't notice the reaction, or if he did, chose to ignore it.

"He was stockier than his pictures show, a good three inches shorter then I, with a massive head shaped like the onion domes of the Orthodox churches in Red Square. It was all I could think of when I walked into his office that first time. Lenin was created by an act of the Tsar. If Nicholas had known what he was inventing when he signed the order to execute Alexander Ulianof for revolutionary activity, he would have issued a full pardon. Instead Alexander hanged and his brother Vladimir became Lenin.

"Here was a man I knew I could do business with—a revolutionary committed to the goals of Communism, *but* a pragmatist first. He saw the famine spreading from the peasants of the Volga to the working men in the cities, the backbone of his power. The danger of a second revolution was a persistent worry. Trotsky would never have veered from the single-minded course of pure Communism, but Lenin embraced a capitalist. I believe he liked me personally, but that was incidental. I offered what he needed—a way to feed his people ... Forty miles in sixty minutes." Merriman clicked off the odometer. "Do you think you'll be able to do as well at eighty-eight?"

Pointer laughed. "I'm not at all sure I could keep up with you now, sir."

Merriman beamed, pleased to receive the answer he deserved. "I'm going to relax in the sauna now. Never give the muscles a chance to start aching—that's the secret."

He leaned close, as if he was going to confide another vital secret, and Pointer smelled the sweat already beginning to stale, the familiar odor of a universal locker room. It always smelled like old corn to him. The only worse odor was the aroma of talcum powder and perspiration—powdered feet or genitals damp with sweat, powdered balls of one kind or another, powder balls, and old August Merriman was having himself a ball between the workout he was getting and the workout he was giving.

"I think I'll go for a swim." Pointer excused himself. It was the one sport in which he had ever excelled.

"Meet me after you swim then."

"Yes, sir." Pointer felt like saluting but checked the urge and turned instead, pushing through the glass doors that led to the pool. A private health club, membership limited to one. Guests accepted. He couldn't picture Prudence using the gym in spite of her slender figure. Angelica, maybe, although she'd never mentioned it, and the staff—definitely not.

Stripping off his sweat suit, he dove in, swimming furiously for the first few minutes, then easing into laps, one after the other, steady, tireless, never more relaxed than when he was swimming, thinking of Angelica, floating over her, under her. One day, they'd swim together in Maine, if he didn't wake up from the dream of her too soon. Summers in Maine at his grandmother's house, his now... they were his fondest memories. He wondered if Angelica was a good swimmer, not that it mattered. It was impossible to imagine her being awkward at anything... ever. She must be waiting for him, wondering why he was taking so long with her grandfather. On second thought, she probably knew the old man well enough, knew how long he spent in the gym working out the few days in a month that he was home to enjoy it.

"So much for so little a man." The thought kept coming back to Pointer, and with it, the certainty that there was something about August Merriman he must be missing. Some depth. Some rare power. Merriman said it about himself with the most accuracy—he made things happen. That was his gift. He believed he could make things happen, and he did... One man could make a difference...

All Merriman bromides. Pointer was collecting them, like rings around the collar. He tried to check his irreverent impulses. After all, he had much to be grateful for. Merriman's generosity had paid for MIT and Livermore. An ASF scientist on loan to the government. It was a way to get around the Congressional cuts in the research and development budget. All the government money could go for defense research, with the scientists compensated privately. It was a way to increase the budget without openly flaunting Congress. That's how Pointer looked at it, and he didn't much worry about who footed the bill so long as he could continue his work without anyone looking over his shoulder.

Lifting himself out of the water, he took a towel from the warming rack that ran the width of the pool, dried himself, then wrapped it around his waist, hoping that he wouldn't find Merriman stark naked in the sauna. The only truly old body he'd ever seen was his grandfather's. He always slept naked in the twin bed in David's room when he came to visit. Pointer had been eight when his grandfather died, but the memory lived on, the skinny white legs, the flesh hanging in wrinkles. He'd dreaded the visits, dreaded the nights, dreaded the early mornings most of all when the old man would push back the blankets and dangle his legs over the side of the bed while he felt on the table between them for his glasses and his teeth.

Pointer never wanted to see another old man in his shriveled glory, or become one himself, he thought, tightening the towel around his waist as he padded into the sauna. In the first minute the heat always got to him, so that he felt lightheaded, uncertain.

Merriman was lying on a stone slab of a bench as if it were an embalming table—flat on his back, eyes closed, arms folded across his chest. For a moment Pointer thought he was dead, until a bromide reassured him.

"Pouring oil on troubled waters . . . that's what I've tried to do all my life." Only his lips stirred.

"A noble ambition, sir," Pointer murmured respectfully, sitting on a nearby slab and continuing to stare at Merriman's nakedness. No visions of his grandfather were conjured by the sight. If age had wreaked its expected havoc on August Merriman's body, it would take a team of barbers to discover it, because he might as well have been wearing a hair shirt . . . or suit. From his shoulders to his ankles was matted with thick white hair as curly as a sheep's, and when he sat up, Pointer was sure the back would be just as thickly covered.

The sight was stunning—a wolf in sheep's clothing. Beside him, Pointer felt as if he'd been waxed. He wanted to laugh out loud, not because he'd never seen a hairy man before, but because of the picture that sprang to mind—Prudence, elegant, impeccable Prudence—married to a three-ply wall-to-wall carpet, putting out for a man with more hair on one shoulder than Pointer had on his entire body. What a shock it must have been the first time he took her to bed.

"That's why I'm so damned interested in this Star Wars project you're working on." Merriman's lips were moving again. "Do you know what I'm saying, Davey boy. If it really has the potential for eliminating nuclear war, if there's even a chance it could do that, then, by God, I should be pouring every dollar I've got into your program. But I'm the kind of man who likes to know what he's paying for. These vague descriptions you get in official reports aren't enough for me. That's why the Colonel told me to talk to you. 'Nobody can give you a fuller picture of what's going on out here than David Pointer, our best scientist.' That's what he said."

"Well, Colonel Hancock did say I should brief you on SDI?" Pointer couldn't altogether disguise his surprise at that. Everything at Livermore was top security. The scientists there were an elite clique. They lived and breathed their research. It wasn't work—it was challenge, discovery, passion. They could only talk about it to each other, which was why such a tight camaraderie, an almost fraternal bond, had developed among them.

Merriman looked over at Pointer. "Remember who you're dealing with, David. I presume you know I *am* the American Science Foundation. I am also the fella who put you through undergraduate and graduate schools, six years at MIT, and I pay the annual stipend so you can continue your research at Livermore. I put you where you are—and I can put you out. A strong word from me and you won't get past the barbed wire fences again. And don't expect Angelica to be waiting for you, either. She's my granddaughter first . . . You're afraid you can't open up with me because you're dealing with top security stuff—is that it? What do you think I am, some ham-and-egger? I had top security clearance when you were in diapers . . . when your mother was in diapers, more than likely. And if you don't believe me, when we go back to the house I'll call the big cheese himself in D.C. and you can get it direct."

The heat in the sauna seemed to be affecting Pointer's vision in a strange way . . . he was picturing himself on a direct line with the President, checking on his benefactor. "You'd telephone to—"

"That's right. The fella in the Oval Office, although he said he was leaving for Camp David at three o'clock, so we'll have to call him there."

Pointer visualized the photographs on Merriman's desk in the library beneath the Monet landscape—Merriman in the Rose Garden between the President and the First Lady, the three of them holding hands like actors taking a curtain call, and an autographed one of Merriman and the President at his ranch: "To a great American from an admiring kid." On top of a bookcase beside the desk there were others, with every President since FDR.

Pointer quickly reviewed everything he knew about August Merriman and all the security precautions that had been drummed into his brain until they were as much a part of it as the neurons and synapses . . . and had to conclude none of it was really applicable in this case . . . "That won't be necessary, sir."

Once Pointer did get started he talked eagerly, out of a deep-seated passion for his work . . . "What I'm working on is a third-generation nuclear weapon, much more sophisticated and exact than either the A-bomb or the H-bomb. Both of them are unfocused. They just explode, letting their destructive energy fly in every direction. My nuclear-pumped X-ray laser pinpoints its explosive power at predetermined targets. Imagine a cylindrical device encased in steel rods. At the head of it is a telescope that tracks distant targets and feeds the information to the weapon's computer. At its core is a hydrogen bomb. The computer aims at a target and the bomb detonates, sending out radiation that hits the lasing wires, causing them to emit lethal bursts of X-rays. The beams can fire across space at the speed of light to destroy on-coming missiles.

"Unlike regular light, laser light-waves have the same frequency and direction—they're in perfect synchronization. I'm developing a laser with the shortest possible wavelength, one angstrom—that's about four-billionths of an inch. The shorter the wavelength, the more energy it packs..."

After the first few minutes the technical going got too steep for Merriman. Never mind, he didn't have to understand, every word was being recorded. By the time Pointer was finished Merriman was nodding off and Angelica was waiting impatiently.

"I'm afraid I bored you."

"... Not at all, Davey boy. Fascinating stuff, every word of it. You just about have me convinced to increase my support. I want to hear more, though—next time you visit Angelica."

*   *   *   *

Angelica filled his mind, pervaded his senses. He breathed her, tasted her perfume and sweat, the one made sweeter by the other. A weekend in New York with Angelica. They stayed at the Ritz-Carlton on Central Park South as Merriman's guests. It was small, everything understated except the price, and discreet, but it lacked, he thought, the old world grace of the original Ritz in Boston with its immaculate service and extra-dry martinis.

They walked up Central Park West to the Museum of Natural History. He wanted her to see the celestial show at the Hayden Planetarium, one of his strongest boyhood memories. The resonant voice that had frightened him years before seemed funny now, melodramatic, and the darkness was so complete, the blackness tempting him to take liberties like a kid in the back seat of a movie theater. Only the heavens held the same majesty.

Angelica was as heavenly as any body in the universe, and he was in her orbit. They ducked out when the show was half over and headed uptown, walking in the warm afternoon along Columbus with its jumble of new restaurants, cafes, one indistinguishable from the next, glass and whiteness, with boutiques in between, then west to the slice of park that hugged the river, "Arm in arm over meadow and farm, walking my baby back home." His mother used to sing the song to him, and probably her mother, and he hummed it to Angelica because he couldn't remember the "meadow and farm" part. His first weekend in New York with Angelica. The Big Apple never tasted so sweet.

In Riverside Park she leaned against the iron railing, watching the river and the children—babies in strollers, kids on skateboards, bikes, hula hoops, old men nodding in the sun. A pocket of tranquility in the chaos of Manhattan. A ghetto blaster was playing Madonna's "Who's that girl? Say a prayer and kiss your heart goodbye." Hello. He kissed her neck, on the side below her ear where he knew it tickled.

That night they went to the Bolshoi Ballet at Lincoln Center, box seats courtesy of Mr. Merriman, who with Prudence met them for dinner first at the Jockey Club.

"You know why you can sit in Lincoln Center and watch the greatest dance company in the world? You know who you have to thank for that privilege?" Merriman jabbed his shirtfront. "Yours truly."

Pointer had already thanked him for the tickets, but he decided it was better to sound redundant than ungrateful.

"I'm not talking about the damn tickets." Merriman brushed the air with the back of his hand as though he was brushing away Pointer, his thanks and his pair of reserved box seats. "I'm talking about the ballet . . . the Bolshoi. Remeber, Prudence? 1956."

"Prokofiev's *Romeo and Juliet*. The incomparable Galina Ulanova danced Juliet, and in my opinion no one has surpassed her."

Prudence nodded, smiled in the soft light. Even as a girl she had never been a knockout like Angelica. Her figure was boyish and slim, her features too uneven to be classic. But she had style and class, a glorious smile that transcended physical beauty, and a belief that she could do anything she put her mind to. Time had deepened her faith, and her husband's admiration. Where other women had faded with the years, she had grown more elegant and interesting. She could elevate a man with a smile, cut him down with a glance. He loved her the way he loved himself, and never asked if she reciprocated. He had no complaints.

He slapped the table. "Damn right. Ulanova did more to thaw the Cold War that night than a dozen summit meetings."

"We had seen her dance it in Moscow. It was a confusing time over there—disruptive. Transition periods always are," Prudence sounded as if she were commenting on a family problem instead of history.

"Stalin had died in '53, and Khrushchev was struggling for power," Merriman cut in. "During the intermission I said to Prudence, 'If America and Europe could see this, they'd look at the Soviet Union in a new way . . . the way you and I know it.'" He looked at his wife as though he was reliving that moment. "Do you remember what you said? 'If any man in the world can do it, it's August Merriman.' And the rest, as they say, is history." He was smiling at his wife, basking in self-satisfaction. Prudence was always at his side no matter how many miles he logged, how many deals he implemented. If her body was barren, her mind was fertile. Many of his most lauded ideas were hers—the International Forum for World Peace, the American Science Foundation . . . "Prudence is the only partner I've ever had . . . or ever wanted, Davey boy."

After the ballet, a hansom cab brought Angelica and David back to the Ritz through Central Park, each detail so sharply delineated—the clop-clop of the horse's hooves, the summer lushness of the park, every leaf, every blade the deepest green, the slice of new moon, and Angelica's profile in the dusk.

They held each other without the need for words, only their bodies talking. And he thought of the movie *Beau James*, His Honor, the Mayor of New York, James J. Walker, that fancy talker, in a hansom cab in December.

"Will you love me in December as you do in May?" he asked her, laughing because it was July and they hadn't even met in May.

CHAPTER
NINE

Nora checked her handbag for money, keys and ticket—round-trip TWA to Berlin, a fourteen-day excursion fare, Dulles to Tempelhof. She had obtained the required permission to go on vacation and filled out the necessary paperwork at the Agency, although she knew she wouldn't be missed. She had accumulated months of vacation time through the years, and nobody cared now when she took it.

With a final glance around to make sure nothing was forgotten, she picked up her suitcase and let herself out. Traveling gave her a kick, better than drugs or sex, she decided. It wasn't a moral stand, it was a personal choice. She hated the prospect of losing herself—not to be in full control of her thoughts and behavior. She shuddered at the mere prospect.

Nora had paid a price for her choice in a certain loneliness that might finally have drowned her, if it weren't for the fulfillment she derived from her job. And now Matthias Conrad—her mentor, one of her oldest and dearest friends, a man she had so admired, had risked her life to satisfy on more than one occasion, a man she might even have loved, platonically, of course—knowing all that, seemed to be taking advantage of her, damn near blackmailing her. From now on, Nora decided, she was on her own. Of course she would bypass the Agency's Berlin office. No point in raising an alarm. At least not yet. She had no intention of simply turn-

ing over everything she'd found to Matthias, then going back
to business as usual. She had her own sources, and she was
itching to find out more about Angelica Merriman.

Although the Dean didn't give much away, something
about the girl had clearly aroused his curiosity. Nora was
determined to find out all she could about August Merriman's illegitimate grandchild. Berlin, where it had all begun,
was the place to start her search.

*   *   *   *

"Matthias, what are you doing here?" Charlotte Conrad
was obviously on her way out—and just as obviously none
too happy to see her husband.

"I thought I lived here." He pushed past her to shuffle to
the kitchen and rummage through the refrigerator for a beer,
knowing that Charlotte liked to down a cold one at least as
much as he did. She followed, protesting every step.

"You live in Little Compton, and I live here."

"I didn't want you to be lonely, dear. Anyway, Beth and
Tom are there."

Lady bounded in at the sound of his voice. She was the
only thing they'd fought about when he moved to Little
Compton permanently. A fifteen-year-old Irish setter, half-
blind and semi-crippled. She jumped on him, thumping the
floor with her tail. Conrad leaned over so that she could lick
his face. "At least someone's glad to see me."

Charlotte didn't answer. "It's disgusting, letting her kiss
you like that. It makes me sick."

"Jealous."

"Don't be ridiculous. Now, I want to know why you're
really here." Charlotte stood her ground as best she could.
She was a full eight inches shorter than her husband and had
the face of an aging schoolgirl, a nomenclature more apt than
teenager because she belonged to a time before teenagers,
when little girls grew up to be young ladies.

"If you must know, I came to woo another woman. Nora

Hewitt." He wheezed again. The beer was icy in his throat.

"I hardly think Nora requires any wooing. She's been in love with you for years... Each to his own." Charlotte heaved from below her diagphram, a response she'd perfected to indicate that she was a long-suffering wife, no longer interested in the conversation, or simply pretty well fed up with everything pertaining to her husband. "I have a luncheon date, then my bridge club. Will you still be here when I get back?"

"Does it matter?"

"Certainly. It matters if you intend to disrupt my life for one hour or for twenty-four."

"I'll try not to overstay my welcome." Conrad turned away, beer can in hand, and started toward the bedroom, Lady dogging his heels. He might as well have taken a hotel room. He had no feel for the place, his home of twenty-six years, a modern, ranch-style house on a half-acre in suburban Alexandria, Virginia. It could have been anywhere, belonged to anyone—except for the photographs on the dresser of Beth in a wicker stroller, Beth in a prom dress, Beth on her first two-wheeler, Beth in fishing boots with her father holding up her first catch. He didn't remember so many pictures on the bureau when he'd retired and moved permanently to Little Compton. Maybe Charlotte was lonely, too.

They had never really been a family. Mostly three people sparring, stockpiling grudges, an arsenal of petty grievances to let fly at almost any provocation. If there had been other children, it might have been different. But Beth had always been difficult. Charlotte had been afraid, and he had been preoccupied, wedded to his work. He supposed he had never given Beth a chance, or perhaps Charlotte for that matter. The beer can was empty, and he crushed it in a fist.

As it turned out, Conrad was too late to woo Nora. His flight from Logan was taxiing to the terminal at Dulles at precisely the moment that TWA Flight 625 to Berlin was receiving passengers.

Once he learned she wasn't in her office, it took a single phone call to find out that she was on vacation, her destination and expected date of return. Nora was not the only friend he had left at the Agency, old purges notwithstanding. There were many intelligence officers as dissatisfied as he with the constrictions they worked under now. And they were not limited to Langley.

Virtually every strategic goverment agency was infiltrated by military officers and advisers who had lost faith in the country's ability to conduct effective covert intelligence operations. There were too many leaks, too many oversight committees. In his retirement Conrad had become something of a rallying point for them, a quasi CIA-in-exile—the head of an unofficial, extra-legal intelligence service that provided the Israeli Mossad and British MI5 a network of information sources in the Pentagon, NSC, State and Defense Departments, military research and even Congress.

Nora was not one of these. Her loyalty to the Agency, right or wrong, was like her loyalty to her alma mater—firmly entrenched in her heart. While she regretted the changes in both institutions, in her judgment the obverse of loyalty was intolerable.

Conrad could keep tabs on her through his friends in MI5 and use the time she was away to research the foundations he had marked on the list of Merriman's philanthropies. Charlotte would be unhappy to learn that he was staying in town for thirteen additional days, but Lady, at least, would be glad of his company.

CHAPTER
TEN

Every memorable city has its unique observation post. In Rome it is the Via Veneto. In Paris, the Champs Elysees on the Right Bank, Boulevarde St. Germain on the Left. In Berlin it is the "Ku-damn," Kurfurstendamn, the most fashionable and busiest avenue in town. To sit on its sidelines enjoying dinner at one of its lively restaurants is to watch the Berlin world rush by—prosperous businessmen, youths decked out in metal and leather, frauleins window-shopping arm-in-arm. Quite a change from the ravaged city Nora remembered, and now she was going to dredge up a part of that bitter history. Why, though, would any German welcome her? And yet Peter Braun was genuinely glad to see her—at least for the time being.

By any standards, Braun was a charmer. Basic for a double-agent. Handsome, slightly arrogant, and very clever, he moved through his complex life with the grace of a born aristocrat. It was the perfect camouflage. He had an illustrious genealogy, the right connections, educated at Heidelberg and the London School of Economics. The Student Prince with a serious underside. A lawyer ostensibly working to reunite German families, he crossed from one sector of the city to the other unquestioned.

Nora had met him a dozen years before when both were serving their respective agencies at NATO headquarters.

They had shared information when it served their mutual interest and discovered a common fondness for Handel's *Water Music*. During the two years that their work in Brussels overlapped they were as close as it is possible for foreign agents to be. Now Peter Braun coordinated all of the Landswehr's operations in Central Europe.

"An impressive achievement." Nora was saying to him. They were sitting at a sidewalk table at the Drei Baren in the heart of the Ku-damn over bowls of Halberstadter Kasesuppe, the rich cheese soup, and ice-cold bottles of Doktor. "To old friends."

Braun clinked his beer against hers. "To what do I owe the honor of your visit—business or pleasure? Knowing you, there can only be one answer."

"Actually I'm on vacation, and staying at the Astoria."

"On Fasanenstrasse near the zoo?"

She smiled. There wasn't a detail of the city that Peter didn't know, which made him quite invaluable. "It's good value, an excellent location and quiet enough for an old lady like me."

"You'll never be old, Nora." He reached across the table and pressed her hand as if it were smooth and white instead of a roadway of thickened veins and brown spots. Nora actually felt a flutter of excitement. Foolish, she reprimanded herself. Still, it was almost abnormal not to be attracted to Peter. Neither sex was immune, although she had long suspected that for all the stunning women he escorted to Berlin's social functions, his personal preference was homosexual. He was not conspicuously effeminate, but maybe it was his grace that occasionally gave her pause, or the fact that he seemed subtly yet continually conscious of his body as a desirable object, much the way beautiful women were.

"Gallantly put, Peter," she said. "but eternal youth has always struck me as a singularly unappealing notion. Can you imagine seeing the world in absolutes for an entire lifetime?"

He smiled and sipped the soup. She was a more interest-

ing companion than any of the young agents who had replaced her. "It would be one way to eliminate our
profession."

"How true." Life in the gray zones, Nora thought, where
good is never as pure as Ivory, bad is never Bible-black, and
right and wrong can always be qualified. "But it's your profession now, not 'ours.' I'm semi-retired—technically still at
the Agency but out to pasture for all practical purposes."

"Allowed to graze undisturbed."

"Well put." She laughed. "When the Dean was forced out
I became so much old baggage."

"But Matthias Conrad is far from retired." Braun was eye-
ing her closely now, sifting her answers in his mind.

"Then you have other sources than I. To the best of my
knowledge he's content to putter, and the Agency is busy
trying to bury just about every trace of him."

Braun wasn't prepared to dispute her, because it didn't
really matter if she was lying or truly in the dark. "There are
other services."

"That devil," Nora burst out with uncharacteristic passion
—she *had* gotten old, Braun thought—"you mean Matthias
is in contact with the Mossad, MI5, your Landswehr."

Braun carefully wiped the corners of his mouth. "Let's just
say he keeps a hand in."

"Then you've been expecting me." She should have known
the Dean would at least be keeping pace if not ahead of her
every step.

"Why do you say that?"

The moment he asked, Nora realized her mistake. She had
set herself up, blown, in effect, her own cover. Sitting at a
desk all day shuffling computer printouts had made her
rusty—or was it her age? She was spared from answering
because the waiter had begun to clear the soup bowls. He
served them both Rostbratli, the hearty pot roast that looked
tender and smelled aromatic. Nora tasted it and signalled her
approval with a satisfied sound.

Braun refilled her glass with Doktor. He had turned silver at the temples since she had last seen him, which accentuated his perennial tan. Beside him Nora looked as though she had spent six months in a hothouse. Not far off the mark, because that's what Langley had become. "It would be good to be working again," she said, hoping to recoup her losses. "I miss it." An honest enough sentiment. It was always wise, she knew, to base a lie on truth, give it the ring of authenticity. "Now I work for machines all day, feeding data to computers and waiting for them to spit back my orders."

"Not as lively as working for the Dean."

Peter wasn't convinced, Nora could see. She'd have to give him more, something tangible to make him believe.

"The youngsters there like to listen to my stories about the way things used to be back in my day." She sighed. "I must sound like I'm reciting *The Waverly Novels* to them. There's one particular young man, Rick Thomas..." She smiled fondly. "There are others, too, of course, but Rick is always begging for a story."

A name would be easy for Peter to check, and then he would find that every word was true as far as it went. Her new job was minimal security. If she was on a mission, her job description would be of no value. And just as surely, if she were, she would never give up the name of a colleague.

Braun finished his wine and graced her with his warmest smile. "Enough shop talk for one night, Nora. I thought you were here on vacation."

"You're so right," Nora laughed with relief. "But you know me. I can't get out of the habit of digging. So I'm going to use my time here researching a genealogy for some old friends. They're interested in an English woman who lived here during the war, a distant cousin, I think. She may even have died here. They lost track somewhere along the line."

"What did you say her name was?"

Nora hadn't said, and they both knew it. But if she wanted his help she would have to give that much.

"You forgot already?" She laughed again. "Lynneth Carrington."

After dinner they strolled up the avenue, looking in the fashionable shop windows. Although the evening had grown threatening, they walked all the way to the Tier Garten. It was impossible to pass through the vast park in the heart of Berlin without looking back. The trees were plentiful, but young. They should have been old and imposing, their branches forming a thick canopy overhead. But the winter of '45-'46 was Berlin's bitterest. The bitterness of defeat froze the soul and the bitterness of the weather threatened to have a similar effect on the body. To survive those cruel months, Berliners chopped down the old trees for fuel.

"You're unusually quiet," Braun said.

"Sorry. I guess I was, as they say, lost in old thoughts... memories really. The tranquility here feels, I don't know, unnatural almost to someone as old as I am."

"It's not a question of age. The very soil under our feet is soaked with blood. To walk along these paths is to relive a child's terror—the sounds and smell and fears of war." Peter's voice was so soft Nora had to strain to catch each word. "The guns are silenced, the treaties signed, the debris is cleared away. New cities rise, new governments. But for those who lived through it the war doesn't end. It's the measure for the rest of our lives. For everything we do."

*   *   *   *

Berlin was fixed in Nora's mind as a wet gray city, because that was the way it had impressed her when she first saw it in 1948—bombed-out, bone-chilling, short of everything, especially hope. The weather forty years later did nothing to dislodge that picture. It rained continuously from the moment she got up. The drumming on the windows was incessant, background music to her search, and she found herself humming as she worked, fragments of Handel, brought to mind from seeing Peter again perhaps.

Nora wouldn't have been surprised if he knew all about the Carrington woman. She had been something of a phenomenon, at the least a curiosity piece in Nazi Germany and certainly an oddity in her own country—traitor being too harsh a term for the naïvete she'd displayed in her unfortunate, deluded life. If Lynneth Carrington rang a bell in Peter's mind though, he hadn't shown it except by the faintest flicker in his eye, which could just as easily have been a trick of light or of her imagination.

While Nora combed through the yellowed files, Peter Braun remained closeted in his office mulling over her interest in Lynneth Carrington. Of course he knew nothing would come of it. It was a dead end, literally and figuratively, which was why he allowed her to pursue it. Nonetheless, he couldn't quash a certain apprehension. Premature, he'd be the first to admit, but he'd been in the business of espionage a long time. He understood the rules, and how life had a perverse way of ignoring them.

Nora stuck to her search until the records office closed for the day and told the clerk she would be returning in the morning. With her archaeologist's mind it was only a matter of time before she unearthed whatever records existed on the offspring, legitimate or otherwise, of Lynneth Carrington.

The next day Nora got her first reward—a brittle but perfectly legible birth certificate. More than forty years after Germany's defeat and Hitler's *Götterdämmerung*, it seemed as if Berlin had few secrets. Lynneth Carrington had given birth to an illegitimate daughter in Berlin. August 17, 1940. Name: Klara. Probably out of reverence for her true love, Nora thought. The Führer's mother had been Klara, too. On the line marked father the name August Merriman was there. Citizenship: U.S.A. Lynneth Carrington's death certificate was there too, dated June 22, 1945. Nora's German was sufficient to read the certificate: cause of death, suicide by poison.

Walking through the soggy streets, through a rain too chill for August, she tried to imagine the girl Lynneth had been —a foreigner alone in the eye of a ruinous war, carrying a child out of wedlock, a child she must have believed was August Merriman's to have given his name for the birth certificate. Or had she been prescient and concerned with protecting her baby's future? A few years later the pillar of her fanatic faith crumbled. Klara would have been five at the time of her mother's death. In war-ravaged Berlin clearly no attempt had been made to contact the presumed father. What would have happened to the child, Nora wondered, deprived of family yet heir to a comfortable inheritance. A little girl with what must have seemed a fortune by postwar German standards. Someone would have taken her in—if not out of kindness, then certainly out of greed.

The next morning Nora approached the records clerk boldly and asked if adoption records were available to the public. It was a long shot, but worth a try.

"Nein," he answered, and even that was spoken grudgingly.

"Then I would like to be directed to the marriage licenses, please."

The clerk was a formidable old man with unforgiving eyes and a cruel mouth. Where had he been through the war— on the side of the Nazis? Nora found herself trying to see behind the bland faces of modern Germany. Allegiances were rarely revealed, the past too often glossed over. But the blond, bright-eyed children of Hitler's Youth were the middle-aged businessmen and bureaucrats running the country today. They had come of age in business, politics, law, science, medicine, technology, shaped by that primary and passionate allegiance. None, though, stepped forward to tell the world how he or she had spent the formative years, and yet such a powerful experience must have left its mark. The child is father of the man... but not in Deutschland, she thought. The country was an enigma to her, as much in the present as it had been forty years earlier.

The clerk was pointing a long finger down a hallway. She read the impatience through his thick rimless lenses. Meddlesome foreigners had no business wool-gathering. With her most insincere smile, she followed the finger. Locating a marriage license—even if one existed—for Klara Carrington without any date of marriage or even evidence that a wedding had occurred would be like looking for the proverbial needle in the haystack. Nora wasn't kidding herself that it would be easy, especially given the distinct possibility that the girl had been adopted and given a different name. But Nora's confidence in her ability to ferret out the least scrap of information was undaunted.

When the office opened in the morning she was waiting on the steps. When it closed in the afternoon she left with the clerks. By the fifth day her confidence was dimming, as was her legendary patience. At midday when she took a lunch break, she was bracing herself to accept defeat.

The government buildings are clustered around the Rathaus in the Schoneberg district, the southern sector of the city. Nora bought a Bockwurst from a sidewalk vendor and sat on a bench. The Freiheitsglocke, the Berliner's liberty bell, was ringing out its noon gong. She was the only one taking lunch outside that day. The persistent drizzle had sent the government workers ducking into restaurants or kept them at their desks. Sitting alone, disregarding the dampness that was frizzling the ends of her hair, she decided to give herself the rest of the day. One more afternoon before abandoning the search for Klara Carrington.

As it turned out, Nora only required a fraction of that time to turn up a marriage certificate issued to Klara Carrington of Berlin and Martin Klebehoff of Mollenz. The date seemed to fit: March 14, 1960. By the end of the day, Nora was back where she had begun, combing through birth certificates.

But if the Klebehoffs had any children, they were not registered in Berlin. It seemed as if she had reached another dead end, but Nora was too thorough an investigator to stop there.

Peter Braun took Nora's phone call with a sense of foreboding. The very qualities he admired most were pushing her into a no-man's land. If only there was some other way . . . But he was trapped.

Interestingly, the British had also asked for his help in keeping tabs on Nora, and when he had vacillated they said, "Humor the old girl, she's harmless now."

Braun had no doubt where *that* originated. Retirement notwithstanding, the Dean, was still pulling some important strings. The security services of Western Europe and Israel were nervous about the new, everything-up-front mentality of the CIA. They did not want to read about their covert operations on the front page of the Washington *Post*. There was one American, though, that they knew would keep their secrets. Matthias Conrad was outside the mainstream of the American government, but his connections were as powerful as his sympathies. Nora had been one of his agents, and now she wanted to get into East Germany. . .

"Why don't you forget your hunt and come to the country with me," he said casually.

"You know me better than that. I'm like an old hound. Once I get on a track I can't give it up—even if it's only a genealogical trail for a friend." She added her cover faithfully, knowing Peter recognized the lie. It was part of the game. Agents never revealed their missions to each other, unless their respective governments were working in tandem—and even then, there was a certain reticence. But Peter would help when she needed him, she was sure. There were certain unwritten rules among agents, and that was the first of them.

There was an uncomfortably long pause. "I wish you'd reconsider," Braun finally said.

"I honestly think you're worried about me."

"You've been a friend." His voice was very quiet. "I wouldn't want to see anything happen to you."

She laughed, a little too sharply. It wasn't like Peter to be a nervous Nelly. "I'm only going as a tourist. My professional days are behind me."

"Where precisely do you want to go?"

"Mollenz."

"And you'll be traveling—"

"By car."

"The necessary permits and registrations will be at your hotel in the morning." Braun's tone became as detached as a stranger's. The consummate professional. There was no room for personal feelings.

However many masters he might have, he was a German first, and the war was still a blanket of shame over the nation. Only many generations of peace and national pride would finally lift it. But a third war was a persistent threat. Germans lived each day in a divided country, with the knowledge that nuclear weapons were poised on their doorstep, trained on their homes. The threat came from the East, and the only way to neutralize it was to cooperate fully with both sides.

CHAPTER
ELEVEN

On his seventh day in Washington Matthias Conrad caught the ten o'clock shuttle to New York and took a cab from the airport to an address on East Seventy-Sixth Street between Park and Madison Avenues, a five-story Italianate townhouse of white granite with filigree at the lower windows and a deep bay that bowed above the front door. A brass marker above the bell gave the name American Science Foundation.

The American Science Foundation was fourth on his list of foundations financed by August Merriman. He had already investigated the Inter-American Association for Public Interest, a left-leaning, so the pundits said, think tank located in Washington; the International Committee on the Arts, which arranged cultural exchanges between nations with a record of exporting eastern bloc talent; and the Humanitarian Relief Fund, which acted like an independent Red Cross or Catholic Relief, providing medical supplies, food and clothing to disaster victims. He couldn't take issue with the causes espoused (noble one and all), and his initial investigations of these had not made him curious to probe deeper.

Now a supercilious young man in a fawn-colored suit and four-in-hand silk foulard tie, polished and creased in all the proper places, ushered him into a formal sitting room, glancing at his watch. Conrad's appointment with the director was

11:45, and the time was just 11:41. It was one of those sweltering New York days when every breath of air seems to have been sucked out of town. Conrad had been lucky to get an air-conditioned cab. Still, in the space of time—not more than a few seconds—it took to get from the curb into the house, he had wilted so that he felt, if he didn't precisely look, like the last rose of summer. Wiping the sweat from his face and neck with a hankerchief, he followed the young man.

Inside was blessedly cool, like stepping from a grimy steambath into the cool, hushed tranquility of a mountain lake. Nothing moved. The Foundation retained the aura of the posh private residence it had once been, carved paneling imported from France, crystal chandeliers, furniture made for admiration rather than comfort. The long windows were hung with damask drapes held back by braided cords. Arrangements of fresh flowers failed to give the place a lived-in feeling, or even a feeling that work was accomplished there. The atmosphere was like a museum, the offices relegated to the upper floors, he presumed, most likely the former servants' quarters. The only vestige of science in evidence was a miniature solar system encased in a glass globe on the front hall table, each planet exactly proportioned and positioned in relation to the others. When turned on, the whole system revolved in perfect synchronization.

Conrad sat down on a stiff sofa and lit a cigarette, depositing the match in the arrangement of anemones, snapdragons and roses because there were no ashtrays in sight. He was just flicking his ashes into his pocket when the director came in.

Paul Bayard was facing sixty, and fit. He entered the room as if propelled by a gust of wind—clearly a very busy man, important, too, and impressive. About five feet eleven, as perfectly tailored as his assistant, with a boyish shock of white hair, a freckled forehead permanently furrowed due to the weightiness of the decisions he was called upon to make, glasses framed in goldtone and behind them, winter eyes so pale the color seemed bleached out.

The director sounded like a handbook written to promulgate the foundation. "The American Science Foundation, or ASF as we like to call it, was created after the launch of Sputnik I to encourage American technology. Its aim, if it can be put succinctly, is U.S.-Soviet parity. It was founded and funded by a most remarkable man, August Merriman, the great entrepreneur and tireless ambassador-without-portfolio. It's truly astounding." Bayard shook his head to emphasize his amazement. "Think of it, the man is eighty-eight, and he hasn't slowed down a bit. I don't know how he does it."

Conrad shook his head, too, willing to agree as long as it suited his purpose.

"Now where was I?" The director frowned.

"You were talking about the Foundation... American-Soviet parity," Conrad repeated like a prompter giving an actor's cue.

"Oh, yes." Bayard's smile was so thin it barely disturbed his facial muscles. "Actually the ASF was Prudence Merriman's concept, enthusiastically endorsed by her husband, I should add. Mrs. Merriman is chairman of our board of directors—a wonderful woman, highly intelligent and very committed."

"To what?"

"Why to the Foundation... and her husband... to scientific discovery, to the future. She takes a personal interest in the details of our work."

"Which is?"

"That's what I've been explaining to you, Mr. Conrad." Bayard's annoyance was beginning to show around the edges.

"I was hoping you could be a little more specific." Conrad was trying to keep on his best behavior. "What exactly does

the Foundation do? What institutions or individuals are re-
cipients of its generosity?"

"You might say our work has two arms, the humanitarian
and the purely scientific, although our primary interest is
research. In the humanitarian arena, we support experimental programs at hospitals and medical centers throughout the
world. On the scientific side, we provide direct grants to the
most promising young scientists so they can pursue their ed-
ucation and research without financial worries. There are no
strings attached, no repayment of any kind."

The director had the accent of a certain New Yorker, the
ethnic origin removed but the borough distinctly Manhattan,
slightly nasal, exuberant, educated, as unmistakable in its
own way as a Brooklyn longshoreman or Queens housewife.

"Are you a scientist, Mr. Bayard?"

Bayard laughed easily, a man skilled in the art of imparting
confidence. "The only science course I ever took was The
Fundamentals of Basic Scientific Concepts, an undergraduate requirement, and I grazed by with a C minus. I'm an
administrator, Mr. Conrad, but we have an estimable team of
scouts, not unlike a ball club's, to look over the new crop
each year, always with an eye out for a young Einstein. Just
between the two of us, I believe we may have found one—a
brilliant young scientist working on an ASF grant in the
space-defense program at Livermore." Bayard was getting
up. "Unless you have any other questions..." His time was
carefully apportioned.

Although the thought of being fried on a New York sidewalk held no appeal, Conrad forced himself to face the mer-
cury. Once outside he walked the half block to Madison, then
took a cab back to Kennedy and changed his return flight
from D.C. to San Francisco.

The Lawrence Livermore National Laboratory was forty-
five miles east of the Golden Gate. Once again it seemed
the U.S. was poised at a pivotal point in history. This time

it wasn't the atomic secret the Americans held but the technology of Star Wars. Conrad had studied every side of the controversy, listened to the opponents and proponents and deduced that U.S. research was much further along than anyone was admitting officially. That was the only explanation for the Soviets' obsession, their going all-out to stop SDI with the most sophisticated public relations anti-American campaign in memory. What would they risk— with a new arms-control treaty taking shape? Matthias Conrad thought he knew the answer. Industrial and scientific espionage was a basic component of the Russian research effort. The Kremlin had a laundry list of items to secure and it didn't take any suspension of disbelief to imagine that the Star Wars technology was uppermost on it. Through the ASF and the young scientists it funded, August Merriman was in an ideal position to pass on the coveted information to the Russians.

In San Francisco Conrad placed a personal call to Colonel Paul Hancock, director of the weapons lab at Livermore, and arranged a meeting for the next morning. Back when Hancock was on the NSC staff and the Dean was working his black magic at Langley, they had discovered that many of their fears and goals were identical, and Conrad knew he could still count on the colonel's help.

Eighteen hours later he was driving a rented cream Cougar through the barbed-wire fences and heavy security guards to the personnel office of Livermore, where he identified himself and received a green visitor's pass to wear on his lapel. A private, second class, drove him in an army jeep along a curving road past a fire station, radio towers and a track course to a group of prefabricated trailers joined together to form a complex of offices. Colonel Hancock's office was in the first jerry-made building, a low corner room spanking enough to pass military inspection.

Nursing a paper cup of coffee brewed freshly in a Mr. Coffee machine down the hall, Hancock skipped the usual pleasantries and went right to the point.

"Are you investigating something—or someone—in particular?" He wasn't a man who put value in small talk. "You said this wasn't a social call, Matthias."

"Let's say for the record that I'm here on a personal visit to see an old friend. For you, I'm pursuing an independent investigation, checking into certain—I wouldn't want to call them irregularities at this point—let's just classify them as interesting coincidences."

"Coincidences being the spice of life, and independent being a euphemism for outside the law, or in this case, the Agency?"

"I doubt that I could have put it as well."

Conrad had always enjoyed Hancock's dryness. It was another factor in their friendship, and he was tempted to take his old friend into his confidence if only to weigh his opinion. But the direction of the hunt was still unclear, like a picture of a runner taken with a still camera. Then, too, he didn't want to finger anyone . . . at least not yet, not until he was sure that his desire to see August Merriman crucified was based on professional motives, not long-suppressed personal ones.

"I don't have to tell you that SDI is one of the most ambitious defense programs ever undertaken, an effort rivalling the Manhattan Project. The Soviets would do anything they could to burrow their way through these walls . . . and I'm afraid they may have found a soft spot."

The colonel listened uneasily. "A mole at Livermore? Absolutely not. If there was any question in my mind of the loyalty of one of these men, you know damn well he wouldn't be working here. This is a hand-picked team and I swear by each one of them."

"They were hand-picked at Los Alamos, too," Conrad said quietly.

"Not comparable." Hancock was abrupt, the curtness of his manner reflecting a quick mind rather than a short temper. "I'd go to the wall for these boys, Matthias."

The seconds ticked by while Conrad digested that. "Okay, so they've all got red, white and blue stripes on their asses. I'm not sure it's your scientists' loyalty that's the question. I'm wondering which of them have ties to the ASF."

"The ASF?" Hancock's echo was guarded. "The very best of them. I could give you the names of a dozen off the top of my head."

Conrad sucked at his cigarette, inhaled and coughed and inhaled again. "Spare me the litany. Is any one of them particularly involved?"

"I'm not sure what you mean."

"Neither am I." He laughed, easing the tension that had grown up between them. "But there's some indication that the Soviets are using the ASF to gain access to our weapons research. The suspicion could be wrong, but you know the way the game is played. Any suggestion that SDI has been infiltrated, and Congress will cut your funding down to zero. I don't want that to happen anymore than you do. That's why we need to work together. As I understand it, the ASF is funded by August Merriman, along with enough other hospitals, schools, charities and assorted worthy causes to fill a phone book. So he couldn't possibly get personally involved in any of them . . ." Conrad was fishing—floundering, actually—but he hoped it wasn't obvious to his old friend. "A man like that probably doesn't know half the things his money supports. He wouldn't have time to come out here, look around, get to know any of the staff . . ."

"As far as I know he's never been out here," Hancock conceded.

"Do the ones supported by ASF grants have to go through

an annual review, any formal testing to make sure they still meet the grant requirements?"

"Sure. Each grant is reviewed annually, but not by Merriman himself. Personally, I've never met the guy, although I'd be pleased to shake his hand for the brilliant young men he's sent my way. The review's a fairly routine thing, as I understand it, usually with one of the foundation's officers. Oddly enough, this year is the first time I've ever known Merriman to conduct one himself. It was with David Pointer, our resident genius—and I'm damn glad the old man did."

Conrad did not attempt to interrupt, just let Hancock sing.

"Pointer was moping around here, not getting any work done, just thinking about the girl who jilted him when he got the call for his annual review, this one at Merriman's own place in upstate New York. It seems that Merriman got some help from his granddaughter, though, because Pointer came back a new man. From what I hear, Angelica Merriman is some considerable looker, and I couldn't be happier about it. This is no ordinary romance."

"You can say that again." Conrad laughed with his old friend, congratulating himself that his instincts were still sound. "Sounds like you're getting yourself a blank check."

"Don't jump the gun, Matthias. I'm afraid to think about it. Pointer hasn't nailed the girl yet, that's what I keep telling myself, but I'm pushing hard for the gold band."

"I never took you for a matchmaker, Hancock. I'd like to meet the boy. Sound him out—"

"Not Pointer." Hancock was instantly sober. "There's no way."

"I'm not suggesting anything. I just want to give him a little quiz... if you'll ask him to cooperate."

The colonel knew Conrad was right... any hint of Soviet penetration and Star Wars support would be compromised. "I'll talk to Pointer, but I've got to tell you, I think you're barking up the wrong tree this time."

"I hope you're right. Now how about showing me around the place. I'm curious to see what kind of ship you run out here."

"Unconventional. It takes a continuous supply of soda and popcorn to get these wizards ticking. Once they're pumped up, though, anything can happen. We're on the cutting edge of something here—something very big indeed."

CHAPTER
TWELVE

David Pointer, however he might not look the part, was an alchemist, a twenty-first century high-tech Faust working amid the vineyards and ranch land of Livermore Valley to channel the power of nuclear explosions into beams that would flare through the heavens to destroy enemy missiles —to surround the New World with a shield of weapons, supercomputers and communication devices that would act on hostile nuclear invaders like Excalibur on evil.

Now Conrad was sitting opposite him in an office cubicle, more a warren. Crammed into the bookshelves were an eclectic collection of books and tapes; Dos Passos' *U.S.A.*, *The Age of British Romanticism*, *The Annotated Shakespeare*, three volumes, *The Dream Songs*, *Confessions of a Mask*, Bach's *Six Suites for Solo Cello*, software, empty soda cans, popcorn boxes, notebooks, a squash racquet, odd pieces of clothing, conch shells and loose change collected on every surface, floor, tables, bookshelves, cabinets, chairs, desk. Through the debris, the computer terminal stood out clean and pure. Conrad wasn't sure what he'd expected, but it definitely wasn't a freckle-faced kid in scruffy jeans and a T-shirt that said, "I believe in Crystal Light."

"Do you believe?" Conrad said dryly.

"Do I what?"

"Believe in Crystal Light."

"Poison. I wouldn't touch the stuff unless I was lost in the Sahara with a one-humped camel."

"Dromedary," Conrad corrected.

"Have it your own way . . . but I don't necessarily believe two humps are better than one."

A humorist-scientist, yet. "I share your sentiments."

"What are you doing out here, sir?"

"Perhaps a search and destroy mission."

"Sounds unpleasant."

"It shouldn't be, if you cooperate."

"Me?"

An incredulous, foolish face, Conrad thought. A young genius should be brooding, intense, thick eyeglasses, sallow skin, gaunt, a little stooped, perhaps, and shy, compulsive, his communication skills limited to computer games and mathematical equations. David Pointer looked more like an animated Howdy Dowdy with his freckled face, turned-up nose and reddish brown hair that he was constantly pushing out of his eyes. The impression was caused by the mouth, which was too wide, so that when he smiled, his lips all but disappeared. Five foot ten, skinny and disarming—an all-American whiz kid. He was difficult to take seriously, unless you looked at his accomplishments.

"Hancock tells me you have a new girl."

"And we're supposed to be security-conscious around here . . . What can I do for you, Mr. Conrad?"

"Talk about Angelica Merriman."

"Why? Do you know her?"

"Indirectly. Is she as beautiful as Hancock says?"

"More so, but—"

"You wouldn't have a picture."

"I took some in New York." He pushed a pile of junk around his desk and pulled a color snapshot from under the glass.

Pointer was not exaggerating. Angelica Merriman was even more beautiful than Conrad had feared. She was smil-

ing into the camera, the golden Prometheus in Rockefeller
Center behind her blurring with the gold of her hair. Conrad
shook his head, dragged the last smoke from his dangling
stub. "Damn the old bastard," he muttered under his breath.
There was no place for sentiment in his business, and the
sooner Pointer woke up to the facts of life, the less harm
done.

"What old bastard are you referring to?" Pointer was sliding the photograph back under the glass for safekeeping.

"August Merriman. When will you see Angelica again?"

"In Venice next week. I'm going to take some vacation
time. Angelica will be there with her grandparents for a couple of weeks and she invited me—" Pointer stopped short.
"Why in *hell* am I telling you all this?"

"Because Colonel Hancock told you to cooperate with
me."

Until that moment Pointer could have bumped into
Matthias Conrad the next day and not remembered ever
meeting him. Now he would never forget the small, round,
cloudy blue eyes behind the large, round, tortoise-shell
glasses; the thin lips, the cigarette stub stuck to the lower
one; the high forehead, thinning hair still a sandy brown; the
slouching shoulders, pot belly, the expression of perpetual
bemusement that covered his true thoughts and emotions.

The old spymaster himself. Something large must be going
on to bring him out of the woodwork. Once Colonel Hancock
had jogged his memory, Pointer remembered reading about
"the Dean," an oblique figure forced into the spotlight by the
Intelligence Committee hearings twelve, fifteen years ago.
Pointer had been in high school then, but he remembered
the photograph on the front page of the Boston *Globe*, the
remarkably alert face peering out.

"This is a business visit?"

"An unofficial business visit," Conrad said.

"To discuss Angelica?"

"And her grandfather."

"Are you nuts?"

"I've been accused of worse. And hard though it may be to believe, I was in love with a young lady once, too. It didn't end happily ever after. In fact, it involved a most unsatisfactory fun-while-it-lasted kiss-off."

"You're telling me that's what I should expect from Angelica? Why, you old bastard, you don't even know her or anything about her."

"Call me, Matthias, dear boy—and save the characterization until you know me better." He coughed and wheezed, but Pointer barely noticed.

With a sickening sense of *déjà vu*, he realized what had brought Conrad to Livermore. All along he had been afraid that it was too good to be true. There had to be some mistake somewhere. Girls who looked like Angelica Merriman and acted like Angelica Merriman were never interested in the David Pointers of the world—the nerdy guys, too short, too skinny, too brainy. It would be like Cinderella falling for Peanuts' Linus Shroeder instead of Prince Charming.

"What exactly do you want from me, Mr. Conrad?"

"Patience." The Dean took a fresh cigarette and lit it from the old stub. "I don't suppose you've ever heard of Jedburgh. It's the name of the abbey that gave sanctuary to Mary Queen of Scots, and the code name for the Allied intelligence officers who were dropped behind enemy lines just before Normandy. Across the Channel in Southampton the invasion force was stranded on crowded transports waiting for the weather to lift enough to make the crossing. Many of those GIs would die on the beaches. The tension, the anticipation on the night of June 6, 1944, was indescribable. The Germans knew the invasion was coming. Rommel guessed Normandy. The rest of the Nazi high command said Calais because it was the closest point of land to Britain. One division was left behind, the rest moved south. Hitler was convinced by the majority, and by our disinformation—only we didn't call it that at the time." Conrad wheezed. "The history of Western civilization turns on such misinformed gambles..."

Pointer tried to interrupt. Old men telling old stories... he didn't want to listen anymore, but Conrad held him off.

"You're going to tell me that you don't need a history lesson from a frustrated professor, and you're right. But you may as well bear with me, because I'm going to finish my story one way or another."

"I believe it." Pointer snapped.

Peering over his glasses, Conrad looked like an aging bad boy. "I'm glad you accept the inevitable with good humor. It will be easier when we get to your part."

"And when will that be?"

Conrad chuckled. His laughter was a physical exercise, shoulders and belly shaking but little sound emitted.

"We're just to '44, and we've got forty-four more years to go. So, back to the night of June 6. I was one of the Jedburghs. As the transports started across the Channel, we slunk behind the German lines, harrassing the rearguard to divert attention from the beachhead. The Jedburghs and the Resistance fighters worked together, three to a team. Tanks burst into flames, tires blew off jeeps and trucks, mines exploded. The Germans thought a platoon of demolition experts had infiltrated their ranks. My team was lost before we began. One man's parachute tangled in a tree, he was dead before his feet touched French soil. The other stepped on a mine. He tried but couldn't go on, and rather than be taken by the Nazis he swallowed the L-pill we all carried. I didn't try to stop him. The fate of OSS agents taken by the Nazis was a badly kept secret. I went on alone and set my sights on a Tiger tank. Destroying it would be my personal tribute to the team I'd lost. Just as I got in striking distance, a masher stopped me.

"I remember a white flash, an orange lick of flames, and then I was listening to my own screams. It was easy to be a hero then. All you had to do was get behind a Sherman tank or in the way of a German one. The kind of war we're fighting today is rather more subtle."

"I presume we've come to my part." Pointer tried to sound unconcerned but couldn't pull it off. The old boy was a sonofabitch—a very sharp sonofabitch. Whatever point he was coming to, Pointer wished he'd never reach it. He'd heard more than he wanted to know already.

Conrad rolled right on like one of the tanks he kept talking about. "It's a clandestine contest of wits, more elusive than conventional warfare, but just as brutal, and it's very possible, dear boy, that, like it or not, you are in the thick of it. The Soviets would do anything to get their hands on your nuclear-powered laser research."

"What does any of that have to do with Angelica and me?"

"Do you spend a lot of time together?"

"Most every weekend."

"Do you talk about your work?"

Pointer didn't answer... he didn't have to. Sitting across the desk from Matthias Conrad, his feet stuck in the open middle drawer, his favorite way of sitting, he tried to rationalize.

He had spent the past six weekends with Angelica, usually in Durandana, once in Washington, once in New York, shuttling back and forth to the coast. When he was in California he didn't remember what it felt like without jet lag. When they were together, he forgot such a thing existed. There was a certain routine to his visits that had never worried him before. In fact, he had never even noticed it, it had evolved so gradually.

"Suppose, for the sake of argument," Conrad said, "the Soviets want a favor—information on a particular research project that a young scientist is conducting for the U.S. government. They turn to a long-time American friend, a man beyond suspicion or question, who enjoys having other men and governments in his debt. And suppose he turns to his granddaughter for a little help... to sweeten the task, you might say. Friendship blossoms, romance is in the air. In the natural course of events the grandfather discusses the young man's work, drawing him out, which is his special skill, and brushing aside the young man's scruples about confiding classified information. After all, the grandfather is an intimate of premiers and presidents, a regular guest at the White House..."

Pointer felt punch-drunk. He hadn't slept in thirty-six hours or changed his clothes. He hadn't had time, or more truthfully, hadn't wanted to take the time. His computer had been humming non-stop. And now Matthias Conrad was inventing preposterous tales with a disconcerting ring of fact—as if he'd been there in the sauna with Merriman.

"Are you suggesting—?"

"I'm not suggesting anything. I'm just giving you food for thought, to chew on while you're in Venice."

"I don't believe it," Pointer insisted, and at the same time thinking that it would explain why a woman like that was in his bed. And hadn't he briefly had an intimation of being set up when they first met... a feeling her presence snuffed out?

It seemed as though Conrad had read his mind.

"Look at yourself, David. No offense, but what have you got to make a rich, beautiful young woman want you so badly? A face, a body, money, fame? You've only got two things worth putting a price on—your brains and your job. You're the company whiz kid here. Hancock couldn't stop bragging about you—and you've got some tough competition. Do you know what I'd do if I were the Soviets? I'd put the best looking girl I could find in your bed, then I'd have her introduce you to her grandfather, who just happened to have a yearning for scientific knowledge. You can't resist her when she asks you to talk about your work with the old man, take him into your confidence."

"No. It's not like that. You've got Angelica all wrong," Pointer insisted, but kept thinking about the predictable pattern that went with his visits. Angelica would be away when he arrived—close enough to be expected back any moment but not immediately available. Prudence would greet him, and then he'd meet with Merriman, usually for an hour and always to discuss the work he was doing. When they finished, Angelica would be waiting, like a reward almost, a gold star from the teacher for a job well done ... except that she was always so happy to see him, so vibrant, her excuse for not being there the second he arrived to fall into his arms so convincing, and the way she made up for keeping him waiting and saddled with her grandfather again was so complete, awesome, that it was impossible to question her or fault her or think anything except the most glorious thoughts about the most glorious girl, woman, he'd ever even fantasized meeting ...

"I don't have to tell you that the Soviets would just as soon steal scientific information as spend the time and resources to develop it. More than any other scientist in the country, you are in a position to give them what they want most—access to the latest SDI developments."

"What are you telling me to do?" Unsophisticated about the labyrinthian ways of Langley, Pointer assumed Conrad's visit was official, and the Dean saw nothing to gain by correcting him. It was safer to be considered legitimate, and potentially more promising. The weight of the Agency gave credence to his suspicions.

"Nothing, really. Just play along with Merriman and report back to me. Keep your eyes open—and don't give your heart away, if you can help it ... I envy you. Venice is one of the truly great cities of the world ... very beautiful, and Angelica is very beautiful, and a beautiful name ... angel, angelic. You're not in the movies with good and bad marked clearly white hat or black. If you're tempted to forget it, just remember that Lucifer was the most beautiful of God's angels before the Fall. Try not to take one in Venice, and for your sake I hope I'm all wet and she's one of the good ones."

He put a card on the desk with two telephone numbers written on it and an address someplace in Rhode Island and stood up. "Memorize the numbers, then burn the card. All part of the game, right?"

"You've really got to be nuts..." Pointer wanted to convince himself. "August Merriman is practically a national monument. His face will no doubt be chiseled on Mount Rushmore one of these days, or put on the first thousand dollar postage stamp. Angelica is his granddaughter—August fucking Merriman's granddaughter, and you're accusing—"

"Friends and enemies often take on the same protective coloration. I suggest you refrain from mentioning our talk to the girl or her grandfather... or anyone else, even your associates here, if you expect to stay on. A suggestion that you're less pure than Galahad and the amazing research facilities at your disposal will be closed off. Don't trust anyone."

"Does that include you?"

"Myself least of all, dear boy."

Pointer stared at the scribbled calling card suspended between his thumb and forefinger. Nuts. He lit a match, ignited a corner, and dropped it into an empty popcorn box, watching the ends char and curl. He called Angelica and got Joseph. Miss Merriman was away but the message would be "transmitted." Joseph, like a sinister voyeur... thinking of him made Pointer uneasy. He tried to concentrate on Angelica in New York, Riverside Park... "Say a prayer and kiss your heart goodbye." The words were Madonna's but the sentiment was Matthias Conrad's. "Will you love me in December as you do in May?"

It was December now, and he didn't want to think about the answer anymore.

CHAPTER
THIRTEEN

Nora rented a white convertible Volkswagen Rabbit. And why not, she didn't have much fun in her life anymore, stuck in a routine desk job. And after all, she was supposed to be on vacation.

"You only live once," she told the bewildered Hertz salesman, who was much too young to have discovered the comfort in clichés. Thanks to Peter, she breezed across the border as easily as if she were crossing from New Hampshire to Vermont and took the *autobahn* west, only stopping to put the top down. Once out of Berlin the sun was strong, strengthening her private conviction that it only shone outside the city limits. Her reservations were at the Magdeburg Interhotel, one of the chain of government-owned tourist hotels in the G.D.R. Although she would have preferred a local inn, she knew she would be less conspicuous sticking to the accepted tourist route.

Magdeburg was not without interest. There was a handsome Gothic cathedral, one of the oldest in the country, a charming puppet theater and it was an easy drive from there to Mollenz, a town not even indicated on a map of Germany with the tiniest dot to mark its location.

When she reached Magdeburg, Nora settled herself in her room for the night. It was clean if stark—an ideal base for the daily forays to Mollenz that she planned. Klara Carrington, daughter of Lynneth and August Merriman, had married a man from Mollenz, Martin Klebehoff. There was no prohibition against moving from West Germany east, the constrictions flowed the other way, so Martin Klebehoff could have brought his bride home. If he did, their children would be registered in the town, probably live in the town still, and certainly if one of them went to America to live with her grandfather, everyone in the small town would know about the good fortune.

The next day Nora went to great pains to give the impression of an ordinary tourist. Certainly she looked the part with her camera, guidebook, sturdy walking shoes and a sun visor to protect her eyes.

By comparison with the West, time seemed to have stood still here. To drive from Berlin into the rural east was to step back, to wipe out the post-war years. Whatever oppressiveness existed was not overt. She was free to travel into the countryside, to explore the evergreen forests of the Harz Mountains and stop for lunch at the single hofbrau in Mollenz. The fare was simple country cooking, which in either Germany, regardless of political distinctions, means substantial dishes that adhere to one's innards.

Even if Nora had no ulterior motive for being there, Mollenz, held, as it were, in the embrace of the hills and meadows of the Harz, would have made a congenial vacation site. And even if she never found the answers she was looking for, the Pinkelwurst and ice-cold Korn Schnapps served in the beer hall would have made the trip worthwhile. The establishment was owned and operated by the Leidensdorfs, a couple whom she put on the far side of middle age—sixty, give or take a couple of years, she guessed. The place was as simple as they were ... a single room with long, bare wooden tables and benches, occupied by the regulars, men for the most part, broad burgher faces and light eyes, looking as if they'd stepped out of a Franz Hals portrait, occupying the same spots each day, drinking from the same steins. The light that slipped through the shuttered windows was the only variable in the room besides Nora.

When she complimented them on the meal, Herr Leidensdorf and his wife were easily drawn into conversation. The next day she returned for lunch and was welcomed like an old friend. Then and for the next couple of days Nora limited her curiosity to the town and found in Frau Leidensdorf a veritable motherlode of history and gossip, the one, as she said, too dry without the other.

Mollenz was a modest imitation of Goslar, just across the border in Lower Saxony—a poor cousin rather than a sister city. Both were medieval towns that the war had missed. Local men had been killed in combat, but the cities themselves went untouched, a phenomenon acknowledged as a miracle on both sides of the border. The people of Mollenz were as removed from politics as the town, their lives unchanged for centuries in spite of the philosophical and social upheavals.

Mollenz never achieved the splendor of its wealthier cousin. Without the great silver mines that had made Goslar an imperial city six hundred years before, it had little to recommend it other than its own modest and peculiar charm—the stream rushing through the center of town, narrow labyrinthian streets, cobbled squares, the fifteenth-century guild house, and the old timbered homes, not as intricately carved as those in Goslar, but still ample evidence of the architectural wonders that can be performed on a simple wood-frame house.

Frau Leidensdorf was willing to talk as long as she had an audience. But nowhere in her stories was there a mention of Klara Carrington or a family of Klebehoffs. Nora felt that she'd gained the woman's confidence enough to venture a hint.

"You know, Frau Leidensdorf, I had neighbors in New Hampshire who came from this area." She waved a hand vaguely as if to include the whole of Lower Saxony. "It was a long time ago. Their name was Klebehoff, I think." Seeing the glimmer of recognition in the good *hausfrau's* eye, she repeated with greater conviction, "Yes, Klebehoff."

"There are plenty of Klebehoffs right here in Mollenz. The plumber's one of them and the old man over there—" she pointed to a very old, very heavy man hunched over a far table—"He used to be the schoolmaster, but now his mind..." She tapped on her forehead and shook her head. "The Klebehoffs are hard workers, always were."

"I wonder if there's any record of my neighbors."

"It's all written down in the church—everything there is to know." The discovery of a mutual bond made Frau Leidensdorf even more voluble than usual. "In other towns the family records were lost in the war, you know, even the churches bombed to nothing." She shook her head. The opium of the people still played a central role in the life of Mollenz. "Our town was lucky, sixty-four men killed, but not a single bomb."

The next day when she was out for her daily stroll through the village, Nora ducked into the church. The pastor was playing the organ, liturgical music filling the nave. It was the last thing she expected to hear in East Germany. The shaft of light from the open door distracted him, and he turned eagerly.

Her visit was expected. The town being close-knit, both news and foreign visitors were equally sparse, even in the height of the tourist season when Berlin and Munich were swarming with strangers.

"I'm sorry to interrupt." Nora smiled. "Bach's 'Magnificat,' isn't it? It's one of my favorites, and you play it beautifully."

The pastor smiled back with an attractive mix of embarrassment and self-approval. An earnest young man to whom war was a subject for history books not memories, with pasty cheeks and a physique melting to soft fat. He was eager to help.

"You are looking for the church records of your friends."

"The Klebehoffs. They moved to the United States some years ago . . . to New Hampshire."

The pastor had gotten up and was leading Nora to the sanctuary. A large black book that looked like a cross between a bible and a ledger was closed on a lectern. He opened it without hesitation. The page listing the Klebehoff family was marked with a worn red satin ribbon.

"You've been waiting for me," Nora said.

The pastor's smile flickered. "Which Klebehoffs are you looking for?"

Nora scanned the page. "Gretchen S.—that sounds right." She frowned for the pastor's benefit, as if she was searching her memory for a forgotten name. Actually she was reading carefully down the page.

"I don't think it could have been Gretchen S. She only died last year, and I know she never left Mollenz, even to go ten miles to the south. That's true of many of the people here. We are very parochial."

Nora was nodding in agreement, but her mind had skipped ahead of the pastor. Three spaces below Gretchen S., the names Martin and Klara Carrington were inscribed, "Parents of Angelica, born September 6, 1962." There was an asterisked notation squeezed in at the bottom of the page. It was not clear enough for her to read. Maybe with the magnifying glass she always carried in her pocketbook, but then the pastor might think she was more than an eccentric tourist. If she could only get rid of him for a few minutes, but there was virtually no chance of that. A visitor was such a rarity—someone who recognized Bach's "Magnificat"—and he'd been waiting all morning to help her.

"Gretchen S. is buried right here in the cemetery. I per-

formed the service myself. Is there anything you would like
to know about her?"

"I guess my memory must be playing tricks with me.
You're right, of course. It has to be someone else." She tried
to disengage herself without rudeness. She's gotten the information she came for. August Merriman did have an illegitimate granddaughter named Angelica, born twenty-six years
ago. All the parts fit exactly, except one—Prudence Merriman's. If a wealthy American woman came to Mollenz within
memory to adopt a local girl and bring her back to America,
Frau Leidensdorf would have poured out the whole fantastic
story at the first mention of the name Klebehoff. But she
hadn't said a word about it. Most peculiar, Nora thought. At
lunch she would make a few discreet inquiries to draw the
hausfrau out. For now, though, she had to thank the pastor.
She closed the black book and turned to him, her camera
swinging against her chest.

"You've been so helpful, I was hoping you'd let me bring a
little remembrance of you back to America."

The pastor's pasty cheeks colored. He hadn't anticipated
such a request. "I don't know what . . ." he began.

Nora touched his arm to calm him. "Would you let me take
your photograph, to remember you by?"

He beamed, honored by the request, and stood straighter.
"Where would you like me to be? Here at the lectern?" He
leaned an elbow on the stand to give the effect.

"I was thinking more of the organ. You could be sitting
there, getting ready to play."

"Perfect." The pastor was already starting back. He arranged himself at the organ with care. To have his likeness
taken back to America was an offer of immortality. No
wonder he should see it as such, he was in the business of
peddling immortality. A salesman for eternal life, insurance
against death. Who could say what would become of his picture, how many strangers would view it with interest, fasci-

nation even—breadth and exposure he'd never imagined for himself.

Nora positioned herself midway between the organ and the door, adjusted the lighting, focused. "Say cheese."

She snapped the picture and waved goodbye. At the door she looked back. The pastor's hands were arched over the keys again, the cheese smile still frozen on his lips.

"I'll just take a walk through your cemetery while I'm here," she called back.

The pastor waved an airy benediction, his mind still basking in the Kodak light. "The Klebehoffs are toward the back, by the wall. You'll find all our history buried there." Nora wasn't sure whether the remark was intended humorously or as a philosophic truth. She'd take it either way.

The grass in the cemetery was dry. The sun high and hot for such hilly country. She picked her way through the stones and crosses, lingering to read the inscriptions or snap an occasional picture. Wild flowers had sprung up here and there. Clearly tending the graves was not high on the pastor's list of duties. Nora was careful to insure that if anyone was watching, her visit would appear aimless, prompted by nothing more than general curiosity, cemeteries being popular tourist stops. Actually, she didn't expect to find anything. She was, in fact, preoccupied with framing the questions to ask Frau Leidensdorf. Very probably, Klara and Martin Klebehoff were alive and well and living right there in Mollenz, because there was no notation of their deaths in the church registry. If she played her cards right, she might even wrangle an invitation to meet them. But first it wouldn't hurt to double check the graves.

Just as the pastor said, in the far corner by the wall were several generations of Klebehoffs. One stone in particular engaged Nora's interest—a granite marker engraved with a wreath of flowers. Set in the center of the wreath was an inscription:

ANGELICA CARRINGTON KLEBEHOFF,
BELOVED DAUGHTER OF
MARTIN AND KLARA KLEBEHOFF,
SEPTEMBER 6, 1962–NOVEMBER 14, 1964.

Nora had a day to kill and nothing more to keep her in Mollenz. She crossed the border below Goslar and drove west toward the Weser River. If she followed it to Hanover, she could pick up the *autobahn* there, double back to Magdeburg, then continue on to Berlin—a scenic detour and joy ride. She would reach Berlin by early evening and catch her return flight in the morning.

The Wesberglad in Lower Saxony is fairytale country—a region of hills, castles and deep forests where the scenery is as fabulous as the stories that sprang from it. The hills rise on both sides of the river, giving rise to fantastic imaginings. In the height of summer the Wesberglad was at its thickest and greenest. Nora felt like abandoning the car and letting her body sink into the lush countryside. But, of course, she would never act on such an urge.

She passed through Bodenwerder, the town where Baron Munch Hausen, teller of the world's tallest tales, once lived, and stopped for lunch in Hamelin, home of the Pied Piper. Just to the south in Hesse was Sababurg Castle of the sleeping beauty, and now there was a new fairytale to add to the others.

The tale of the resurrected Angelica Merriman, née Klebehoff.

Back at the haufbrau for the last time, pumping Frau Leidensdorf about the dead infant, Nora had learned that the Klebehoffs still lived in Mollenz. More than twenty years later, Klara Klebehoff was still mourning her baby—the only one she ever had.

Then who was the eye-catcher passing herself off as August

Merriman's granddaughter? Nora pondered the question as she drove through the fairytale country. The name was honest, but little else. Most likely the girl was a gold digger. An old man like Merriman, childless and filthy rich, was a perfect target for an enterprising, greedy woman. But Merriman must retain a battery of lawyers to keep such scavengers at bay. And if that weren't sufficient, Prudence Merriman had investigated the claim herself. How could the girl have fooled them all? And then there was the question of her name. Was it a coincidence or did Angelica Merriman know about the dead baby?

Nora was still ruminating over the mysteries when she got back to her room in Berlin. She had just taken her shoes off and loosened her skirt when Peter Braun telephoned to invite her to a concert that evening. It was her last night in Germany and she was tired from the long drive but she didn't want to refuse an old friend, as she thought of him now, any more than she wanted to ask how he knew she was back.

The concert was held in the courtyard of the Jagdschloss Grunewald, a hunting lodge in the heart of the park. It was a balmy night, one of the few clear evenings Nora could remember spending in Berlin. The air was cool, the sky above the park dotted with white stars.

"It's not every night I have a date with such a handsome fellow," she said, a touch of pleasure putting a glow in her plump cheeks.

Peter took her hand and wrapped it around his arm. "I think this concert was planned especially for you. The program tonight is all Handel."

"Perfect." And it was. They sat outside in a courtyard lit with candles. The Water Music with its preponderance of wind instruments was composed for open-air performance, and Nora had never heard it played better. Peter had been

quiet during the drive out the Ku-damn, but under the spell
of the music his mood seemed to lighten. During the intermission Nora described her trip. He listened, thought about
it, the way a father preoccupied with office work listens to his
child. Nora went into the details of Mollenz and her scenic
drive through Lower Saxony and the Harz Mountains, only
touching on her search in the most oblique terms.

The concert concluded with the mad scene from "Or-
lando," the hero imagining himself in Hades. Although she
didn't realize it at the time, she must have held her breath
through most of the performance. As the audience rose to
applaud, she leaned over to Peter. "A smashing finale to an
exciting evening."

He stared at her intently, as if he was committing each
feature to memory. "It was unforgettable . . . as you are." Her
cheeks were flushed with pleasure at his remark and from
the wine they'd drunk, her eyes bright in the candlelight.
She wore a green linen suit, a string of pearls around her
neck and matching clip-on earrings. "Tell me something," he
whispered for her alone, "did you find the girl you were
searching for?"

"Yes—although I'm afraid it was something of a dead end.
It seems she died in infancy. I found where she was buried.
My friends will be disappointed, I'm sure."

"I'm sorry to hear that," Peter murmured, taking both her
hands in his. "More sorry than I can tell you."

"She died twenty-six years ago," Nora pointed out. "You
sound as if you're giving your condolences to the family."

Leaning across her, he blew out the candle that illumined
her eyes. "Maybe I am, dear Nora. Maybe I am."

CHAPTER
FOURTEEN

It was approximately eight o'clock when Nora let herself into her parlor-floor flat. Depositing her luggage in the bedroom, she turned on the lights and opened the windows to give the place a thorough airing. Nora was a firm believer in brisk walks, clear heads and fresh air.

She put a teakettle on to boil, then went back to the front door to pick up the mail.

When the tea was made she sat down in her favorite Hepplewhite chair to enjoy it. Traveling always invigorated her. She never felt more vital than she did when she was winging it, so to speak, still, it felt good to be home. She smiled at her own poetic flights and flipped through the envelopes. Not much of an accumulation for ten days—the expected bills, a catalogue from Talbot's, a few pieces of junk mail, a solicitation for "Jerry's kids," a Bryn Mawr alumnae report and a note from Matthias saying that he would come calling around nine. Nora read it with a mixture of annoyance and amusement. The old bugger. He wouldn't get anything more out of her. Finally there was a package, wrapped in brown paper and small enough to slip through the letter slot. Nora always saved the best for last, anticipation being one of the pleasures of an unsatisfied life.

The package was so small that a tag was attached to it with

the mailing address. In the upper lefthand corner printed clearly was Mr. R. Thomas, 1400 Corcoran Street, NW, Washington, D.C. 20009. The only R. Thomas she knew was Rick, a bright young researcher on the Soviet desk who was fascinated by the olden days. She had coffee with him once in a while and let him pick through her memories.

Rick Thomas sending her a present? Pulling off the paper, she found a white card, such as one might be given in a florist shop or department store. It read, "Welcome home, Rick." Nora was surprised and touched. What a sweet gesture, she thought. She couldn't quite remember anyone sending her a welcome-home present before. In fact, there was always an edge of sadness about coming back because there was never anyone waiting for her.

She knew from the box what it was. Chanel No. 5. A thoughtful gift for a maiden lady. Personal, but still quite staid, altogether respectable, she thought, measuring the care he must have put into his choice. Smiling, she opened the white box piped with black and the familiar "C" trademark and took out a purse-size black and gold atomizer.

Nora felt a warm glow as she pulled off the top and sprayed the cologne behind her ears, on her throat, her wrists. All the pulse points, she could remember her sister instructing, wreathing herself in a cloud of mist. She inhaled deeply, expecting to savor the familiar fragrance. Instead there was a vague, slightly fruity smell. Nora sprayed again and inhaled. The scent still eluded her. Putting the top back on firmly, she shrugged off her surprise. She was probably coming down with a cold after being cooped up in an air-compressed 747 cabin for hours, and she was tired, more tired than she'd realized.

She rubbed her eyes. They'd begun to ache, and the room seemed to be blurring. Familiar objects with fuzzy edges. She tried to drink the tea, but it was difficult to coordinate her hand and mouth, the way it is after novocaine. She wiped the corner of her lips with the back of her hand to catch the drooling. The room felt hot, suffocatingly hot. She'd just go into the bedroom and lie down.

Face it, Nora told herself. You're not as young as you used to be, able to gallivant around the world and not feel anything except exhilaration. She tried to reassure herself that she was only tired, but when she stood up, she felt her chest constrict. The recalcitrant left eye twitched wildly. Each breath was more difficult than the one before. She began to sweat.

"Dear Jesus," she murmured. The pile of mail fell on the floor as she stood up. She didn't notice. The room was a carousel at high speed. She staggered, reaching out for familiar objects to steady herself. The glass doors separating the bedrooms were open. Just a few more steps and she could lie down. Rest. She fell onto the bed, hitting the corner of her suitcase. Her body jackknifed. Her head throbbed. The nausea was a tidal wave gathering in her gut. She leaned over the side of the bed, clutching the spread to keep from falling. The bathroom might as well have been on another continent. It must be the weather . . . the flight . . . something she ate on the plane. But the night was balmy for Washington, the flight smooth, and she hadn't really eaten much of anything except the bread and the butterscotch pudding.

When her stomach was empty, there was nothing left except an immense tiredness. Nora lay back. Each second it was becoming more difficult to breathe. She was gasping as if she were still in the air-compressure cabin and a leak was sucking the oxygen out. Nora tried to hang on—to remember what had happened, where she'd been, who she was. Her mind was a jumble of broken thoughts, distorted images, divided cities . . . loyalties. She could feel the ties loosening, slipping away, vague, elusive.

Her mind was stuck on one thing. Before she fell asleep, she had to get the film . . . more film. Pushing herself up, she fumbled with the clasps on the suitcase. Tomorrow, she told herself. You can do it tomorrow. But some inner force propelled her on. The suitcase opened. She began to feel through the clothes, forgetting what she was looking for. Her mind was a labyrinth—a carousel, like the room.

Her wrist banged against the hard edge of the lens cover. Nora grasped it and pulled it out. The suitcase fell off the bed, upturning on the floor, the clothes spilling into the pool of her last meal.

CHAPTER
FIFTEEN

Matthias Conrad was sure of the exact time that he parked Charlotte's light blue Fiesta because the radio announcer had assured him that it was exactly 9:32 in a tone that chimed with authority. It had been years since he'd paid a call on Nora, but in the shadow of evening the neighborhood and house looked much as he remembered them.

A two-family frame house off Dupont Circle, architecturally undistinguished but sturdily constructed. A childless couple, both civil servants, lived in the upstairs flat. The small details of Nora's life came back as he went up the steps onto the circular porch and rang the bell. The parlor window that fronted the porch was open and the lights shone through.

Conrad rang again. He'd expected Nora to be miffed still, but not so angry she wouldn't come to the door.

"Nora." Stooping over, he called in the window. The house was so quiet. A breeze plastered the glass lace curtains against the screen. No one but Nora still had glass curtains, he thought. He called again, and was met by silence. An unwelcome visitor.

"Damn it, Nora. I have to talk to you." Conrad called through the window. The breeze picked up again, bringing with it a certain odor. The wind was coming from the north through the house. He tried the door. Locked. The screen.

It lifted easily, and not so easily Conrad pushed his way through, upsetting a table. A pot of African violets crashed to the floor. He swore and pulled the screen down behind him. Inside the room the odor was unmistakable. He took in the place, trying not to breathe.

Because it was built somewhere around 1910, it had the features considered luxurious in a new apartment—double parlors with a bay window in the front room, a tiled fireplace in the back; beyond that, a dining room and kitchen, each the size of a contemporary master bedroom. Off the parlors separated by glass doors were two bedrooms with a bath between them. Inhabited by a more austere personality, the flat would have appeared roomy. But crammed with the relics of Nora's sixty-odd years, it was cramped.

The parquet parlor floors were covered with Oriental rugs, considerably worn but just as obviously genuine. The furniture was an amalgam of family pieces and oddities she'd picked up during her peripatetic life—a high secretary and mahogany library table, a hand-tooled leather hassock that appeared to be Indian, a distinctly Peruvian hammock suspended from the ten-foot ceiling, a highback chair that could easily have been a Hepplewhite with a woven blanket draped across it. Surprisingly, since it was Nora's forte, no effort had been made to pull the disparate elements together. The result was a confusion of American antiques and native crafts of a fairly primitive order. Overflowing on, around and under this interior designer's nightmare was an equally eclectic over-abundance of books and journals.

Conrad saw the half-empty teacup, the mail spilled on the floor, the brown paper wrapping, but he didn't stop to investigate. With almost a spring in his step, he went through the glass doors into the bedroom. He stopped in the doorway, took out his handkerchief and covered his mouth and nose before going in. Nora Hewitt was not a pretty sight. She was still dressed for traveling down to her tasselled Pappagallo shoes, but she was not going anyplace. Ever.

The old-fashioned four-poster bed was neatly made, the crocheted spread still pulled up. Nora lay on top of it, her face the color of pea soup. She must have lost control of her muscles because the spread and her clothes were stained.

Conrad turned away. There was nothing he could do except try to make her decent. Taking the blanket from the Hepplewhite, he went back into the bedroom and covered the body. As he pulled it up over her face, already set in death, he saw the camera. Her arm was half under her head, the camera strap caught between her fingers. Gingerly, he pulled it loose, then finished covering her. He did not search her luggage. Nora was too good and experienced to have written anything down.

Back in the living room, Conrad wrapped the camera in his handkerchief and squatted on the floor to sift through the mail. He left the bills, the solicitations, junk mail, Bryn Mawr; pocketed his own note, the wrapping paper, tag, card and perfume box. Then he let himself out. At the door he stopped and turned back.

"So long, old girl," he said aloud. He would miss her.

The funeral for Nora Hewitt was a sad affair, even as such things go. A dry-eyed group of eighteen or twenty to see her lowered into the ground: A brother Conrad didn't know she had, the next of kin; a couple of old college friends by the look of them, dewy-eyed at best; a few old-timers from the Agency who'd dredged themselves up for the occasion; three of the new breed; her upstairs neighbors. On the way back to the cars, Conrad drifted away from Charlotte and fell in step beside one of the younger men.

"Rick Thomas, aren't you?" The young man nodded in surprise, although he knew he shouldn't be surprised at anything that came from Matthias Conrad. The man was a fucking legend.

He held out his hand. Legends don't require introductions. "It's an honor to meet you, sir."

Conrad put an arm on Thomas' shoulder. "You're probably wondering how I know you. Nora spoke about you often."

"She was a fascinating woman. I could listen to her talk about the old days for hours."

Thomas' feelings were sincere, Conrad felt. An average young man—average height, average build, dark hair, pleasant face, dark-rimmed glasses, sincere, earnest. Either he'd toughen up or be eaten alive. "Is that all?" Conrad's tone sharpened. "I mean, were you close friends?"

"She was considerably older than I . . ." Clearly Thomas wasn't sure what he was driving at.

Conrad wheezed. "You mean she was a creature from another world, another planet . . . an alien."

"I only meant—"

"And I meant did you have a particular fondness for Nora Hewitt, such as a young man might have for his grandmother or a favorite aunt?"

"We weren't close, if that's what you're getting at." The boy's uncertainty was increasing.

"Not close enough to send Nora a present, then? A welcome-home gift, a modest perfume spray, Chanel No. 5, perhaps?"

Thomas was looking at Conrad curiously, almost sadly as if he'd suddenly realized that the mythical "Dean" was all too human—an old man, now. "To be truthful, sir, I didn't even know she was on vacation. You know, a woman of her years. I thought she might have come down with something. There are so many bugs going around D.C. . . . ."

When Charlotte went out to her bridge club that evening, Conrad tested Nora's gift, making sure to aim it away from himself, as if he were testing a bug repellant instead of a fine perfume. No sweet fragrance rose to fill the room. Conrad dropped the spray in his pocket and went to the kitchen, where he scrubbed his face and hands thoroughly. He went around the house opening every window so that it would be thoroughly aired by the time Charlotte got home. Only then did he go outside.

Lady wasn't waiting at the front step.

"Lady?"

He called, whistled, called again. Reluctantly he unlocked the door, not wanting to go back in the house. Lady had been sleeping behind the living room couch, her favorite spot. Charlotte must have forgotten to let her out.

He knelt down beside her and stroked her snarled coat. Lady was the one thing he had fought his wife over when they separated, he to live in Little Compton and she to remain in Alexandria. He wouldn't have fought so to take Beth with him, even if she had been a minor, knowing that his daughter belonged to her mother, not to him. He had been mostly an uncertainty in her life, nothing more. But he would have gone to court over Lady if Charlotte hadn't finally agreed to let him have her once she got over the fright of living alone for the first time in her life. What he had found extraordinary was that Charlotte had such strong feelings about the dog. She had kept them well hidden through the years, habitually complaining about Lady's—and her master's—foul habits.

Lady be good... Conrad stroked the dead dog one last time, then went into the yard and began to dig in the darkness.

CHAPTER
SIXTEEN

At 2 Dzerhinsky Square the KGB counter-intelligence chief leaned back in his new black Italian leather chair. The contours of his body had not shaped it to his comfort yet, but he was a patient man who recognized the value of time. A man who couldn't wait had no business in his line of work.

"Drawing a fine line is an essential part of espionage," Anatol Dostankov lectured his aide. "The difference between a good officer and a superior one is judging the exact point when waiting becomes counter-productive, or worse. This case is a perfect illustration." He picked up the dossier in front of him and tapped it against the rim of the desk. "The case of the U.S. scientist David Pointer—a brilliant operation by its very simplicity, and one that has evoked the personal interest of the General Secretary."

Dostankov was given to lecturing on everything from the fine points of espionage to the beauty of fifteenth-century ikons to the smoothness of the finest vodka. He was, in his fashion, a cultivated man with esoteric tastes. Five-ten, slender and dark, sensual without being good-looking, eyes deep-set. He was also a hungry man, hungry for power and position. To his good fortune KGB Chairman Viktor Chebrikov's learning was limited to his profession.

Dostankov was also a man who enjoyed his work. And why not? It provided the best his world had to offer—membership in an elite club, an unlimited fund of inside information, money, and freedom to think and speak as he wanted within a limited, private circle—without fear of the secret police. When one *was* the police, one enjoyed an unusual liberty, though not to be abused regardless of the temptation. Lavrenti Beria, for all the power and fear he commanded, was executed when he made the mistake of thinking he was untouchable. Dostankov looked to history to guard and help realize his ambitions.

Opening the dossier on Pointer, he nodded in the direction of his aide without looking up. "That's all. But remember what you've learned today." Dostankov needed to be alone to think about the American Star Wars' scientist—a case with an historical precedent. In 1934, when the Kremlin was anxious to obtain the A-bomb, a White Russian emigré, Peter Leonidovich Kapitsa, working on a project to liquify helium at Cambridge, was invited to a scientific conference in Moscow. When the conference ended, Stalin ordered the KGB to seize his passport. A year later Kapitsa was named head of the Institute of Physical Problems of the U.S.S.R.'s Academy of Sciences. When he wasn't working on experiments to find the absolute zero temperature where the structure of atoms could be observed, he enjoyed a large flat in Moscow, a country dacha, two chauffeur-driven Chaikas and all the other fringe benefits of the privileged.

Dostankov had based his operation against Pointer on the Kapitsa incident—and staked his future on its success. An audacious scheme, Operation Counterpoint.

His faith in it was such that he had already begun to imagine replacing Chairman Chebrikov, when the report came in from Germany. A dotty old CIA agent was digging up records in Berlin and snooping around Mollenz in a sun-visor like an American Miss Marple. Dostankov unwound by reading British mysteries, and occasionally picked up a useful idea. The vintage ones were his favorites, Agatha Christie and Eric Ambler. On a recent trip to London, though, he had found a newcomer—P.D. James. Smashing, as his friends in MI5 would say.

The report from Germany was in the front of the dossier but he did not reread it. No need to. He knew each word by heart, and what they added up to was that the CIA was onto the operation, or getting close to it. There had been no leak, he was sure of that. Counterpoint was limited to a select handful of his own choosing: the Soviet General Secretary, the KGB Chairman and himself—all above suspicion; the girl and her control—he was confident of them both; and the old man, August Merriman—although he had dealt with both sides before, Merriman was under the strictest observation. Only one possible answer remained and it made Dostankov shudder to think of its implications—the scientist, David Pointer, that he was trying to compromise, was himself CIA. He, Anatol Dostankov, had, it seemed, proposed to entice an American operative to the Soviet Union and give him access to the country's nuclear secrets. It seemed the only explanation for the old agent sniffing around Germany. And how clever of them to use such an old, presumably discarded agent, someone least likely to arouse suspicion...

Dostankov paced his office, his long manicured fingers pressed together just under his nose. He couldn't accept defeat. There was more at stake here than the success or failure of a single operation. There was his reputation, his future. The General Secretary was taking a personal interest in the operation... He fingered the lapel of his Saville Row suit, the moisture smirching the tan gabardine. He favored English suits—a little tweedy, pleated slacks, classic tailoring. They'd go, too, along with everything else, probably even his wife... Dostankov couldn't imagine Natasha allowing herself to be dragged down for something as insignificant as fidelity or love. She was already considered one of the most promising molecular biologists, and her ambitions rivalled his own. The Dostankovs belonged to the new breed of Soviet professionals—confident, self-absorbed, acquisitive, as far removed from the patient proletariats who stood for hours in the lines at GUM as the tsar from his peasants.

Natasha... she had an Oriental cast to her features, a throwback to some forgotten Mongolian bloodline. Petite, with long straight hair as black as her eyes and a linear face, a flat plane disturbed only by the short straight line of her nose flaring slightly at the nostrils, her enthusiasm for scientific experiments extended beyond laboratory tests to their sexual forays. Inventing novel ways to perform a basic and fundamentally crude act aroused her, leading her beyond unconventional positions to experimenting with a variety of mechanical devices. Whenever he traveled to the West, Dostankov brought a present home to his wife, purchased in the Times Square district of New York or the Red Light district of Hamburg in places called the Treasure Chest and Erotic Tricks 'n Treats.

Natasha's lovemaking was exciting but detached, as if the scientist responded and the woman remained beyond reach ... Thinking about it led him back to Angelica Merriman and the perverse case of the American scientist. Dostankov believed with absolute conviction that there was not a man worth his balls—CIA or not—that Angelica couldn't turn. Once she had made love to him, this Pointer would sell out his honor, his country, his mother to have her again. *Any* man would, but how could he convince Chebrikov?

Being a thorough professional, Dostankov had tested Angelica personally before entrusting her with such an important assignment, and she had passed unforgettably. Even now, more than a year later, he would wake up in the night with a hard-on that could stand up to the Ivan the Great Bell Tower. She was so good at her work that she had made him believe it wasn't just a sexual exercise performed with skill. In the heat of the night she had convinced him that she had fallen in love for the first time, that nothing she had learned in her three years at the KGB training school for sexual operatives had prepared her for Anatol Dostankov, that she had learned to use her body in a thousand different ways but never her heart until *he* touched it. She wanted *him*, Comrade Anatol Petervitch, again and again. Her thighs were long and spread wide to encompass him, and between them . . . he could never remember being so hot in Moscow in January.

Only in the morning when Angelica asked for his evaluation as coolly as if she were expecting her grades in marksmanship did he realize that she had been playing a part. Outwardly Dostankov was as brusque as she, although looking at her standing in front of him, all naked and glowing, he would have crawled on his belly around Red Square to have her again. He had asked her to dress and wait in the next room. When she did he went through her hamper and masturbated with a pair of her panties.

Was David Pointer a stronger man than he—superior in character, a more astute judge of women, a more dedicated patriot, a more experienced lover? To accept such a premise was to deprecate himself. Even knowing in advance what Angelica was, he had been taken in—and he was clever, worldly, cosmopolitan, sexually sophisticated and not without a healthy skepticism. With those thighs wrapped around his waist, David Pointer would beg to be compromised.

Yes, Dostankov was sure of it.

Still the risks made his stomach contract with fear. Natasha had told him one day he'd get an ulcer, and now she was probably right. If Operation Counterpoint failed, his ass would be on the line. On the other hand, if he sat on the report from Germany it would give Angelica time to complete her assignment. Meanwhile, there were certain sensible precautions he had already begun to take. The old CIA agent had received a homecoming surprise. There would be another for her esteemed control and former boss. And he was dispatching a special agent to Venice to assess and monitor Angelica's performance.

For that last assignment, Dostankov felt he had just the

man: Leon Ivanovitch, an instructor at the Leningrad school for sexual services, *and* Angelica's fiancé. Dostankov had used him before on special assignments and found him to be most efficient. His special skills were physical, but in this case he was uniquely qualified to make a judgment.

CHAPTER
SEVENTEEN

"That will be Pointer now. Just in time to go to the party with us." Merriman stepped into black formal trousers. An exhibit of his Russian ikons opened in Venice in the morning, and the U.S. Consulate was giving a white-tie dinner in his honor to kick off the six-city European tour.

"I'm sure he won't want to look at anything except Angelica tonight." Prudence turned in front of the mirror, considering her reflection. The same goes for you, my dear husband, she thought, and swept out of the room to let Pointer in.

"Welcome to Venice, David." She offered a thin smile and her hand. "That will be all, Joseph."

"Thank you," Pointer said, already wishing he had stayed at Livermore. Joseph had been waiting to take charge of his luggage and his person the moment he walked into the hotel. There was no time to check in, take a leak, see Angelica.

"You're late, and Mrs. Merriman doesn't like to be kept waiting." Joseph's arm had been raised to emphasize his words, the cuff pulled back to display his watch.

Pointer thought of Matthias Conrad, the routine unchanged even here . . . report to Merriman and get Angelica as a bonus. It had seemed relatively innocent before, but now . . .

"My husband is in the bedroom getting dressed. You can

go right in." Prudence closed the door behind him, cutting off any possibility of retreat. "August will be pleased to see you again. He takes such an interest in your work."

The Merriman's suite was bigger than Pointer's apartment. The sitting room, which was warmed by the glow from a Venetian glass chandelier, was decorated in gold and white. A formal room without being formidable with arched doorways, a marble mantel, and above it, a large gilt-framed mirror. Pointer's reflection looked tense, Prudence's composed. She didn't sit so much as glide onto a Regency loveseat, her dress falling into graceful folds around her ankles. The light of the chandelier caught her diamond earrings. They were the only jewelry she wore, but with them, nothing more was needed.

Pointer followed her finger to the bedroom to meet Merriman. A long black dress splashed with bold orange-red flowers—poppies or peonies—long tight sleeves, a high neck that accentuated her aristocratic neck. He tried to imagine her at twenty-six.

"Davey, boy." Merriman's greeting was predictably effusive. "Will you give me a hand with this damn thing?" He was standing in front of the mirror trying to work a monogrammed platinum stud into his starched shirtfront. White tie and tails. Pointer was impressed.

"Same suit I've had for fifty years." He patted his belly to show off his youthful figure.

"I hope I can say the same one day," Pointer answered, fastening the stud.

The bedroom was as large as the sitting room, a harmony of lemon and peach, both refreshing and restful. Pointer wouldn't mind catching five.

"We're having a little party at the Consulate to open the August Merriman Special Collection of Russian Ikons. I picked them up little by little over the years . . . literally picked them up in the twenties and thirties. Nobody else wanted them after the Revolution. Now each one is worth millions. You're invited to the shindig of course, but Prudence accused me of getting old. Can you believe it—me? She said you'd rather be alone with Angelica tonight than see Michelangelo unveil the Sistine Chapel. It's up to you, Davey, boy. The important thing is you're here with us. How's the work coming?"

For the first time, Pointer backed off. "I've just been tying up loose ends so that I could take a week off. Putting my house in order . . . you know, nothing really." He didn't feel convincing.

Merriman's plan for Pointer was proceeding smoothly, no need to rush things. The boy had gotten comfortable visiting them at Durandana, and now they were including him in their foreign travels—Venice first, because it was a city like no other, next London or maybe Sorrento where it all began, then maybe Moscow. He'd get a kick out of introducing Pointer to the Soviet General Secretary and the rest, as he liked to say, would be history.

Merriman didn't bother to listen closely. He'd never had time for technical details. He had the idea, made the contacts, set up the deal. He couldn't be an expert on everything—agriculture, mining, nuclear science, furs, construction . . . What man could? His mind fastened on the exhibit. It was a demonstration of pride, of culture, of his unique power and position—a citizen of the world, master of brinkmanship, a philanthropist, humanitarian, art patron, a man to be respected, admired, emulated. The guest of honor couldn't be late. There'd be plenty of time to pump Pointer.

"Hand me those shoes over there, will you, Davey?" Merriman pointed across the room and sat down on the edge of the bed, not even an excuse-me for interrupting. "You know, I've never had a valet. I never could understand why in hell a grown man needs someone to dress him, just because he's managed to put some money in the bank. If you can do the one you damn well should be able to do the other. That's my philosophy. Of course, Joseph or somebody lays everything out for me."

"I think I'll pass on the party," Pointer said, "if it's all right with you, sir. The flight was long—"

"Don't apologize. You haven't seen my granddaughter in more than a week. I know just how you feel, Davey. The ikons have been around hundreds of years. They'll be here tomorrow, and so will Venice. If you miss them here, you can always catch them in the next city. The August Merriman Special Collection is going from here to Paris, Brussels, Vienna, Rome and Madrid. And if you don't get to any of those cities, you can have your own show . . . at Livermore, if you like. Science and art. Not a bad idea. Maybe I can do something with that . . . A world class museum, that's what I've got, so why not open it up for the world to see. Share the beauty—and I confess the publicity never hurts. There's no place like Venice to open the show. It's one of my favorite cities, and you want to know why? Not because it's romantic or has spectacular palazzos, pigeons, St. Marks, canals, gondolas—not for any of the reasons you think of when you think of Venice. But because this city is living proof that the twain does meet—East and West in harmony in one city, Byzantium and Christianity. If it can happen here, it can happen all over the world, and anyone who tells you that we have to have a Cold War is full of so much self-serving bull. That's what I've been doing all my life . . . meeting East with West. It's why I think of myself as the merchant of Venice— not some Shylock, a *true* Merchant of Venice.

"While I'm here I *am* the Merchant of Venice . . . Think big, Davey, boy, and you'll make it big. It's always worked for me. It can for you too."

CHAPTER
EIGHTEEN

On his first night in Venice, Pointer took Angelica to Harry's Bar, hangout of the Hemingway-Fitzgerald set in the thirties and of the Beautiful People ever since, and tried to forget Matthias Conrad at least for one evening. Harry's has a small crowded bar on the ground floor and upstairs a slightly larger, equally crowded dining room with fresh flowers and superb food. Although it stands on the Grand Canal, it could be a splendid understated restaurant anywhere because the curtains are always drawn upstairs and down, eliminating the view.

In the pleasantly crowded dining room it was easy to pretend that they were just a man and a woman, lovers like any others. Pointer leaned closer so that he could feel the smooth length of her thigh brush against his and slowly sucked in the silver spoonful of sherbet Angelica held out for him to taste. The orange sherbet at Harry's was bright red, made from the blood oranges of Sicily, and indescribable, she had said.

"I didn't exaggerate, did I?"

"About Venice, you mean?"

"About Venice in general—and the sherbet in particular."

He considered her question as if the future of the western alliance depended on his measured response. "You're right. It's delicious and sensual—almost as good as sex, but not quite."

"Spoken like a true connoisseur."

He wasn't sure if she was serious or mocking him. But she was beautiful. His memory hadn't been playing tricks. Beautiful and so soft. Designing women were supposed to have a hard edge, but her eyes, mouth, her skin when he reached over and touched her throat was soft. Like candlelight.

Conrad's warning lingered in his mind: "You're not in the movies with good and bad marked clearly white or black. If you're tempted to forget, remember Lucifer was the most beautiful of God's angels."

Angelica had taken his hand and was kissing each finger. "I missed you, David."

"Can I believe you?" He hadn't meant to say the words out loud.

"You must, because it's true," she said, but a shadow came into her eyes.

Angelica had allowed other men to make love to her often enough, one especially. With David, though, everything was different. Her points of reference were askew, and it frightened her. She gave herself too completely to him. They made love everywhere and anywhere with abandon and a lack of inhibition that, in moments of reflection, she realized was dangerous. She never knew before what it meant to feel vulnerable. It scared her but she couldn't hold back. The rest of her life, even her reason for being in America, everything seemed eclipsed by the days and hours they spent together. He was funny and sweet and gentle, things she'd never expected to find in a man.

"Is that all? You just missed me?" Pointer was studying her.

"It isn't enough?" She seemed to falter, or was he imagining it.

"How could it be when there seems to be so much more left unsaid?"

Angelica finished the last of her wine, avoiding his eyes.

* * *

Gliding down the Grand Canal in a gondola, the black hull barely stirring the water, Pointer watched the elaborate metal blade at the prow glimmer in the black water and waited for Angelica to tell him more. The gondola was becoming an endangered species like bald eagles and blue whales, Pointer thought, impractical beside the *vaporetto* and *motoscafo*. But then a gondola had nothing to do with practicality. It was a thing of beauty and a local treasure, despite the haggling *gondolieri*.

When they got out at the Gritti Palace she took his hand and they walked without talking from the vaporetti station there at the hotel through the Calle Largo 22 Marzo, one of the wider thoroughfares, that ran behind the Grand Canal hotels and that some soggy beaureaucrat decided would look good in green carpeting; past the travel agencies and antique shops, some as old as the merchandise; by the much maligned facade of San Moisé and across the mouth of the narrow Calle Valaresso, where Harry's Bar was, back where they had begun, the unmistakable moldy smell of the place, the odors of age and dampness dogging them every step of the way.

At the entrance to the piazza they stood for a moment to take it all in, the immense arched set and at the far end the glorious Byzantine theater. Piazza San Marco never failed. Each hour had its special shade. They walked through the arcades on the right, passed Florian's, cafe of Wagner and Goethe, by the small jewelry store where they paused to window shop. Pointer pretended he'd never heard of Matthias Conrad and Angelica was only what she appeared to be, and chose a sapphire ring to match her eyes, Venice being a city of make-believe.

Around the corner in the Piazzetta they stood at the water's edge between the columns on the Molo, the very spot from which Venice launched her empire, and saw the Benedictine Church of San Giorgio across the lagoon, pale gold in the unusually clear evening, and the black gondolas and immense sky. Instead of a barrier their silence was a bond, intensifying their closeness, deepening their awareness of each other. Only their hands touched, but the reverberations didn't stop there.

The Riva degli Schiavoni beyond the Doge's Palace was deserted. They walked slowly by the Ponte dei Sospiri, the Bridge of Sighs, the water a great tongue lapping at the edges of the city, the night as empty as the street. He took her in his arms there and kissed her, her body gracefully arching into his.

"Again," Pointer said, holding her.

She drew away. "I'm afraid..." Her voice was a stranger's whisper. She had never wanted him more—and not for anything that had to do with duty, obeying orders, or a job well done.

Pointer stared out across the lagoon, the *campanile* of San Giorgio etched against the sky. In the mornings from his hotel window the sun glowed on the slender gold angel atop the bell tower and on the red brick of the church, turning the white marble trim pink. Brick and marble, the one so common, the other so rich. What extraordinary mind imagined that the two would be ideally mated on a spit of land in a gray-green lagoon, he wondered. Perversely, his mind strayed back to Conrad. "Venice is one of the truly great cities of the world," he'd said. Not surprising, Pointer thought. It was Byzantine, eccentric, unpredictable. A city that matched the Dean's mind.

He turned back, a certain wariness insinuating itself between them now. "What are you afraid of?"

"I don't trust myself anymore."

Taking her in his arms, Pointer felt her shiver. He didn't trust her anymore either, but that didn't mean he'd stopped wanting her.

Lying in the hull of a boat tied up beside the Ponte dei Sospiri, invisible in the disguise of night—hair, jersey, slacks, Converse sneakers as black as the hour—Leon Ivanovitch had felt Angelica's kiss as if it was his body she was leaning into and not the American's. He was full of anger. Pointer was a poor excuse for a man with his grin as broad as the clowns' Leon had jeered at in the Moscow Circus. And she was his prize student. He'd trained her—and more than that, selected her for himself.

After they had gone into the hotel, Leon still lay in the boat, his anger as dark and opaque as the lagoon. Angelica had not used any of the tricks he had taught her. She kissed the American as if she wanted to . . . worse, as if she *meant* it.

True, he was on a fact-finding mission for Dostankov, but if the facts proved seriously detrimental to the national interest of Russia . . .

He fulminated, turning and twisting his options until a plan began to take shape, a plan with the pleasurable double-edge of duty fulfilled and sweet revenge. A burly, rough man with a taste of power, now he took his job as a license to strut, to boast and, when circumstances permitted, to inflict pain. Neither a lackey like Joseph following orders without question, nor capable of holding a commanding position like his superior Dostankov, whose viciousness was applied through the agency of others—his hands always clean— Leon was a petty officer with illusions of self-importance.

Yes, he reminded himself once again, his instructions were to observe Pointer and Angelica and report back. Dostankov wanted to save the Operation, but now he, Leon, was the point man, the agent in the field. Like a good line soldier he needed to exercise judgment according to the circumstances. And the circumstances were clear—the operation was compromised and beyond repair. Once he explained all this, Dostankov would understand and be grateful. Pointer would be taken care of, and Angelica would have learned a most valuable lesson.

Leon stretched in the boat, invigorated by his comforting rationalizations. He was looking forward to the new day.

CHAPTER
NINETEEN

Gray skies notwithstanding, the morning was bright with promise, Pointer thought, as he went down to the lobby to meet Angelica. They were going to spend the day playing tourist, all cautions ignored and warnings put on hold. But he was early by almost an hour. Turning up his jacket collar, he went out and walked along Riva degli Schiavoni, away from San Marco toward the point of the island.

The lagoon water was murky, morning light filtered through the overcast, gondolas and motorboats dancing at anchor, hulls knocking against each other. He whistled as he walked, hands in his pockets. The stretch of land was a finger in the Adriatic with a park at its point. Toward the second knuckle, Pointer stopped.

Washed against the wall at his feet was a drowned body, half-dressed and cast in bronze. An island's memorial eternally deluged by the sea. There was no plaque to mark the spot or explain the sculpted figure. Ahead, a motorboat was pulled up by the park—a vague outline that grew clearer as he stared. He could make out three people in it, two men and a woman . . . her scarf slipped down, and he saw a blur of golden hair.

Angelica? Impossible, but he called anyway. One of the men turned. Joseph, for all the world. Merriman's man. Pointer called again. The motor revved, swallowing his voice. The boat sped into the lagoon, the prow standing out of the water, white crests rising like waterfalls on either side.

"He saw us." Angelica had to shout over the noise of the engine.

"What if he did," Leon said. "Your orders stand. Have Pointer at the bridge at one o'clock."

"I only take orders from my control . . ." She was miserable as she screwed up her face against the bite of the wind and the spray. Joseph had awakened her at dawn and brought her to the boat where Leon was waiting. There had not been time to contact her control, he said. Anatol Dostankov was very worried about the operation, and he, Leon, was his man—sent *personally* to check up on her. Leon . . . She hadn't thought of him in months, and now he was giving her orders she could not follow—could not refuse . . .

"I told you. Today you're taking orders from me, and if for any reason you fail, tomorrow you'll be on your way back to Moscow to answer to Dostankov personally. That can be considerably less pleasant than the old gulags."

"I've followed my orders—"

"You lie even to yourself, darling. The American has turned the tables on you. You believe he loves you?" Leon's jealousy was feeding his cruelty. "You're a device to him . . . *Pointer is working for the CIA.*"

"I don't believe it. I know him—he's too gentle, naïve—"

"Have your forgotten *all* your training? Appearances mean nothing in our business—"

"Neither should jealousy."

Leon's anger surged. "We have proof against Pointer. The CIA has been in Germany checking up on *you*. Matthias Conrad himself has come out of retirement. Pointer *has* to be their source. It isn't Merriman. He's been collaborating for years—and your control watches him too. There's only one other answer, which is far worse. If David Pointer isn't work-

ing for the CIA, then you are. Which makes you a double
agent—"

"*Stop* it. I am not a traitor, you must know that . . ."

"Prove it. Stop protecting Pointer and carry out your
orders. It's now a test of your loyalty. If Pointer is not at the
bridge . . . Well, you know the punishment for treason."

Angelica was waiting in the hotel lobby when Pointer got
back from his walk.

"Have you been waiting long?" He was surprised to see
her.

"I just came downstairs two minutes ago." She leaned to
kiss his cheek.

"But I thought I saw you when I was out walking, in a boat
with Joseph and some other man?"

Angelica shook her hair back over her shoulders. "No. Impossible."

She sounded merely annoyed, but her face was strangely
tight. Her lips had felt cold on his cheek, and when he took
her hand it was cold too. He tried to shake off the uneasi-
ness. Damn it, this was supposed to be a special day. All
suspicions, Conrad's and now his too, put aside at least for
the moment . . .

"Are you ready to give me my tour?"

"Yes . . . all ready."

"Where do we start?"

"There's only one place to begin and end in Venice—Piazza San Marco. From there we'll go to my grandfather's
exhibit. He's so proud of it. He'd take you himself if he
weren't so busy."

When they reached the exhibit Pointer almost wished he
had asked Merriman for the guided tour; Angelica knew so

little about some things he cared about, less than he knew, for example, about ikons. There must have been over one hundred of them, representing the work of four or five centuries, the spiritual expression of a people placed by an accident of geography and culture on the edge of Europe and Asia. The more he looked, though, the more clearly the singular beauty of the ikons came through. The earliest were flat, without perspective or shadow, one layer of paint superimposed on the other, light on dark, clear, primary colors, and in the center the luminous mandorla, the all-embracing halo of the Christ figure, light of the world, hope of mankind, savior of sinners. The essence of the Christian faith was captured in His large expressive eyes and in the glistening halo, not perched like a crown but circling the entire head. Later the technique had become more sophisticated. The figures were elongated and refined, the details better defined. The ikons, like the faith of the people they reflected, were both simple and complex, Pointer thought, the cumulative effect of art, history, religion and poetry too. Merriman hadn't exaggerated. It was a collection any museum would be proud to own—priceless in every sense of the word.

Later in the morning they shopped on the Rialto. Pointer bought Angelica a long oblong scarf, an abstract swathe of gold and green. But when he gave it to her, she pushed it back at him, startling him.

"No, David. I can't accept it."

"Why the hell not? Don't you like it?"

"It's not that."

She tried to turn away, not wanting to make a scene... Joseph or Leon, or both, might well be following them.

He held her shoulders. "I didn't think you were so old-fashioned. Did you mother tell you never to accept anything except candy and flowers from a man? It's not, for God's sake, a diamond tiara. Just something to remember Venice by."

He opened the scarf and put it around her neck. She didn't protest, but seemed almost grim as she stroked the silk.

"Thank you. I'm sorry. It's just that I'm not feeling well. I'll treasure it always."

Her voice wavered. Were those tears in her eyes? She turned away from him and walked on, looking briefly in every store window along the bridge at the silks, the hand-blown glass, the leathers. Pointer was forever stopping to take a second look. From the crest of the Rialto bridge there was a sweeping view of the Grand Canal, ancient palaces lined along its edge.

Crossing the bridge to the markets on the other side was like walking into history... Housewives and servants crowded around the open stalls for their daily purchases, picking through the heaps of tomatoes, zucchini (their succulent yellow flowers gone with the summer), the first pears of autumn and fiery orange persimmons, not even the wonders of refrigeration able to break the habits of centuries. Here the daily trip to the marketplace was a ritual and social occasion.

In the afternoon, Angelica took him sightseeing. She led the way, repeating to herself Leon's charge, trying to make herself believe he was right. David was an American agent using her as coldbloodedly as she had set out to use him. That meant every word was programmed, and when he made love to her, that was programmed too. As in the beginning it had been with her. But he was so tender, so eager...

She refused to think of what was going to happen to him. She would just shut it from her mind, leave him at the bridge, then go home to a new assignment that would not compromise her heart. Never again.

She walked slowly, reading aloud from her guidebook to cover her uncertainty, each step bringing them closer. He loitered, gaping at thirteen centuries of history on a stretch of marsh melded into a single work of art—a city.

Venice was a stage set, Pointer thought, a spectacular stage set, not a real, sweating, teeming city, and the girl at his side was not real either, and Conrad's story was a fairytale—by Grimm, who else?

"Where are we now, Angelica?" he asked, half expecting her to say "the second act."

"On the Ponte dell'Accademia, which leads to a museum famous for its Titians, Tintorettos, Giorgiones and Veroneses," she said, consulting her guidebook. "It's a simple wooden bridge but it has become something of a landmark printed on the face of the city. It was erected fifty years ago as a temporary measure. Venetians took a fancy to it and it still stands as sturdy as the first day. It was never intended to be permanent..."

"Sounds like me."

She turned away, remembering the question he had asked her, teasingly she had thought: "Do you ever get more than you bargained for?" She had set out to disarm *him*, and instead... She shivered, thinking of Joseph... of Leon and his warning. She knew it was no empty threat. She shivered again and pulled her jacket tight around her.

"You never told me how you feel about me, David."

He thought of seeing her in the boat that morning and of Conrad's warning not to give his heart away, although it had come too late... "Some things don't have to be said."

It wasn't the answer she wanted to hear. But it didn't matter... Because when it came down to it, she could *not* go through with Leon's plan—no matter what the consequences.

"Let's go back, David. I'm tired and cold, and I really don't feel too well..."

It was the siesta hour, quiet... She glanced about but saw only grayness, no lurking shadows. Still her voice sank to a whisper.

"We can come back tomorrow. The museum's closed now. Everything in Italy takes a siesta."

"How about us?"

"If you come right now." She forced a smile and started back. "Please, David . . ."

Pointer lingered another minute on the bridge, poised between her gradually receding voice and the dramatic view. Black hulls gliding over murky water through the gauntlet of grand peeling palazzos . . . "Her palaces are crumbling to the shore/ And music meets not always now the ear:/ Those days are gone, but Beauty is still here." . . . Lord Byron, and yes, Angelica was right, he thought, I am a romantic. But, I hope, not a fool.

Reluctantly, he pulled himself away to follow her—and heard the footsteps behind him, too rapid for the place, the time of day. He glanced over his shoulder just in time to see the metal bar raised. Slight and quick, he dodged so that instead of cleaving his head like a coconut, the crowbar caught him on the skull an inch or two above the left ear. His head exploded. The bridge, the whole beautiful town went up in starbursts like the Fourth of July. His body felt like a star-spangled banner at half-mast, waving uncertainly on the bridge, faltering, crumbling.

He tried to call for help . . . for Angelica, although he knew she must be out of hearing already, and what came out was only a whisper. Angelica, angel—but Lucifer was the most beautiful of God's angels . . .

"Leon . . ." The name passed through his fading consciousness like a stab of pain. Then he felt his body rising, like a car on a hydraulic lift that needed new shocks. The top rail of the wooden bridge scraped his back, and he was on a projection course, hurtling down . . . sinking in the most famous sewer in western civilization.

The cold water shocked him back to semi-consciousness, and he burst through the oily darkness. His head felt as if it belonged to someone else—somebody with a much bigger body to support it. He blinked to clear the oily slick, and saw reflected like an Augustinian vision the huge white balloon

domes of Santa Maria della Salute, the baroque church anchored at the entrance of the Grand Canal. It was a distant
goal to strive for, like the beatific vision, and at that moment
it seemed just as unattainable. Santa Maria della Salute—the
Blessed Mother of health and salvation, both of which
seemed to be slipping away from him fast in the filthy canal
water.

All along Pointer had had the eerie feeling that none of it
was real. He was in a play... *The Merchant of Venice*... or
maybe he'd gotten his authors confused... it wasn't the
Bard's words he was acting out it was Thomas Mann's *Death
in Venice*... He kept his eye on the domes and swam. One
stroke, maybe two. A black, shiny mass floated alongside
him. A rubbery hand reached out and clamped around his
neck, pulling him down, holding him under.

If his head belonged to him, he might have a chance, he
thought. But like this, his skull bursting, lungs filling... if he
didn't surface soon it would be too late... He remembered
all the pools he'd swum in, lap after lap, miles piling up
through the hours. Clear, Olympic pools, his body jackknif-
ing with precision, long even strokes cutting through the
water, not daring to look to either side and risk losing a fraction of a second... and his mother had worried about what
so much chlorine would do to him. So much chlorine and
now so much Venetian shit...

Swimming was the only sport a kid as puny as he was
could go out for, and now he was drowning. He could beat
the frogman in a crawl, a backstroke, breast stroke, freestyle.
But there was no freestyle here, no free anything, and no
contest. If he could get away, gain a few yards, he knew he
could outswim the frogman. He needed time... those few
precious fractions of a second that meant winning or losing a
meet.

Out of the murky depths of fear Pointer remembered
Louise and her laundry lists of causes—world peace and
Central America and the integrity of her own space. Her

self-defense classes had almost killed him because she'd
honed her skills on his body. He forced himself to relax.
Feeling the limpness, the frogman loosened his stranglehold,
just slightly but enough . . . Pointer allowed his body to drift
closer in a dead man's float. Suddenly he lunged and hugged
the rubbery body around the waist, jerking his knee up
sharply. The frogman's stranglehold broke. His body doubled
up, somersaulting. He tried to scream and swallowed water.
The Louise defense: first a knee to the groin, followed fast
with two fingers gouging out the eyes. Easier on dry land
when your opponent wasn't wearing goggles. But Pointer
made a stab for the mask, trying to get under it.

The two locked together and went under. Pointer felt as if
he were trapped in a steel embrace. The other man's arms
were tightening, pushing the breath out of him. All he could
do was keep on groping for the eyeballs. When they surfaced
again Pointer was on top, riding the slippery, thrashing
body. . . A motorboat flashed by, further down the canal a
pair of gondolas drifted, the city was waking up from its nap.
The frogman was trying to shake him off, fumbling to unsnap
the sheath at his waist . . . Pointer saw the edge of a blade, a
silver gleam through the murky water slashing at him. In
another moment he'd be scaled, boned, filleted. The thought
induced the same knee-jerk reaction. He bore down on the
frogman, slamming into his groin, cold terror giving him a
desperate strength.

The frogman flayed wildly, his face, his body twisting in
pain, the knife leaping and darting through the water like a
silver fish. Pointer ducked and came up on the other side.
The current was carrying them back under the bridge.
Through an oily blur he saw the wooden pilings just a few
yards ahead. Reaching out, he caught the frogman under the
chin in a life-saving hold and swam with all his strength and
speed in a straight line. Three seconds . . . five—that was all
he needed. The frogman slashed with his knife to break the
hold. Pointer's shoulder numbed, and they were swimming

in a red sea. He could feel the strength seeping out of his arm with the blood. But the piling was so close . . . if he could hold on another moment . . . the frogman's head was a battering ram on a collision course with the bridge's foundations. There was a flat thud like water slapping a hull as the black skull smashed into the piling, splintering against the wood, pieces of flesh catching onto the barnacles that crusted it. Pointer released the body and watched it sink slowly, one blackness swallowed by another, and only a thin line of bubbles to mark the grave.

Blood and cranial tissue and brains like sweetbreads floated on the water mixing with the rest of the debris, cigarette butts, scum, pigeon feathers. Pointer was shaking so that his teeth chattered, and he couldn't stop them. A man was dead, a stranger—he didn't know anything about the guy—and he had become a killer. There was a baseball on the back of his head, and blood streaking down his chest, dissolving in the slime, and he was a killer.

He treaded water and retched the slimy bile. He did not look back at the bloodied bits of flesh and hair sticking to the piling. If the crowbar up there was coming after him, he didn't want to know it. Instead he thought of Katharine Hepburn in "Summertime." If Kate could do it, so could he, goddamnit. She had always been a favorite, Yankee-straight and uncompromising. He couldn't swim, not with his shoulder, so he turned on his back and kicked off, trying to put as much distance as possible between himself and the bridge, kicking and concentrating on Kate to keep from thinking about the centuries of shit he was floating in, and the feel of the cold rubbery hand on his throat, and the killing.

CHAPTER
TWENTY

The Edgewater Arsenal in Maryland—a high-security instal-
lation. Behind its electrical wire fences the silent weapons of
war were being tested and refined, chemical and biological
killers transforming war from a science to a nefarious art.

Lieutenant Colonel Marcus Engels was chief of defoliant
testing operations, but he had enough expertise in other
lethal chemicals to satisfy Conrad's questions. Of equal im-
portance, Conrad trusted him. A tall, imposing man, thick-
ening around the middle from being trapped too long in
Research and Development, Engels was one of the disgrun-
tled professionals who had rallied around the Dean when he
left the Agency. He had a cropped military haircut, round
fleshy features and an unexpectedly soft voice that retained
the good ol' boy accent of his native Georgia. Conrad had
worked with the colonel from time to time, and it was on
those earlier contacts that he based his opinion. A thorough-
going professional, competent, well versed in his field—the
kind of individual Conrad could respect.

"For the record, sir, what brings you out of retirement?"
Engels greeted the older man with a salute and handshake.

"Not a thing, Marcus. Nothing could." Conrad stated his
position flatly. "I'm in town for a funeral—one of my old
team, Nora Hewitt. You may have heard about her death."

"Hewitt." The colonel rolled the name around his tongue,

making it sound several syllables longer. "What happened to her?"

If the Agency had come to Edgewater about Nora's death, it was too early to elicit that information from Engels. "The immediate cause of death is listed as asphyxia brought on by a constriction of the respiratory muscles."

"Any previous problems?"

Conrad shook his head.

"No unanswered questions, loose ends?"

"Plenty, in my mind at least."

"That's why you're here."

"To pick your brains, if you're willing."

Engels grinned. When Matthias Conrad asked for permission to pick your brain, there might be nothing left of it by the time he finished except splinters of skull.

"I want you to run a test for me." Conrad took the black Chanel atomizer out of his pocket and set it on the table between them. "On this."

"You think Edgewater needs to sweeten its image, or you're trying to tell me I don't smell as good as I used to?"

Conrad laughed. The colonel picked up the perfume case and turned it over in his hand. "How soon do you want to know?"

Conrad took a squashed package of cigarettes out of his pocket and offered one to Engels although he knew the officer didn't smoke. "I've got all day, if you need it."

The colonel weighed the atomizer in his hand again before dropping it into his pocket. "Just for you, sir. We both know you're not supposed to be here, so don't go wandering around."

"My wandering days are behind me," Conrad assured him.

Watching the metal ashtray fill with butts and Conrad tried not to think about Nora. He had sent enough agents to their deaths, but none rankled more than hers. Nora, charging off like a rogue elephant, trying to pass herself off as a tourist, retired and breaking every rule in the process—Peter Braun, always helpful, had filled in the details for him. But none of that made it any easier to swallow.

The Dean was still working on the pack of Camels when Engels came back. He closed the door behind him, sat down at the table and placed the atomizer between them.

A quarter-inch butt stuck to Conrad's lower lip. "Nerve gas?" he said so that the colonel wouldn't be in a position of compromising himself by giving out classified information.

Engels nodded. He knew better than to ask Conrad why he was walking around town with a perfume spray of sarin in his pocket or where he got it, but it was a pretty safe bet that it had belonged to the dead woman, Nora Hewitt. "GA—one of the deadliest. It can be absorbed subcutaneously."

"If a woman sprays herself with the gas believing it's perfume?"

"Doesn't have a prayer. A tiny drop—no more than a single milligram—is all it takes. If not removed immediately it will seep through the skin and cause death in approximately ten minutes. It's quick, but not painless."

"Death by asphyxia?" Conrad seemed to be looking directly through the colonel, as if there was someone else behind the officer visible to his eyes alone.

Engels fingered the atomizer for a moment. "The symptoms are the same as with GB or VX. Eye irritation, drooling, sweating, then the cramps and nausea come, headaches, confusion, the chest constricts. Finally there's loss of muscle control causing incontinence, drowsiness and finally suffocation."

"Asphyxia by any other name..." Conrad pushed his chair back to get up. "The Soviets are familiar with GA." It was a statement more than a question. He knew the Russians were as committed as his own side to an expensive and active chemical warfare research program. Twenty-five years ago, at least twenty percent of their arsenal was chemical, and the figure had only one way to go.

The colonel was nodding. "One of their favorites. We know they captured the German supply during the war and transported it back home. Since then GA has been their principal nerve gas, although they've added more sophisticated ones, just as we have. It's not a subject anybody's comfortable talking about . . . on either side of the fence. Including me."

"Don't worry." Conrad reached over and took back the atomizer. "Handy little gadget though, if not exactly a Christmas stocking stuffer."

CHAPTER
TWENTY-ONE

The Royal Danielli, which fronts the grand lagoon of Venice, had been the palace of the Dandolo family. In the conversion from private palazzo to de luxe hotel as many details as possible were kept—the exquisite Venetian glass chandeliers dripping flowers, the edges of the petals tinged with pastel pink and blue; the carved panelling lining the rectangular lobby and sweeping up to form a gracious stairway and balustrade; the aura of refinement and gentility.

Prudence Merriman was sitting in the lobby sipping a Brandy Alexander when Pointer burst in, dripping fetid water and breathless. She took in every detail with a glance: his clothes plastered to his body, his hair slick with slime, the wild look in his eyes.

"A memorable entrance, David, if something less than grand. Are you always so conspicuous? If you wait outside on the quai I'll send Joseph to make you presentable."

"No, *not* Joseph. I mean, I'll just go up . . ." As he spoke he realized Angelica was sitting with Prudence, in a high-back chair so that she was half-turned from him. She was sitting absolutely still and white-faced, her hands clapped over her mouth, and he was staring at her and his voice was rising. "The quality of mercy . . . that's what's lacking here, ladies. And all this time I thought we were assembled to play *The*

Merchant of Venice. By the way, where is the august merchant? No gentle rain from heaven dropped here, but a very ungentle crowbar to the back of my skull—"

"Cut the drama, David, and get on with it." Prudence Merriman's commanding voice sliced out at him.

"Your guess is as good as mine." Pointer knew he was shouting but he couldn't seem to control his voice or his emotions. "Maybe somebody knowing what a champion swimmer I am wanted me to have a tryout in the Grand Canal. Or maybe we should let Angelica explain what happened. Why didn't you stick around to find out, darling? Or did you already know what was going to happen?"

"David... please... I thought you were right behind me, and when you weren't I started back. There was no sign of you. I could see the bridge and there was no one on it—"

"It didn't occur to you to look *over* the bridge—?"

"David," Prudence interrupted, "what are you saying?"

"... I don't know..." And he didn't.

Either Angelica honestly had nothing to do with it or she was everything Conrad said she was. In either case accusations weren't going to get him anywhere.

"I just got back, David," Angelica was saying. "Ask Prudence."

"Of course, Angelica's telling the truth. What would she have to lie about?" Prudence's deep, no-nonsense voice almost made Pointer's fears seem foolish. "You've been working yourself too hard, David. A brain like yours has to be pampered, cared for—otherwise it can snap." She snapped her fingers at the word, startling him, and her eyes seemed to look past him.

Before he could begin to answer he was being given a genteel bum's rush, not out the front door but through the manager's pristine office to the service elevator.

"Where the hell are you taking me?"

"To your room, *signore*, but privately, so as not to embar-

rass you or the Royal Danielli. You understand." The manager had handled worse. Dealing with the wealthy, the
powerful and the famous he'd become shock-proof.

Pointer was too weak to protest, and he had no more fight
in him. What the hell... maybe Angelica *was* telling the
truth and Conrad's suspicions were an old man's fancies. But
goddammit, no one just falls into the Grand Canal while
strolling across the Ponte dell'Accademia. And there aren't
frogmen everyday in the canal. *Someone* wanted him in
there—and permanently.

Alone in his room, Pointer stripped, deposited his clothes
in the wastebasket and turned on the shower full-blast. It
would probably take days to rid himself of the stench and the
slimy feeling that clung to him like lichen on a rock. As for
the rest... He closed his eyes, too tired to even begin to
make a stab for the truth, and began a priority list in his
head. In cases of extreme fatigue, frustration or distraction,
his mother had always sat down to make a list.

First: shower. He checked it off. It was always a good idea
to begin a priority list with something you could check off
right away to give yourself a feeling of accomplishment. Another pearl of maternal wisdom.

Second: head. Ring for an icebag.

Third: shoulder. Check wound, bandage. As he made the
mental note, Pointer gritted his teeth and turned so the
steaming water beat down in the knife wound and washed
out the sewage.

Fourth: sleep. No additional notation necessary.

Fifth: Angelica... police... Merriman... Conrad...

He was still trying to get his priorities right when he heard
a knock on the door. Pointer knew he had locked it. After his
afternoon swim he didn't want any more surprises, and there
was absolutely no one—with the possible exception of his
mother and she'd been dead for two years—he wanted to
see now. He ignored the interruption and continued his list.
The next knock was louder and closer—too close for com-

fort. The bathroom door eased a crack, and Prudence Merriman's distinctive voice rose above the rush of water.

"Are you decent?"

Pointer swore under his breath and shouted, "No." His answer may have been garbled by the noise of the shower. In any case, it wasn't a deterrent.

"Here's a towel." She stuck one through the curtain. "Turn that damn water off and come out here. I'm going to have a look at your shoulder. Then you're going to tell me exactly what happened today, omitting the high drama and tragic lover's laments, if you please."

In such a compromised position the only course of action open to him was obedience. Turning off the shower, he wrapped the towel around his waist and grabbed hold of the faucet. The hot water had made him woozy. He must have lost more blood than he realized. The bathrooms in the Danielli were veritable throne rooms, ample in size with flowered tiles, deep tubs and a choice of fragrances to scent one's bath. The towels were thick and warm, and there was a bell to call the maid in to scrub your back. In spite of these amenities, Pointer felt distinctly uncomfortable to be sharing one with Prudence Merriman.

She took in his body with a practiced eye. "Well, don't just stand there. I'm not going to tear off your towel. I said I want to check your shoulder. The Grand Canal is a nasty place to soak an open wound."

"I appreciate the concern, but I'm okay." Pointer obeyed even as he protested. Only then did he notice the small bag on the edge of the sink. Prudence had come prepared.

Her hands were quick and sure as she took out a sterile package, unwrapped it. Inside were swabs, Betadine antiseptic, alcohol wipes, tweezers and a roll of gauze. She opened the edges of the wound and swabbed it clean. Pointer stopped breathing to keep himself from screaming. The bathroom swam around him.

"It will only sting for a minute, and believe me this hurts

considerably less than an infection would. And if it got into the bone..." She wrapped his shoulder in the gauze as she talked. "You're lucky, David. It's just a surface wound—and a fairly neat one at that. The thing to do now is keep your shoulder clean—your nose, too."

"I know it sounds crazy, but I *was* just walking across the Ponte dell'Accademia when a crowbar met my skull."

"That's the other thing I want to see. Turn around."

"It's nothing...."

Her hands were on his shoulders, turning him. Prudence Merriman brooked no resistance. A formidable general. It was difficult to picture her taking a backseat to anyone, even her husband, and yet their marriage had been a long and apparently happy one. Pointer heard her snort, but couldn't decipher it. Her face never gave away a thought although it was far from bland. High cheekbones, small straight nose, distinct chin (a little too pronounced for beauty), eyes like a northern lake that rarely thawed, a sweep of white hair.

"Nasty," she said, "but you'll survive with no permanent damage to the national treasure inside."

Prudence Merriman had the knack of making him feel awkward, over-rated. He never knew which way she'd blow, and right now he felt the towel slipping. The last thing in the world he wanted was her critical eyes appraising his naked body.

"If I get out of this—this whatever it is—I'm never not going through the rest of my life looking over my shoulder."

Prudence shrugged. "Welcome to the human race, David. How do you think other people live? With their heads in the clouds like you? When you have to worry about surviving, that's the only way you can live. It's what we're all about. You can't let the fellow behind you catch up or he'll take what you've got. Get your own and hold on tight. That's the American way."

Clearly she didn't approve. For an instant he glimpsed the

fire banked behind the elegant facade, the passion that must have been there in her youth, involving her in so many causes. Just for a moment.

"I didn't know the Merrimans cared."

"It seems to me you don't know much of anything for a young man who's supposed to be the Einstein of the eighties. You don't even know how you fell into the Grand Canal. Now that your wounds are taken care of, I want you to tell me exactly what happened out there by the Accademia this afternoon. August is not interested in an international incident, and the Italians are mercurial people. The officials here can be difficult when they want to, just for the sake of being difficult." She led the way out of the bathroom.

Pointer followed, clutching his towel. "I'd like to change into something more comfortable."

"Drop the towel if it will be easier for you," she said over her shoulder. "Just get in here and start talking."

Pointer made a beeline for the nearest chair. His legs were as insecure as the towel. Sitting down he didn't have to worry about either of them betraying him.

"Begin at the beginning and try to remember every detail. August and I feel responsible for you, David, not just because you're a fellow American in obvious distress, but because you came here to see our granddaughter. You're our guest." She stood over him, smiling.

Pointer felt the sudden warmth. For the first time he appreciated the extraordinary power of Prudence Merriman. No wonder her husband had never had another partner since their marriage. Who would need one if he had Prudence? A vibrant, exciting woman still, and she hadn't forgotten. Her sternness seemed to be melting some. She was still slender, graceful. Why hadn't he noticed until this moment? The straight pink linen skirt, straight over the hips, kick-pleated at the bottom, a matching linen camp blouse, a coral rose pinned to the collar—simple and perfectly tailored. She was bending over him, her arm reaching behind him, lifting him up out of the chair. Her perfume made him dizzy, or maybe it was the pain sharpening as he moved.

"You must be exhausted and aching. You should be lying down, David. You're very pale suddenly."

He could see the concern on her face. She was actually worried about him. He let her walk him over to the bed and waited by the side while she pulled the covers back. He sat on the edge and eased back onto the pillows. The bed felt better than any woman—better even than the treacherous Angelica. He felt his body easing and shut his eyes.

"That's better, isn't it? Much better..." Prudence sat down on the bed beside him. "Don't sleep yet, David. Turn over now. I'll work out the soreness while you tell me your story. There'll be plenty of time to sleep after."

Pointer turned over. Obedience was becoming a habit. Prudence started at his neck, circling the area of his wounded shoulder. Her fingers were strong, working out the pain. The hands of a woman at ease with a man's body, that knew men, understood them, knew when to be gentle, when not to be. He moaned into the pillow. It hurt, but it hurt wonderfully. He never thought he could feel good again.

"Did I ever tell you, I used to massage your friend Matthias Conrad's back like this. He was young once, too, and almost as foolish as you. Even then, I'm afraid, he wasn't a man to be trusted. Do you understand, David? You can't really trust Matthias Conrad, no matter what he tells you. You're surprised I know so much about your friend...or you're surprised I know you're friends? No matter, you were going to tell me your story."

Pointer lay perfectly still. How could Prudence know about Matthias unless Matthias told her himself? Told her what, though? To watch out for David Pointer? Watch out for her husband? Why hadn't Conrad ever mentioned their friendship? Friends, enemies, lovers...all distinctions seemed to dissolve. If a true and false test were put in front of him, Pointer was sure he would flunk.

T or F: August Merriman is a good man and real patriot, and Matthias Conrad the last holdout of the McCarthy Era?

T or F: August Merriman is a tool of the Soviets, and all Conrad's suspicions are real?

Pointer felt Prudence loosening the towel, discarding it. He didn't move, didn't breathe. She was old enough to be his mother . . . older than his mother. And his body hurt. Still it was responding . . . perverse, out of his control . . .

"Good buns," she murmured. She was grasping his ass, stroking it, the length of his body, all the way down his legs. She knew exactly what she was doing. "Go on, David." Her voice was husky now, her touch compelling. He knew what was happening, and he couldn't hold back, couldn't stop himself. She was releasing all his secrets, all his lusts. A wet dream. He shuddered and lay still, trying to remember the last time he'd had one . . . when he was a kid, probably, before he met Louise. He always made his own bed so his mother wouldn't notice the stains on his sheet.

"You can sleep soon, David, as long as you want. But now you're going to tell me everything that happened. I'll help you remember. You were on the bridge with Angelica, the Ponte dell'Accademia. I know it well."

"Angelica started back. She'd been reading from her guidebook. I hung back, admiring the view and wanting to see the paintings, thinking about the miracle of this place, and of Angelica . . ." Pointer droned on, Prudence listening, the rhythm of his voice and her hands like a duet. "There were two men, one on the bridge and one in the water."

"What did they look like?"

"I never saw the one on the bridge."

"And the other?"

"Black and rubbery on the outside and steel under that, but only an average swimmer."

"What did he have? Tanks? A snorkel?"

"No, just the wet suit, a mask, flippers, and the knife—

that goddamn knife... I've got to go to the police." Pointer
came alive, agitated. He saw the head smashing into the piling again. "I killed him. I killed a man and I don't even know
who. Leon something, I think. Do you realize what that
makes me? You're rubbing the back of a wanted man, a murderer—"

"Wanted, maybe. A murderer, no." She rubbed without
speaking, easing his conscience along with his body. Louise
would have made him give himself up immediately. "You
can't turn yourself in. You have to consider August's reputation. He does not, as I said, want an international incident—
a man in his position. You're not just an American tourist,
you know. You're in Venice as his guest."

"But leaving the scene of a crime, failing to report a
murder..."

"You're in Venice, not Los Angeles. Have you any idea
how impossible the Italian police can be when they want to
be, or what the prison here is—the dampness, the layers of
mold, the water rats? Venice may be an international treasure—a miracle, as you say—but the police aren't as sophisticated as the place. They're provincials. First the body has
to be recovered, then there'll be the investigation. You can't
afford to hang around here waiting for that. It could take the
Italians months at least. No, David. We're leaving Venice the
day after tomorrow, very early. That will give August time to
take care of this unfortunate accident. And you'll leave too.
Joseph will make the arrangements for you to fly home."

Maybe she was right, Pointer thought. A mildewed cell
under the canal didn't sound inviting. And if there was a
murder rap over his head he wanted the Dean to be the first
to know. Conrad had gotten him into this mess, he damn
well could get him out. Still... "Someone tried to kill me. I
want to find out what's going on around here—and what
Angelica..."

Her hands felt harder, and he groaned. Her voice sounded
harder, too, when she spoke. "Angelica is in shock. She cares

very much for you, David. I don't know how you could have accused her, except that you were so upset that you had to lash out at someone. I don't come to Angelica's defense often. After all, she's my husband's grandchild, not mine— and she usually doesn't need defenders. But this time I think you're being unfair to the girl. It's absurd when you think about it. Why would she want to hurt you? Do you beat her? Do you cheat on her? Are you walking out on her? Unless there's something I don't know..."

Pointer shook his head.

"Don't you think you're being unfair, then, and, I might add, a touch melodramatic?"

"You make it sound that way now. But it was my head, and believe me, when you've got a steel hand locked around your throat and you're gulping sewage, it *isn't* melodrama, it's the real thing."

"I'm not trying to play down your experience. You're much too valuable to us—to our country—to let anything happen to you. I'm trying to put it in perspective. Most likely it was a case of mistaken identity, and whomever that crowbar was intended for is probably grateful that Leon whoever has gone to his just reward. Another thing, David, how do you know the dead man's name?"

For an instant, lulled by Prudence's hands, her closeness, Pointer considered confiding in her. She was an old friend of Conrad's, after all, and she genuinely seemed concerned. Maybe he should tell her everything, tell her how he was supposed to mistrust Angelica and her grandfather but play along with them, keep his eyes open and report back to Conrad. If he could stay awake he'd lay it all out for her, but his bone-weariness caught up with him and he gave in to it, and to the enveloping, relieving sleep that followed.

*   *   *   *

When Pointer woke up the room was dark and he was naked. Angelica was kneeling on the bed where Prudence had been. She was wearing a navy blue silk dinner dress. There were gardenias in her hair and tears in her eyes.

He looked at her over his shoulder, although the slight movement hurt. "What are you doing here?"

"Prudence sent me with these." She held out two capsules, orange and cream-colored. "Antibiotics for your shoulder. There's water on the table."

He turned over, took the pills and pulled himself up, resting midway to gather more strength. The ache in his shoulder was bearable, but his head was threatening to fly into orbit. Dropping the pills on his tongue, he reached for the water, gulped, and fell back, relieved that nothing more was required of him. He wanted to believe Prudence had been a dream, but he was naked and the sheet beneath him stained.

Angelica was looking at him with eyes as deep as the Adriatic. "I'm sorry, darling, I'm sorry," she kept repeating.

"I should never have left you, if I'd stayed beside you..."

"What could you have done? Slapped the crowbar with your guidebook?"

"Don't make jokes. Not now, David."

Angelica was leaning over him. Her voice was a whisper. Her tears were wetting his cheeks and his lips. He tasted the saltiness, inhaled the sweet fragrance of the gardenias. Her skirt was a full circle, and she raised it over him, stroking his body with the silk. There was nothing underneath. The straps dropped over her shoulders. Her breasts seemed ready to spring out. He tried to reach for them, tried to reach under her skirt, and winced.

"Lie still, darling."

He was becoming a yes-man, and liking it. Conrad was right. He was out of his element. He should stick to laser beams and particle atoms. Much simpler than a beautiful woman. Stick with Louise, even. At least he knew what to expect—heated arguments and lukewarm ass.

The silk was doing strange and glorious things to his skin. He tried to concentrate on the changing textures, knowing it was a losing battle. There was the silk of Angelica's skirt and the silk of her hair wrapping around him, the smooth gardenia petals, the satiny lips. And there was the moisture of her tears and her tongue, and then there wasn't any resistance . . .

"What do you want from me, Angelica?" he asked when he could breathe again. He was angry with himself for being so easy.

"To stay with you tonight. We'll be leaving—"

"I know." He brushed the tears with the back of his hand and held her against him. So what the hell. A few more hours with her couldn't hurt him more than he already hurt, and she was crying again. Maybe she was telling the truth, had been from the beginning. Innocent until proven guilty —it was the American way, after all.

She smiled through her tears, making him believe that his new judgment was right and Conrad was nuts. Except that was what had gotten him into trouble in the first place. He watched her get up and reach behind her back for the zipper. The dress became a dark circle on the rug, and he closed his eyes. He felt her weight on the bed beside him. Then she curled under his arm, a perfect fit, holding him lightly just to make sure.

CHAPTER
TWENTY-TWO

Pointer walked through the streets, looking over his shoulder every step of the way. It was the first night he had been outside the hotel, and the last time he would walk the streets of Venice. In the morning the Merrimans would disperse. The party would be over—and quite a party it had been. Since Prudence interrupted him in the shower, he hadn't been left alone for a moment. Angelica was at his side, lover or warden... he still wasn't sure, not sure of much of anything or anyone anymore.

He breathed deeply, taking it all in—the light and shadows, the *calles*, the singular beauty—just as he remembered except for a shadow of sinistry that seemed cast over it all. They crossed the Rialto bridge, circling around behind San Silvestro with Tintoretto's Baptism of Christ, following the curve of the city to the vast and columned Palazzo Rezzonico, ostentatious imprint of an eighteenth-century *nouveau riche* banking family, drawn irresistibly to that other bridge of death and rude awakening.

"Will I see you again, David?" Angelica sounded tentative —shy, he would have thought if he didn't know with certitude that there wasn't a shy bone, muscle or anything else in Angelica Merriman's fantastic body.

"I have to work." Pointer sounded disagreeable even to himself, out of character.

"We'll be in New York, D.C., Sorrento...I don't remember where else. Bonn, London... Joseph can give you our itinerary for the month."

"Yes, but they're not Venice. It's easier to pretend here—"

"Pretend?"

He ignored the question. "And the hell with Joseph. I can make my own dates." He knew he sounded almost petulant, and unreasonable, nothing at all like the brilliant "star warrior" he was supposed to be. So what else was new? "Let's get an *espresso* at the Florian. We can't leave Venice without a last drink at its oldest cafe."

Angelica fell in step beside him, and he put his arm around her shoulder, casually like a friend. Friends and lovers. That's all. Sure.

They walked in step in the direction of Piazza de San Marco, back across the treacherous bridge, Pointer still looking over his shoulder, through the deserted square of Campo San Maurizio, and along Calle Largo XXII Marzo by the antiques, silk and leather shops. By the time they passed through the arcade into San Marco he felt easier. Directly ahead of them was the piazza, grandiose proof that East and West can meet, as Merriman was fond of saying, and something solid to hold onto when every other certainty seemed to be slipping away.

Each view in Venice was dramatic by night, he thought. The dark cover hid the signs of decay and slow poison caused by the urban wastes dumped regularly into the waters from the industrial centers just to the north, dooming the city centimeter by centimeter. In the illusive moonlight Venice was restored to its legendary grandeur. Maybe it would restore whatever had decayed between Angelica and him—lost or lapsed love. To one side of the square was the *orologio*, to the other the *campanile*, the ornate clock and soaring bell towers, so different as to be opposite extremes, yet together creating a marvel of unity and harmony.

By night, emptied of tourists, the piazza was awesome. A

stray pigeon or two, cocky and overfed, pecked for crumbs. A few couples leaned against the arcades embracing. Otherwise the square was theirs. They headed for the Caffe Florian in the southern arcade. On good days the tables spilled out into the piazza. Tourists relaxed and drank in the scene with their *aperitivos*, and in the afternoon a band played favorite Italian songs. David and Angelica sat inside on a leather banquette at a small table covered with a pink cloth and drank espresso from steaming glasses set in silver holders.

"Did you know Wagner sat here at the Florian?" Angelica said.

"Thinking of *Das Rheingold*, no doubt. You've gotten to be a walking guide book. I should remember to pack you whenever I go on vacation."

"Proust sat here and corrected his translation of Ruskin." She went on undeterred. "And Henry James sat here—"

"Thinking of *The Turn of the Screw?* I'd rather think about taking another turn screwing you." Pointer did a terrible Groucho Marx imitation, which was lost on her anyway, and which made him feel foolish. He was tired. His head had receded to a dull ache, the kind you get from a boring old friend who drones on, and his shoulder hurt if he moved suddenly. Trying to be on guard all the time was exhausting . . .

"How did you get so far when your mind is set on only one thing?"

"Slept my way to the top. How about you?"

She touched his cheek with her fingertip, wanting to tell him so much.

"What shall we talk about?" He was watching her closely now.

"Whatever you like."

"Good. Then we'll talk about you."

"What do you want to know about me?"

"Everything."

"I thought you knew." She laughed lightly, as if he was joking although she knew he wasn't. "There isn't much—"

"Whatever there is then." At least he'd have something concrete to bring back to Conrad. They could swap stories.

Angelica turned the silver holder in both her hands. "It isn't a very interesting story. I was a funny looking little girl, tall and skinny with hair tied up in two tails. My clothes were always hanging off me or above my knees. I don't remember my parents at all, and the woman who took care of me had little . . . a pig, a few chickens. We lived in a small house. Erika was always old, and her eyesight got so poor that all she could see were shapes and shadows. She couldn't take care of me any longer so I was put in a school. I guess you'd call it an orphanage, only it was a very happy place. Full of light. I had clothes that fit, and books, and plenty to eat. The rules were strict—"

"Where was this school?"

She looked up and met his eyes. "In Berlin."

"I think I can finish the rest," Pointer said. "The ugly duckling turned into a beautiful swan, and one day out of the blue, a king as rich as Croesus rode up to the door and claimed the swan as his long-lost granddaughter."

Angelica was laughing. "Not exactly, but you're close. I studied hard, obeyed the rules and was rewarded with many privileges."

Pointer wondered if he was one of Angelica's perks. But there was no point in asking or listening anymore. The story was like a bullet-proof vest, tailored exactly for her. Or was he being too damn suspicious, courtesy of Conrad . . . except what about the little incident on the bridge? Because she was there, did it prove she'd set him up? Just a coincidence . . . ? The possibilities made him dizzy . . .

Angelica drained the thick sugared dregs of her coffee. The waiter was watching them anxiously, hoping they'd leave so he could close up. There was no one else left in the cafe.

Outside in the vast empty square he leaned against a column and studied her again. "It was a marvelous story, Angelica."

Her anger flashed. "I didn't confide in you to have you mock me."

"I'm serious," Pointer insisted. "And I'm not mocking you. I'm just sort of... marveling at it all. I mean, it's hard to believe you're for real—a girl as incredible as you, in a city as fantastic as Venice, and now I find out that you actually did step out of—or into—a fairytale. A poor German girl wakes up one morning and discovers she really is a princess— American-style, anyway."

Angelica smiled. She didn't want to be angry, and it certainly wouldn't help. "Is that really how you see me?"

He nodded. The answer was really half and half. "Tell me one more thing." He took both her hands and brushed his lips against them. "Is it true what you said in New York?"

"What did I say in New York?"

"That there is only one man in your life. There are no others beating a path to your door?"

"Oh, there are hundreds in every city in the world." She laughed. "But I refuse them all." She was glorious when she was laughing.

He took her in his arms, forgetting, blocking out, his doubts and fears.

In the shadow of St. Mark's they kissed as if they were discovering each other for the first time. His breath was cool with a slight sharpness, aftertaste of the acrid coffee. There was a hint of the sea air on his lips and the promise of the sea, enduring and enveloping, in his kiss.

"I'll see you again then, David?"

There was never any question in his mind. Even if he didn't want to—and he did—Conrad would insist on it to get to the bottom of the frogman incident. Anyway he was in too deep to pull out now.

"Will you come to Maine with me?"

Maine, Pointer thought, the temperament of the place was inimical to fairytales, much too matter-of-fact for them to seem like anything but hogwash. Everything would somehow come clear in the bracing New England air.

"It's the closest thing to home I've got and there'll be only you and me—no Joseph to keep watch with champagne, and no bridges to cross."

CHAPTER
TWENTY-THREE

KGB head Victor Chebrikov was cast in the old mold by which most Westerners still viewed the Soviet leaders—thick and balding with a peasant's broad face as glacial as a Siberian winter and a massive chest stuck wall-to-wall with medals. His office reflected the same severity—the big desk and highback chair behind it, two chairs in front with curved wood backs, not even a seat pad to provide comfort, heavy hemp curtains of an undefinable color somewhere in the spectrum between gray and olive drab, a row of gun-metal filing cabinets against the inside wall, fluorescent lighting overhead. The only other items in the room were three telephones and the papers set in neat stacks on the desk. The desk was built as solidly as he was, and he stood behind it, waiting for an explanation from his counter-intelligence chief Dostankov.

"Comrade Anatol Petervitch, your operation to persuade the U.S. scientist David Pointer to share his scientific wisdom with us has engaged the interest of the General Secretary himself. And now"—Chebrikov shoved the report he had just received from Angelica's control across the desk, "what am I to tell him?"

The intensity of color in the KGB Chairman's face was proportionate to the degree of his impatience—and right now his head from the bull-neck up was purple.

Dostankov was exhausted. Natasha had kept him up most of the night watching the contraband video cassette she had borrowed from the director of her laboratory, then reenacting the choicest frames until he was too limp to respond to any stimulation, however inventive. To own a VCR was an estimable achievement. To have something to watch on it, an occasion as memorable as May Day was supposed to be. Wishing he had foregone the erotic night for a sound sleep and clear mind, Dostankov picked up the report and studied it intently.

It was succinct and pointed. Angelica's control had been bypassed and had retaliated by bypassing him . . . a matter of internal politics, which he could settle in due time. The more urgent question was the future of the Operation, and Chebrikov was waiting for his reply, the color progressively brightening in the chairman's face as Dostankov stalled for time.

Dostankov knew his man was dead. Joseph had just filed a detailed report accusing Pointer of compromising Angelica and murdering Leon. Added to the information from Germany, the evidence had appeared conclusive: The American scientist was a CIA agent. Now, though, Angelica's control was contradicting that evidence: "Pointer is *not*, repeat *not*, working for the Central Intelligence Agency. He has been approached but he has not committed himself and remains very much open to Angelica's advances . . ."

Dostankov read the new report, weighing each word. He had over-reacted to Peter Braun's report from Germany. The girl was performing as he knew she would. Everything had been proceeding exactly as planned until Leon's arrival. Now Pointer was suspicious . . . Angelica nervous . . . her control furious . . . and Leon was dead.

The counter-intelligence chief was shaking his head, intended as a gesture of regret, even sorrow. In fact, Leon was fortunate to be floating in the Grand Canal and thereby spared from experiencing the measure of Dostankov's displeasure.

"Leon Ivanovitch," he was saying now, "has paid the price for going beyond his orders. A regrettable accident, but at least I have been spared the task of punishing him for his lapse. He was to check on Operation Counterpoint and report directly to me. Word had come through Germany that Pointer might be more than a scientist. I passed the report on to you, of course, but in all these papers—" he waved toward the desk. "It may have been mislaid. No matter, I will send another copy."

Dostankov was back-pedaling as adroitly as he could, buying time to collect his thoughts and decide how to redirect the Operation.

"A CIA agent was in Berlin and Mollenz asking questions. She died, conveniently, within an hour after returning to her home in Washington."

He paused to allow the Chairman time to digest the information, to appreciate his associate's skill, thoroughness, decisiveness.

"By now her control should have followed her to Paradise."

Dostankov permitted himself the small touch of humor. A new idea had begun to take shape; the only flaw was that he hadn't thought of it sooner. He was confident that his revised plan of operation would overcome any reversals.

"I am particularly pleased to report this to you, Comrade, because he is your old nemesis—Matthias Conrad."

"Matthias Conrad . . ."

When the Chairman echoed the name, Dostankov thought he detected the suggestion of a smile on the dour face. He was prepared to discount it as a mirage produced by his extreme state of tiredness, until Chebrikov added, "I wish you luck, Anatol Petervitch."

The barb reached its mark. Dostankov flipped the report

back across the desk, sat down without being asked, ignoring the Chairman's deepening color, and crossed his legs.

"Now I should like to answer your initial question. The General Secretary should be pleased to hear that in spite of certain unfortunate complications, the Operation regarding David Pointer is proceeding even better than I had anticipated. A small adjustment is in order, though. Pointer will no longer be recruited. No, I have a much more satisfying future in mind for the American—as the husband of our beautiful and talented agent, Angelica Merriman. Instead of being forced into defecting, Pointer will come to Moscow for love."

Dostankov beamed, considering what he would do to Chebrikov's drab office when he moved in.

"Comrade and Mrs. David Pointer. We will arrange the perfect honeymoon for them . . . with your blessing, Comrade Chairman."

CHAPTER
TWENTY-FOUR

By dawn *The Prudent Angel* was sliding down the lagoon into the Adriatic, and the chopper was hovering at the mouth of the canal. Pointer could see it from his window, an enormous silver-winged pigeon, and it was waiting for him. He packed quickly, thinking it might be safer to slip away and take the train to Milan. He would leave a message at the desk for the pilot, he decided as he opened the door.

Joseph was waiting. Pointer should have known. Merriman, it seemed, wasn't taking any chances.

"I was thinking, Joseph—"

"That's not necessary, Mr. Pointer. All the thinking has been done for you. Your bag please, sir."

Pointer, wanting to throttle him, handed it over. He'd been on the losing side of too many arguments lately. And whether or not you put faith in the stories of Matthias Conrad, it didn't seem reasonable to think that someone would push him out of August Merriman's silver chopper. Too obvious.

He followed Joseph, wondering how the man was going to meet up with the yacht. As they stepped outside the hotel the chopper skimmed across the water. Joseph opened the door. The wind from the blades and the noise made it impossible to hear or be heard. Pointer shook hands and climbed aboard. Joseph pushed the tote in, then climbed after it. The chopper lifted.

"Where the hell do you think you're going?"

Joseph seemed more watchful than ever. "Mr. Merriman wants to be sure you catch your flight."

The chopper turned over the city. The roofs of Venice became a line of color. Then that, too, was gone.

The staterooms of *The Prudent Angel* were like continuations of the sea, decorated entirely in blues and greens. Angelica opened her dresser drawer and felt under the stack of underwear. Although she seldom wore any, she kept a full supply in every Merriman domicile. A complete wardrobe down to accessories. It was easier than packing, Prudence had said, as if everyone lived in a dozen different places.

Angelica went along. Life as August Merriman's granddaughter was enviable. Her friends had not been so lucky— a maid in the U.S. embassy in Moscow, a secretary in Prague, a field officer in Cuba. As long as she obeyed...

In the beginning it had been easy. She got her orders and followed them...enjoyed them. SEDUCE AMERICAN SCIENTIST DAVID POINTER. GAIN ACCESS TO STAR WARS SECRETS. She had already received the assignment when Merriman asked for her help: "Make him fall in love with you, Angelica. You can do that with any man."

And it was true. Her body was a sophisticated weapon. She had been trained in its uses at the KGB school for sexual operatives in Leningrad, just as she had been trained in languages, explosives and conventional weapons at a school for espionage agents in a suburb of Moscow.

In the beginning her assignment had seemed so simple. Pass herself off as August Merriman's granddaughter and obey his wishes—make David Pointer fall in love with her. But now the lines were tangled. Angelica felt the hard edge of the cassette with relief. The yacht had been anchored off the lagoon for two weeks, ample time for her control to make the plant. Inserting the tape into her Sony Walkman, she adjusted the earphones and stretched out on the bed to listen.

By training she was supposed to obey without thinking or feeling, both of which interfered with performance. And David had been so easy, so naïve—and such a surprising lover—tender, generous, leading her into dangerous areas of the heart. Now she was no longer just carrying out an assignment. She wasn't sure when it had begun, but she'd realized it in Venice. And, for once, she couldn't help herself. If she could talk to someone . . . But there was only her control— an altered voice on a cassette. They had never spoken, never met. Her instructions were to relay any questions through Joseph, and he would pass them on.

Angelica lay very still, listening, her body tense. She was not sure if Merriman knew that Joseph was more than his secretary, or that she was not his granddaughter. He certainly treated her as if she were. She could ask for anything she desired and receive it. The archetypal doting grandfather. But Merriman was also a superb conman, it was his greatest skill. He could make you believe anything.

Angelica pushed the review button and listened to the whirr of the tape rewinding. Something had gone wrong in Venice. Joseph had warned her, then Leon arrived. It was the first time she had received orders from anyone except her unknown control. A breach of the rules. She had checked her dresser drawer in the Danielli every day. Eventually there had been one cassette. She found it the day David arrived. It was short: VENICE IS MADE FOR LOVERS. USE IT.

Venice was a romantic stage set, except at some point, maybe it was over the orange sherbet in Harry's Bar or when David kissed her near the Bridge of Sighs—wherever, whenever, she had stopped acting. Stopped following orders because she was following something stronger, more irresistible.

Enter Joseph and Leon with their deadly message: *There was no time for her control to make contact. The order would be confirmed, but not in time. You are supposed to be leading the American, and he is leading you. He must be eliminated. Note the view from the bridge.*

She had tried to stall, to avoid carrying out the order, hoping even as they started that day on their walk toward the bridge that something would happen to stop them. But in the end she had done her best to warn him, pretended to be ill and tried to entice him back to safety. If Leon ever knew what she had tried to do . . . And Joseph would be no easier on her. As for David, of course he was suspicious now, after what happened to him . . . But what about *him?* Was he, a CIA agent? She didn't trust herself anymore . . . didn't trust him. . . .

And now she had new orders. For the third time she ran the tape, uncertain whether she was being given a sentence or a second chance. It was a two-word message: MARRY POINTER.

CHAPTER
TWENTY-FIVE

Beth Conrad inched the vintage Wagoneer jeep along the two-lane road and turned with relief through the opening in the stone wall onto the rutted path that was her father's excuse for a driveway. Her palms were wet on the steering wheel, her fingers cramped as an arthritic's. It had taken three hours to make the hour-and-a-half trip from Boston's Logan Airport—as if it weren't upsetting enough to be kissing Tom goodbye after five goddamn years. "A little space to grow in," he called it, a thirty-seven-year-old ski bum talking as if he was one of her father's tomato plants. She would have given him a couple of miles, a state even—but the whole frigging continent...

After a lot of stuff she wished she had never said, Beth had given him a month before she went back to California. She had even taken the bus to Boston with him to show there were no hard feelings and to give him one last chance to appreciate the kind of superior person he was trying to ease out of his life. It worked out for her anyway. Her father wanted his car picked up at the airport, so she wouldn't have to take the bus back.

All the way home, Beth cried and cursed Tom for walking out on her for something as nebulous and unfair as personal space, as if she had gained fifty pounds and spread into his square footage... The rain started about ten miles from the airport, a rush of water that never slackened... One thing Beth was goddamn sure of. She wasn't spending the next month listening to her father belch and predict the end of western civilization. She'd go to Washington and stay with Charlotte.

Fathers are always there when you need them—an American myth, by Conrad family standards. Matthias Conrad had never been there, and when he was it was mostly to criticize. Whatever he'd expected from his only child, Beth knew she hadn't provided it, a disappointment from her earliest memory.

The rain was relentless until she crossed the Tiverton Bridge. The fog was gathering on the other side, like enemy forces blocking the way. By the time she reached Little Compton the road was slick and the visibility zero. Scrunched over the wheel, she tried to steer by the white dividing line, her speed never going above twenty-five. In the best of weather the jeep felt like a tank after driving a subcompact for ten years. When it was new and she was younger she'd torn up the byways of Sakonnet in the four-wheel drive, screwed Jeff Wrightson in the back among her father's fishing gear and laughed 'til she cried when he rolled over and landed bareassed on Matthias' hand-tied fly. Quite a catch.

It all seemed so long ago, those bright summers when she and her parents came to Little Compton like a regular family. Matthias commuted from Washington for long weekends that he stretched out into as many days as he could, and she played tennis at the club while Charlotte golfed. In the lengthening afternoons they sat on the verandah drinking Tom Collinses, although she was under age, she hoping Jeff would notice her.

Jeff... Beth hadn't thought of him in years. He was a tax lawyer now, pompous and bald, the crown of brown curls that had been his pride gone with the lazy summer days when they were seventeen and suffering from hot pants and angst. Everything looked whiter then—tennis whites, white teeth freed from braces for the first time in years, the patches of white skin where a tan stopped and discovery began, the white heat of first sex . . .

Beth pulled up behind the house and cut the engine, remembering her father's warning, and wishing she hadn't. "If you see anything unusual, call me right away," he had said when she telephoned the night before.

"Unusual like a purple cow or a team of Libyan assassins?"

The Old Man had hung up only to call again a few minutes later. "I don't like you being there alone."

"Tom is free, white and a lot more than twenty-one. I can't tie him to a vegetable stake."

"You can ask him to stay—at least until I get back there."

On the third call in less than an hour he'd said, "Your mother is lonesome, Beth."

"Tell her I'm coming as soon as I get myself together. Nothing could keep me here. After Labor Day this place becomes so godforsaken. How do you stand it?"

"I wallow in solitude . . . sort of what you and your ski bum do with sex."

"Really, dad."

The Old Man was being so clandestine all of a sudden, downright paranoid, calling from different pay phones as if he'd never sworn off his old habits. Beth remembered him saying, "I'm only keeping the good habits . . . smoking and drinking. They destroy my body but leave my peace of mind intact." The Old Man was something else, she thought with a certain grudging admiration, only admissable because the fog was enveloping, making her feel as if the rest of the world had dropped off the edge.

Matthias's foul-weather gear was stuffed under the front seat of the jeep. Beth put on the yellow jacket, pulling up the hood as she got out of the car. The fog was lifting. She could see it rushing across the fields, rolling, swirling, somersaulting toward the sea as if it couldn't wait to plunge in

the surf. As she watched, it seemed to be a living force, yet
ghostly. The house, the fields, the gardens—the most familiar sights, all the work of her father's hands, as much a part of
him as she was—appeared eerie, meancing, unknown and
unknowable. This must be what madness is, she thought.
Terror of the known. The familiar suddenly turning hostile.

Her teeth chattered and she slammed the car door and
sprinted toward the house. The rain was reduced to a drizzle. She fumbled with the back door. The dampness made it
stick. It wouldn't budge even when she pushed into it with
her shoulder. Swearing at the entire frigging world, she tried
again. The top was giving, but the lower half wouldn't move.
Beth stepped back to kick it in, propelling all her strength
into the effort.

She never knew what hit her, or that she was thrown forward against the stubborn door with such force that it burst
open. Her body fell across the doorway. There was no one to
hear the thud or to answer the phone that began to ring a
few minutes after she fell. The caller was persistent, allowing
the telephone to ring for several minutes before giving up,
convinced that no one was available to take a call.

CHAPTER
TWENTY-SIX

Matthias Conrad had never felt like a legitimate candidate
for retirement until he got home from Washington and found
his daughter sprawled on her face, the door banging against
her skull. Where the back of her head had been, there was a
jagged chasm, stuck with scraps of bright yellow rubber and
yellow hair.

Later Conrad could not tell the police what he had done,
although each action had seemed precise, controlled, and
above all necessary while he was performing it. His tears had
melted her dried blood—he remembered that—and the
white bones of the vertebrae that had held her head were
shattered into thin flecks like bleached pencil shavings. And
he had fallen going up the stairs to make the phone call because all he could see in front of him was a blur of moving
treads and the blackened blood and bright flecks of yellow, as
if the sun had shattered. Not son, daughter, he remembered
correcting himself. Oh, what a stickler for getting it right was
he . . .

These were the things he remembered—none of them
what the police chief was interested in. He only made the
one call to the police. He couldn't tell Charlotte over the
phone that Beth had the back of her head blown off. Charlotte had always been so careful to keep a protective hand
behind Beth's head when she was a baby, to brush the few

hairs over the delicate spot until they glistened, to put a bonnet on her before taking her out—all that care wasted with a single shot.

"Had to be a dumdum, Matthias, to do such a job." That was all Sam Daniels could say at first, and he had to swallow several times before he got that out. In his thirty years as the Sakonnet police chief, Daniels had never been faced with a murder before. He had seen a number of drownings and his fair share of automobile accidents, but never murder. All he knew about handling a homicide was what he'd seen in the movies on or TV, and at that moment the reality of dealing with Beth Conrad's blasted-out skull seemed as far removed from "LA Law" or "Miami Vice" as he was from Don Johnson.

Daniels was small and leathery, a horned lizard with alert, darting eyes and jutting brows too heavy for the rest of him. He remembered Beth when she was still playing with a pail and shovel at Briggs Beach. Now her body was rigid, already beginning to decompose in the midday heat. He turned away from the sight to give his deputy orders. With only nine years on the force, Sgt. Mark Tanner was a rookie in his chief's eyes. The other three members of the Sakonnet police were twenty-year veterans.

"Tanner." Daniels' bark lacked its usual bite; the rookie was in the tall grass behind Matthias' garden emptying his stomach. Daniels knew how he felt. Tanner had known Beth, too, way back when, probably seen her out on the Point when her old boyfriend Wrightson used to go slumming with the townies, flashing false IDs and swilling beers. She'd been a wild one, all right, before she went out west—bold as brass and always ready with a smartass answer. Tough to think of Beth Conrad as middle-aged, but anyone over thirty these days qualified. Even tougher to see her dead.

Daniels had lost track of her when she went to California to college. Nobody local had killed her, he'd bet on that. One of those California nuts, most likely. A Charles Manson type.

Seemed as though they bred weirdos out there with the freeways and the surf and the Hollywood stars. Too bad they didn't stay where they belonged instead of bringing their craziness back here, where the madness was more deeply rooted, predictable—like Lila Tillingwood parading to the Village Green in her birthday suit whenever there was a full moon, or Bayard Sturgison saluting the flagpole in his front-yard every morning with his grandfather's Civil War sword. A civilized, manageable insanity that didn't get in anybody's way.

"Tanner." He barked again, glad of an excuse to keep his back to both Conrads. "Get your ass over here." They'd have to get the body to Providence for a coroner's inquest, search the area for evidence, ask around town if any strangers had been seen. After Labor Day a stranger stuck out like a dandelion on a golf green. Conrad might even want to bring the FBI in. Hell, a man like that could probably get the President to work on the case if he wanted to.

A good man, Matthias Conrad, a real American. Daniels had known him as long as he could remember, since before the war—the big one, not Korea or Vietnam. Once in a while they went fishing together, out in Conrad's old outboard at 5:00 A.M.—nothing fancy, no airs about him, nothing phony. That's what the chief admired, and Conrad always treated him like an equal. No difference between them. None of the put-on social bullshit of his wife and daughter—the exact opposite. Built the house, too, and damn good job it was, never asking help from anybody but always grateful for a piece of sound advice. Same with the vegetables.

Now the Dean was standing just inside the door at his daughter's head, and Chief Daniels hadn't a word to say. Even if he'd solved every detail of the case he wouldn't have been able to get the words out—not with Beth lying there, and Matthias like the statue of Colonel Henry T. Sissom on the Village Green—rigid, hollow-eyed, a scarecrow with a beer belly, formally dressed in suit and tie as if he was all ready for the funeral.

Daniels turned his cap between his hands. "My condolences, Matthias, and if you could give me any more particulars, it would be appreciated. No hurry though . . . whenever you're ready."

Conrad coughed and cleared his throat, although he wasn't even smoking. "I just got back from Washington. Beth was lying here just as you see her." He was looking at his daughter, not Daniels—staring at the yellow jacket, the key ring closed in her right hand. "How's the weather been, Sam?"

The chief took a deep breath, relieved to be given a break from his grim duty. There was no subject more comfortable or comforting than the weather. "Pretty hot for September. The storm yesterday cooled things off some. A real beaut it was—"

"That confirms the time, then." Conrad cut him off. "Beth was killed some time yesterday while it was still raining."

Of course, the jacket. Daniels frowned. He should have figured that out himself.

"Somebody must have been waiting when she got out of the car."

"A crazy jilted boyfriend?" Daniels began, trying to sound smarter than he felt.

"No. Beth was driving *my* old jeep . . . and that's my foul-weather jacket she's wearing . . . in the storm with the rain and the fog . . ." His voice trailed off.

Sgt. Tanner was coming back from the field, looking as though Little Compton was going to have two deaths to deal with at any moment.

"That's just between you and me, Sam," Conrad mumbled.

The chief nodded. "Will you be around later . . . if we need you to answer any questions?"

"I have to go to Washington and bring Charlotte back. I don't want to break this to her over the phone. We'll bury

Beth here, beside my mother." Conrad's voice broke.

Daniels turned away. His own eyes were wet, and he didn't want to embarrass his friend. "One of my boys can drive you up to Logan, if you want. Quiet around here now without the summer trade." Daniels shuffled his feet for a few minutes and turned his hat, then put it on. Matthias had nothing more to say. The Chief walked to the car. Opened the door. Got in. Started up. Idled the engine. Got out. Started back. Conrad had gotten a blanket from the house and was covering Beth's body. The chief waited until he finished, out of respect and because it was easier to speak up with her body covered.

"One thing, Matthias . . . about what you were saying. The fog was pretty thick around these parts yesterday. I know because I had to put my high beams on to find my own driveway."

Conrad's head came up slowly, thrusting out from his neck, and he peered over his glasses, over the chief's head to the stretch of open fields that had been Conrad land ever since anybody in those parts could remember. There was no mystery in his mind. The fog, the car, the foul-weather jacket added up to an obvious case of mistaken identity—his daughter died for that mistake. Someone had a .44 Magnum carbine trained on the door, expecting him to come home.

"If the killer was waiting with his telescopic sight set before the fog thickened, it would only have been a matter of listening and timing. Once the engine is cut it's ten yards from the car to the door."

Daniels digested the words, syllable by syllable. "The killer could have been set up before the storm started . . . around noon. That's when it really began to get bad."

"Possibly." Conrad's voice was cold. Daniels had never heard it like that before.

"A professional killer is a patient man. We're trained to be," he said, more to himself than the chief.

CHAPTER
TWENTY-SEVEN

Sixteen hours after leaving Venice Pointer was on all fours pulling up the last of Conrad's beets. Matthias didn't seem surprised to see him or interested in what had happened. That night over fresh bluefish stuffed and broiled in the fireplace he listened to the murderous story as if it were a minor incident. A brush with death, however close, becomes insignificant when you've buried your daughter in the grave marked with your name not thirty-six hours before.

"I'm sorry Venice didn't agree with you, but it wasn't a total loss. You're here, only slightly the worse for wear, and the girl told you something about herself at least. A clever enough story."

"You don't believe any of it?"

"It's rather like a skeleton, accurate as far as it goes, but once you add the flesh and blood you get a different picture of the person. She didn't mention that the school was in East Berlin, or that the reward for good behavior was the opportunity to go to the KGB training center outside Moscow, did she?"

"Angelica doesn't fit the role—"

"They never do, you know, in real life. You've seen too many movies. She must care for you, though, because she took pains not to lie. She's taking orders. It's probably all she knows how to do, all she's ever done. You shouldn't judge her too harshly, but it would be just as foolish to trust her. Angelica Merriman is quite probably a dangerous woman."

"I know. Lucifer..." Pointer mumbled.

Conrad got up and cleared the plates, stacking them in the sink. "He who hesitates is lost, dear boy. A truism, but truisms are the only consistent truth. Put your trust in clichés instead of beautiful women and you'll live a much longer life."

The day had long since died, the only light was from the fire. Pointer started to turn a lamp on but Conrad checked him. "We're reading hearts and minds. A lamp won't help." He sat down in his favorite wingchair. He didn't say that they were safer in the dark. He didn't need to. "What are your plans now?"

Pointer leaned back on the couch, feeling the full effect of jet lag. "Go back to Livermore. I need to work again."

"Good. Stay in the compound. Eat there, sleep there. Do what ever you have to do—but do it there. Don't go back to your apartment. I'll see that you're protected."

"How? Will I know?"

"You won't—and you're safer that way. You can't give away what you don't know."

Pointer felt as if an ice cube was sliding down his back. "You believe me then...?"

Conrad ignored the question. "What are you going to do about the girl?"

"She promised to come to Maine with me."

"No. Meet her in a city—New York, Paris, London. Not Maine."

"But it's my home, I invited her."

"Disinvite her." Conrad's tone was sharp. "I can't protect you there. It's too desolate."

"I have to find out something...and I can only do it in Maine."

Conrad sloshed his Scotch. Nora and Beth and almost David... "If you go to Maine, you're on your own. Just you and the girl . . . and I hope she's on the side of the good angels, for your sake. Now, tell me about the bridge again, every detail." His voice sounded calmer. "Why didn't you rush to the police—an eagle scout like you? I would have thought—"

"I was going to, but I wanted to find Angelica first. She was all I could think of. Then I decided to go after I did something about my shoulder. But I never got a chance." He faltered, unsure how much to say. "Actually Mrs. Merriman stopped me."

"Prudence Merriman. How does she fit into this?"

"She was in the lobby when I came in, and then she followed me upstairs to check my shoulder."

"And she was so warm, so understanding, you poured your heart out to her."

"Some, I guess."

Conrad shook his head. Pru hadn't changed. She could still work her magic.

"She knows we're friends," Pointer was saying. "She told me she knew you."

"What exactly did she say?" Even now he relished hearing about her.

Pointer took a deep breath, afraid he might be going too far. "She said, I used to give backrubs to your friend Matthias Conrad and even then he wasn't a man to be trusted. You didn't tell me you knew Prudence Merriman."

"Just old friends," Conrad mumbled into his glass. But his mind had jumped back decades. All these years he'd blamed Pru for kissing him off. What if, unwittingly, he'd done something to make her lose faith in him? It was too long ago to recall all the details . . .

"Matthias," Pointer was saying, "you must have been a helluva lot more than friends because I was . . . I only had a towel on when she said that—and the towel wasn't any too secure."

"Pointer, you're a brilliant scientist, but you're a damn fool about women. Wasn't it enough for one Merriman woman to compromise you? First you let Angelica almost get you killed. Then you let Pru do whatever you let her do . . ." His voice trailed off.

"I didn't let her *do* anything. I mean, she just joined me in the shower—"

Conrad wasn't smiling, not even the usual wry, cynical half-smile. "Let's go back. After, as the tabloids say, narrowly escaping death, you returned to your hotel room to take a shower. A woman old enough to be your mother waltzed in—"

"I locked the door. I triple-locked it. Do you think I wanted a second visit from that crowbar?"

Conrad drained his Scotch and stared gloomily into the empty glass. "The Merrimans get or take whatever they want. It's a prerogative of their kind of wealth. If Pru wanted your door opened it would be opened for her. If she wanted your head on a silver platter, you would be John the Baptist. Even if she wasn't August Merriman's wife, she'd get what she wanted. She always has."

Pointer kept quiet, waited for him to go on.

"The last time I saw Pru face-to-face was in 1944, aboard a hospital ship in Cherbourg. I remember the day, gray, nasty. The wind whipped so that we had to shout to hear ourselves above it. The non-critical cases, anyone who was conscious and could be moved without causing immediate death, were brought out on the deck for a VIP inspection. August Merriman, entrepreneur and power-to-reckon-with even then, was touring the troops with General Bradley. He was a big supporter of the war effort and of those strange bedfellows— Churchill, Stalin and Roosevelt—and he was getting the four-star treatment. I didn't know that Pru was his wife. I didn't even know she'd married . . ." A log broke, sending up a column of blue and orange sparks. "I'd imagined exactly how it would be when I saw her again. None of the scenarios fit. Pru was wearing a navy blue suit and a wide platinum

and diamond wedding band. I remember. She looked as surprised as I was . . .

"She said, 'What are you doing here, Matt?' Her voice was
the same, slightly hoarse and probing."

"'Admiring the seascape.' Dumb, but I had no idea what to
say to her, or her husband.

"'You know this soldier, Pru?' Merriman was short, bandy-
legged, and arrogant, and I took him as a personal insult.

She shrugged. 'More or less.'

"I saluted. 'Lieutenant Matthias Conrad, sir.'" Conrad
raised his glass to Pointer in a mock salute.

"Pru tried not to smile and looked at my crutches. 'What
happened to your leg, Matt?'"

"'Just a scratch.' A hero home from the wars. Bullshit. 'I
was trying to blow up a German tank,' I said. 'One of their
grenades got me first.'

"'Where did it happen—Omaha Beach?'

"'No. I got here early, before the others arrived, and I'm
damn glad they made it. I'm with the OSS.' Merriman had a
dozen questions. I don't remember what they were, or even
answering them. Then Pru was asking, 'There's no permanent damage, is there?' I wanted to believe she was really
concerned and I wasn't just imagining it. I told her, 'The
doctors say I'll be as good as new, not even a limp to remember this by.' I didn't know what else to say, and I could
see that Merriman was getting impatient. I held out my
hand, hoping my feelings wouldn't come out in my voice.
'It's been good seeing you, Pru, and you, sir. I'm sure you
have a full schedule and I've got orders not to stand on this
leg too long.' I can't believe it now, but that's what I said.

"Pru's handshake was strong. I knew it would be, although
I didn't remember ever shaking hands with her before. I
think she said, 'It's been too long, Matt,' but I've never been
sure."

The memory suspended between them was so real that
Pointer was afraid if he moved, he would destroy it. Matthias

Conrad wasn't a man given to confidences. "You loved her."
Pointer breathed the words. Still it was enough, too much.

The cynical, bemused voice came through the darkness. "I
was young. Love is a young man's illusion, dear boy. You'd do
well to remember that."

"You still love her, though." He was afraid he'd presumed
too much, but Conrad was generous.

"Then I'm even a greater fool than you." Conrad got up
with his glass and started toward the kitchen, picking up
Pointer's on the way. Pointer watched the fire and listened to
the sounds from the kitchen. It seemed to take an awfully
long time to mix two drinks.

"Was it Pru who told you not to go to the police?" Conrad
said as he shuffled back carrying the fresh whiskeys, filled too
high so that when the ice clattered the Scotch spilled over
onto his hands. Pointer nodded.

"Just as well for us." Conrad handed him a glass and sat
down. "Pru convinced you to forget the whole unfortunate
business?"

Again Pointer nodded, feeling as if he couldn't do anything
right. Boy genius makes an ass of himself, stumbles over his
own feet, tries to drown himself in the Grand Canal . . .

"What did the great Merriman have to say?"

"Nothing, when you come right down to it. Are you surprised?"

"Not that Merriman wanted to keep it quiet, but that he
made his wife do the covering up. He must pay a staff to take
care of any potential embarrassments. Unless . . ."

"Unless what?"

Conrad went over to the expanse of window and peered
into the night. "Go to bed, dear boy. Young men in passionate affairs need their beauty sleep and old men need to think
in peace."

"That's it?" Pointer was incredulus. "You're going to leave
me hanging, and you expect me to sleep with 'unless' rever-
berating in my brain?"

Conrad glanced over his shoulder. "One other thing. You'll have to grope your way downstairs and undress in the dark. I removed the lightbulbs in your room. Just a precaution. Old men must be humored, you know."

Pointer was sure he would not be able to sleep until his curiosity was relieved. But he clocked eight hours and woke up feeling almost normal for the first time since his swim. By the time he showered and dressed, Conrad was finishing breakfast.

"Unless what, Matthias?" Pointer said, sitting down opposite him.

"Unless August Merriman actually had no idea what was going on." Conrad pushed the coffeepot across the table.

Pointer watched him butter a slice of toast. He cut it in half, wedged the better part of a divided slice into his mouth and chewed deliberately.

"Tell me about Merriman," Conrad said finally.

"He's still sharp, if that's what you mean." Pointer was deliberate. "But I imagine the cutting edge has blunted some. The man is eighty-eight . . . a vital eighty-eight, though. Just thinking about his itinerary gives me jet lag. I can't imagine him slowing down, and if he did Prudence would probably prop him up and push him out there."

Conrad seemed concentrated on the apricot jam he was spreading. "The power behind the throne . . . and you don't like her much."

"I didn't . . . but I'm human."

Conrad slurped his coffee. "She used to be the kind of girl young boys dream about."

"Some things never change, sir." He thought Conrad smiled into his toast at that, but couldn't be sure, and for a while there was only the crunch of toast and the awkwardness between them.

Conrad was thinking about finding Beth's body. The blood

stain was washed away, but that was all. Beth and Nora and almost David. The awful sequence came to mind again. The suddenness and sweep of the violence had caught him by surprise. The timing of Nora's trip must have been critical— more critical than either of them guessed, because the counter-attack had been so swift. Someone in the Kremlin had too much to lose.

Conrad chewed until the toast was pulverized, then took another overly large bite, still turning over the same question in his mind: how did the KGB get onto Nora? The possibilities were limited. Either she had been indiscreet in Germany, difficult to believe from an old pro like that, or she had made the mistake of taking someone at Langley into her confidence before she left.

That didn't explain Beth's death, Conrad thought. Nora would never have implicated him, no matter how annoyed he might make her. He could only imagine one other possibility—the Soviets had monitored her trip the same way he had—through Peter Braun.

Conrad swallowed hard. Charlotte had started back to Washington, driving alone, a few hours before Pointer showed up. She hadn't called to say she'd arrived safely and most likely she would never come back—certainly never walk through the back door again.

"You realize there's an incongruity at the heart of your story, don't you?" he said, coming full circle to Pointer again. "What good are you to the Kremlin dead? All that brilliance, that glorious scientific brain, lost to them forever. Not even August Merriman can pick the brain of a corpse."

Pointer had considered the same question on the plane ride home, in between frames of *Outrageous Fortune*. "They might think that killing me would derail the Star Wars effort," he offered because it was the best explanation he'd been able to give himself.

"No offense, dear boy, but the Russians know us better than that. No one—not even you—is that indispensable."

"Then you *don't* think Angelica set me up?"

"I only said there's an incongruity. Two dead and one near miss. I'd say we're talking about something bigger than puppy love. Finish your breakfast, then I'll drive you to Logan. Not that I'd be much good if it came to your salvation, but at least I know what to watch for."

It was past noon when Conrad got back from driving Pointer to the Boston airport. The rental car looked out of place parked behind the vegetable garden. Everything else was so familiar. Conrad wished again that Nora Hewitt had never come calling. He was too old to have his memories churned up like so much sediment, gold that panned out to be sand.

He started toward the house to change, then stopped. His gardening trowel was stuck in a pot of radishes. He had left it in the row where the beets had been when Pointer finished digging them. The pot was as unfamiliar as the rental car. A poor choice, radishes. He loathed them, and Brussels sprouts. He thought of Beth again. He had wanted to bury her in his foul-weather jacket, but Charlotte became violent at the suggestion. She went to Bannister's Wharf in Newport and bought a new dress, costly and impersonal. A case of mistaken identity to the very end, he said. Charlotte didn't understand what he was saying. That was the story of their marriage, and he dropped it. Minds that never met except to cross. And then there were memories of Pru...and the fucking radishes.

He ground out his cigarette and turned on the hose, dousing the trowel and pot from a cautious distance until he'd created a veritable lake, the water rising half-way up the clay. Ignoring the mud and water, he crouched down beside the pot and began to dismantle it, starting at the farthest point from the trowel just in case it was a detonater. Old as he was and as much as he'd loved Beth in his own peculiar way,

Conrad wasn't ready to join her—at least not before someone paid for her death, for Nora's, too, and Lady's. But first for Beth's. Soil flew out of the pot, spurting in the air as he flicked at it with his penknife, ever so carefully, a few specks at a time, until he saw the first flash of red—wires wrapped around the radishes like roots, a letter bomb to a green thumb. Say it with flowers—or vegetables. When he pulled the trowel out, the radishes would detonate.

"Matthias Conrad, former CIA official, died this afternoon from a lethal radish plant. The radishes were a gift from an anonymous donor. Investigators are still combing through the vegetable patch, trying to pick out the pieces of the former chief of covert activities."

Had the pot been there when he drove Pointer? Conrad couldn't remember, and it was immaterial . . . He got into the rental car and drove to Providence, stopping at the general store first to pick up Nora's pictures. He had dropped the film off on his way home from Washington, but then the business with Beth had pushed everything else out of his mind. He parked in a twenty-four-hour lot beside the bus station, walked over to the mall and caught the Smith Street bus to the new Amtrak station. The train to Washington wasn't due for an hour and a half, and the circular station was deserted except for a boy of nine or ten and an old man.

The old man's shirt had come out of his trousers and hung below his sweater vest. There were moth holes in the vest and the hair in his ears was thicker than the hair on his head. At first Conrad thought the old man was a bum. Then he realized the two were together. The boy wore an undershirt, an open blue windbreaker, dirty jeans and dirtier high-tops. He'd come, apparently, to watch the trains with his grandfather.

Conrad didn't think kids watched trains go by any longer. Trains like silver bullets, the armchairs in the parlor cars and the bell to ring for service. He was dressed in an Eton suit on his first trip to Washington with his mother. She wore a hat with a veil, and the porter had polished his shoes just before they pulled into Union Station. And he remembered the Yankee Clipper, Back Bay Station, Boston, to Grand Central Station, New York, with Pru in pink at nineteen. And now he was reduced to radishes.

He bought a one-way ticket and went outside to wait. Acres of desolation, part of the old city torn up at the cost of millions of federal dollars all in the name of urban renewal. The city the Conrads had helped build was disappearing before his eyes, and Little Compton, preserve of Yankee wealth and class, idyllic meld of country and seashore with no tourist attractions, had become a death trap.

Conrad opened the Kodak envelope and flipped through the prints. There were only eleven. The rest of the film was blank. All the shots seemed to have been taken in a small German town, somewhere in the north by the look of it. The usual tourist shots—children playing on a picturesque street, a couple of shots of what looked like the local beer hall, a substantial building, probably the townhall, a Gothic church, and a clergyman posed self-consciously at his organ.

There were four more pictures, all taken in a cemetery. The prints were so sharp, Conrad could read the markings on the granite:

ANGELICA CARRINGTON KLEBEHOFF
SEPTEMBER 16, 1962–NOVEMBER 14, 1964

When Pointer got back to Livermore there were two messages waiting for him. One from Angelica somewhere in the Adriatic, saying that she missed him already and asking him to meet her at the Augusta airport, Eastern Airlines, Flight 327, September 16, 3:20 P.M.

The other was from Matthias Conrad: "Lucifer destroyed Paradise. Nix Maine."

CHAPTER
TWENTY-EIGHT

Living in California, Pointer had come to realize that Maine was, as many said, a state of mind as well as a place, but he did not tell Angelica that. It was too much to explain and he had other more pressing things on his mind. Dusk was just settling when they arrived. He inhaled deeply, breathing it all in—the coast, the sea, the slate rocks and white sand, the tide pounding in, surf leaping and cavorting urged on by a light westerly wind. It was a place of stark lines and absolutes, each definition clean—the opposite of Southern California, he thought, where life was a special effects trick, truth elastic and much that met the eye an optical illusion.

Turning into the pebbled drive that arched like a cat's back, he pointed to a sprawling, turn-of-the-century cottage with gray weathered shingles and green shutters. "This is it. How do you like it?"

"It's wonderful . . . just what I imagined, so *American*. Like you."

"It's not Durandana but it's all I've got." Coming back was an act of love for Pointer. The house, anchored securely at the crest of a steep cliff, was the closest thing to a home he had ever known. A verandah shaded with a green-and-white striped awning stretched along the back, the ocean view clear and unencumbered. "Come on, I'll give you a tour of the place," he said, wanting Angelica to love it as much as he did, to love him, to be nothing more than met his eye, his touch.

Here on his own turf, freed from the influence of the Merrimans, their overbearing wealth and the shadowy Joseph, he would strip away the lies and find that the real Angelica was the one he loved—an extraordinary but not devious girl. That's what he was hoping, against all odds, but he was nervous. Very nervous. How could he not be after getting Matthias Conrad's warning telegram? Of course Conrad was getting on, maybe he was seeing spies in his imagination rather than reality . . . and maybe not . . . probably not . . . ?

Taking her hand, he led her inside. There were ten rooms, and he began describing each in the detail of an over-zealous guide. The kitchen alone kept him talking for five minutes, and then there was the dining room, living room, sun room, and bath just downstairs. He couldn't stop himself. Angelica, by contrast, was unusually quiet, her eyes never leaving him.

What if Conrad were right and he had walked smack into the plot of a spy novel? What if she really was a Soviet agent and her assignment wasn't just to pick his brain but eliminate him for being uncooperative, for being on to her and thereby a threat . . . ? It had always been a problem with him. Cooperation. His report cards were all the same. "David is a brilliant boy when he puts his mind to it. He could easily be a straight-A-plus student if he were more cooperative . . ." He remembered his mother shaking her head as she read. "You get it from your father, Davey. He walked out when I was eight months pregnant and never sent a penny." Pointer had always thought that was a lot more than uncooperative, but it was the worst his mother ever said. Now, he thought, if he concentrated on cooperation, maybe he could hang on a little longer. One thing was certain—someone had tried to kill him in Venice.

"David, are you all right?" Angelica was staring at him.

"What . . . ?"

"You were telling me about the house and then all of a sudden your voice dropped off and you began to mutter to yourself."

"A long drive." He rubbed his forehead. "I'm just tired."

"I'll make you forget. There must be a bedroom some place around here." She laughed, a delicious sound, full of promise—or threat? "Upstairs...?"

"Yes—I mean no." Pointer thought suddenly of the widow's walk that wound around the top floor and the women who had watched from it through every season, full black skirts whipping their ankles, drawn hypnotically to the churning abyss that had swallowed their whaling men. The railing was low and rotted in places, the ocean waiting below. One slip... "No bedrooms. Upstairs is empty. We never used it because there was just my mother and me." He rushed on, grasping for words. It was going to be a long weekend...

"Where do you sleep?"

"Right here, on the couch." He patted the arm of the old wicker sofa, a familiar friend and the only one he felt he had at the moment. "You can have it tonight. I'll take a sleeping bag out to the porch. That's what I always do on summer nights. I watch the stars. Did I ever tell you I taught myself astronomy, right here, lying out on the verandah. The Milky Way and Lyra, Cygnus, Pegasus, good old Orion—"

"And now you're at war with the stars. A star warrior." Angelica was smiling, a teasing smile.

"I'm not at war with anyone. I'm an anti-nuke"... coward, he finished under his breath. He had always felt the pure *science* of his work, justified being on the project. The freedom to experiment. But he also recognized the inherent conflict. Now he was living out the consequences. "Music— that's what we need." He chose a Bach sonata and slid it in the tape deck to calm himself. And it would have worked, he assured himself, if Angelica had let him listen.

"I've got a better idea," she interrupted. "I'll make some

supper. Just the two of us alone here, cut off from—"

"No." He practically shouted. "Let's go out . . . someplace bright . . ."

"If that's what you want, David." He felt her eyes on him, intent and watchful, and heard the disappointment in her voice.

"Yes, that's what I want. In fact, we can go right now."

"But you haven't finished showing me the house."

"The house can wait. It looks better by daylight anyway, and I'm starving." There was safety in numbers—any number greater than two, he thought. He'd be okay if she'd stop watching him. But she didn't, all through dinner.

Maine in late September was not teeming with night life. The better restaurants were closed for the season, and they ended up at a saloon. The Red Lantern Bar in East Machias was a far cry from Harry's in Venice. In fact, by anybody's standards it was a dive—grizzled old townies in flannel workshirts and young ones in black leather, long hair shining with grease, yellow lights, an old pool table, juke box, the kind of place where you ordered a bottle of beer so you wouldn't have to drink out of the glasses.

The food matched the atmosphere. Pointer didn't care. He couldn't swallow anyway. Angelica played with her bowl of chili and kept her eyes fastened on him. They weren't the cold smoky blue the ocean had been, but a vivid, summer-sky blue. He remembered the bridge in Venice and how she'd walked away, her measured steps receding, without ever looking back. No tender kiss goodbye, no word of warning, no quick hard embrace to take into his watery grave . . .

"Let's get out of here, David." She was leaning across the bare wooden table, trying to reach through his fear.

"No." He tried to smile at her but his face felt stiff—unco-operative. "The night is young, and what you're seeing is the real old New England, not a restoration to bring in tourists. That's taxidermy, this is life."

Louise would have put up an argument and probably

ended up walking out, with him trailing behind after a few minutes wait to cover his embarrassment. But Angelica sank back against the straight hard chair and waited and watched. Whatever she had in mind, he thought, she was so sure of herself she didn't have to rush it. Pointer began to sweat.

"Two more beers over here," he called to the bartender. He was afraid of getting drunk, but they couldn't just sit there staring at each other. Cradling the cold bottle, he pretended to watch the pool players, and Angelica went right on watching him.

The night seemed like a magician's scarf—endless. Finally the barkeep called over. "O.K. neighbors, closing time."

Pointer didn't trust his legs to get him to the door. "What do you want to do now?"

"I thought you were tired."

"Just got my second wind. Anyway, I want you to see Maine . . . that's why you're here."

"I thought you wanted us to be together. Just the two of us." Angelica's voice was a wistful question. He didn't listen —forced himself not to.

They drove around the town, dark empty streets, silence the only presence until Pointer could not delay the inevitable any longer. For the first time in his life he drove home wishing he could be some place else. The night was cold, stars bright. Angelica left him to his astronomy and went inside. The first floor burst with light. A few minutes later the upstairs lit up. Empty rooms . . . a stupid lie. Pointer looked up and his breath caught in his throat. Angelica was standing on the widow's walk bathed in starlight, her nightgown clinging like a second skin. A Valkyrie. Brunnehilde— she was supposed to be German, after all. She waved to him, then disappeared.

The light went out. He started in, there was no escape. The wicker couch was empty, the house silent as the night. He tiptoed, avoiding the boards that groaned the loudest as carefully as he used to step purposely on them when he was

a boy, found a sleeping bag and carried it out to the verandah, shivering. A Maine night in mid-July was like November anywhere else, and this was September. Pointer was
sure he wouldn't sleep a wink. But when he closed his eyes
he was gone. Escaped...

He woke up to Angelica's kiss and a day that was a gift of
brilliant light and primary colors. She looked as fresh as the
morning. It was just about impossible to be *afraid* with such
a girl on such a day or to believe in subterfuge and gray
designs. Matthias Conrad, in the light of this Maine morning, with this wondrous girl, became a twisted, bitter, med-
dling old man, and the only believable fantasy was pure love.
He unzipped the sleeping bag and stretched to work out the
kinks and aches. Here in Maine, at least, he was on home
ground. In the darkness even the familiar had seemed
threatening. But in the morning light with the scrub pines
and wild roses, the blueberry bushes and weathered shingles
clearly defined, he felt the serenity and security of home.

"What shall we do today?" Angelica was waiting expec-
tantly. Mata Hari in sneakers, jeans, and over-sized pink
sweater, her hair pulled back in a ponytail. Pointer laughed
out loud for even believing the crazy story for a minute.
Whatever happened in Venice just had nothing to do with
her.

"Can you ride?"

"I love to."

"Great. The Hammond Stable is just up the road. We can
rent horses there and ride to the lighthouse at the point. I'll
pack a picnic lunch and we'll take a blanket. It can be cold by
the lighthouse."

The horses snorted and whinnied as the cold white foam of
the surf swirled around their hoofs. They pawed and side-
stepped in the sand, impatient to run again. A fine layer of
sweat made their coats glisten.

Angelica spurred her horse. "Come on," she called, "I'll race you to the point."

Pointer's horse whinnied, eager to follow. He held back, shortening the reins, and watched her go. She was so different from the others—girls like Louise were all variations on a single theme, loose tits, loose ass, and a mind like a steel trap. Angelica a killer? Only if he got a heart attack from pumping her too hard . . . and what a way to go.

Watching her further contradicted his fears of the night before. She was an expert rider. It excited him to watch her magnificent body become one with the horse, her legs opened wide, thighs hugging the powerful back, moving up and down with the animal's thrust. He was sure, as so many said, that young girls' love for horses was sexual, though they might not realize it at the time, and he wondered with growing excitement if Angelica ever fantasized about it. He raced after her, a hunter hungry for the chase, feeling appropriately primitive. Jealous of the horse. He wanted her smooth thighs wrapped around him.

Galloping along the beach, the surf pounding with the horses' hooves, the water spraying, salty wind wetting his face, Pointer licked his lips to taste the salt and thought again of tasting Angelica. He remembered each line and muscle of her body, the touch of her hand, the scent of her skin, the way she smiled suddenly when she was pleased and grew distant when he was intrusive. And, of course, he knew the bare facts of her life, both versions of them: the one according to the Merrimans, the other according to Matthias Conrad.

But he wasn't thinking about either now. He wasn't thinking at all. He was remembering how Angelica had taken possession of him at Durandana above the Hudson. It had been urgent and exhilarating as only the first time could be. And it had gotten better. She made love when he least expected it—in the bathroom, on the beach, in the car—as if she couldn't resist him . . .

It was a long ride to the lighthouse. Three hours if they took their time, and they were almost there, at the point where the open Atlantic charged the continent from three sides. Angelica would love the drama of it, he thought, the roar of the breakers crashing over the rocks, shooting spray high in the air, coupled with the impatient cry of the gulls, and as far as the eye could see, white caps dancing.

Pointer had lost sight of her. She was a better rider. In a fair race he would stand little chance of even keeping pace, and in a contest where she had a considerable headstart he was beaten before he began. He rode harder, exhilarated by the brilliant day and by the chase. The ocean was sweeping in on his right; to his left rocky cliffs rose, planted with gun emplacements and cement bunkers, a World War II crop still unharvested though it was harvest season. Late September of an Indian summer day. The sumac leaves gleamed scarlet between the rocks and relics, and in the shade the air was cool enough to cause a shiver.

Pointer reined in his horse so abruptly it reared up, whin-nying in surprise. Angelica stood less than fifty yards away, perched on a rock, a bright blue blanket billowing around her, looking like some mythological sea creature, a Nereid that had been carried in by the tides. She was as glorious as the day, and she was waiting for *him*. Jumping off his horse, he tethered it quickly and ran down the beach to her. She threw open the blanket to embrace him, and he saw to his surprise and delight that she was naked.

"You'll catch pneumonia," he said against the voices of wind and sea and pulled her into his arms.

"Good," she laughed, "then you'll have to nurse me, and I promise I'll be a very demanding patient, requiring all your attention—and the most unorthodox treatment." She took him into the blanket, wrapping it around them. "I want you, David." She was suddenly serious. "I couldn't wait."

He cupped her face in his hands, tilting it up to his. "Never let it be said I deprived a beautiful woman."

They lay on the sand wrapped in the blanket as if it were a womb they shared, naked bodies stretched against each other.

She straddled him, legs splayed wide, and pushed herself down on him, her breath quick and sharp at the first thrust. Reaching up, he flicked at her nipples with his tongue until they hardened too. He cupped her breasts and held them as she began moving up and down on him, riding him as surely, as powerfully as she had ridden the horse, starting at a slow gait and gaining speed, breaking into a canter, a gallop, driving, fine crystals of sweat forming between her breasts, her head thrown back, their cries rising with the sounds of the surf and gulls, a madrigal of love and desire.

They lay together, locked in each other's arms at land's end, near-hypnotized by the sound of the sea, drained by their sex, she cradled in his arms.

"I can't get enough of you," he said. "I'm like an addict."

Angelica's arms tightened around him, and he ran his fingers through her hair. He couldn't entirely dismiss Conrad's suspicions or his own brush with death, but he also couldn't give up on Angelica without making their love a sham. Deep down he could not accept that she was just a KGB puppet making love to him on orders. There was more to her than that, and she was about to prove it to him again. "Which would you rather do? Ride on to the lighthouse or ride me again?"

They laughed in the blue cocoon of their blanket and clung together, kissing and teasing, arousing each other again.

It had never been like this before for Angelica, and she had known so many men in her work. She would somehow have protected herself, insulated herself, if she had ever imagined it could happen, fall in love with David Pointer? A target, an assignment?

She placed him side-by-side in her mind with Ivanovitch —strong, brutal even. She had once believed in him as she had believed in her country, her party, impressed by his strength, excited by his power. Now all that seemed like posturing. But she also knew the risks of what she was feeling, and thinking, and tried to shut her mind to them.

"I've never told you, David, I was engaged."

"You said there was never anyone else."

He held his breath, afraid to hear more yet reassured by her confidence. Confession is a sign of trust, he thought.

"Do you want to talk about it?" A Louise line, he realized the moment he said it, and wished he hadn't.

She arched an eyebrow. "It has nothing to do with us. I don't even know why I mentioned it now." Although they were still officially engaged there was no question of going back. Duty came first—and duty was now David.

"What was his name?"

"Leon."

Overhead the sky was a reflecting pool with a single cluster of clouds mirrored in it. Cirrus, cumulus, stratus, nimbus or none of the above . . . Pointer tried to concentrate on the clouds. Cirro-stratus, alto-stratus . . . The sky in Venice had been gray, too gray for clouds but not for voices. He had heard the whisper before he felt himself pulled under, the name hissed like a warning into the water ahead of him. "Leon." The deadly undertow had been named Leon.

"But it doesn't matter what his name was," she was saying, "because I love you, David, Others have touched my body, but you are the only man who has ever touched my heart."

"Do you mean that? Do you swear you're telling the truth, the whole truth and nothing but the truth so help you, God?" Pointer felt the ocean where his brain was supposed to be. Coincidences really did happen, didn't they? He prayed for blind faith, and felt in answer her warm skin rubbing against his naked side.

She was laughing soundlessly. "I'll never understand you, David. I tell you that I love you and you want to take it to a court of law. All right, then, let's make it lawful..." Her laughter drifted away, and her lips covered his. "Mr. and Mrs. David Pointer."

Pointer tried to concentrate on the clouds again, but they blurred overhead in the reality of the girl whose leg was thrusting between his, and he began to think the name he'd heard in the canal might have been Leo... or Leonard... Louis... All he could really be sure of was the L. L for love, for lust. Whatever, *not* L for lunacy or Lucifer.

CHAPTER
TWENTY-NINE

Pointer leaned against the glass wall of the telephone booth, his hands, cupped around the receiver to block the noise from the highway, and winced at the contempt in the voice that crackled in his ear.

"I hope this is a bad connection, Pointer, because I thought I heard you say that you plan to marry Angelica Merriman."

"Right, sir," he answered, pretending to ignore Conrad's tone. "And the connection's perfect."

"You proposed to her?"

"Well, actually, I guess she did the proposing but—"

"Are you sure she was proposing marriage, not unilateral disarmament?" Either there was static on the line or it was the Dean's phlegm-rattle laugh. Pointer suspected the latter. Conrad always enjoyed his little jokes. "You stalled her, of course, to give us time to figure out what they're up to."

Anger surfaced. Pointer knew he was over-reacting, probably to cover up the fact that he was so unsure himself, but he couldn't control it. "No, I *didn't*, goddamnit. I accepted with pleasure."

"Congratulations. And I suppose you're going to bring your KGB bride to Livermore and get her high-security clearance, or have you already promised to defect?"

"You're going too far, Matthras."

"You're a brilliant scientist, David, and a horse's ass."

"I resent your—"

"You shouldn't. I don't know the first thing about particle beams, but I know people, and most of what I know I don't like. A cynic? Yes, indeed. It's what's kept me from getting nailed all these years . . . So, as I was saying, you're a brilliant scientist and a horse's ass—like Oppenheimer was, and you know what happened to Oppie. I'm *trying* to save you from a tragedy, Pointer, but you're making it damned difficult. Where are you now?"

"I just left Angelica at Duradana and I'm heading for Albany to catch a flight to San Francisco."

"Hang up, drive at least fifteen miles, then call me again from another payphone." Although he was sure his line was safe, mistrust had become a lifelong habit. Besides, he needed time to think for two.

The forest-green Alfa flew along Route 9. To the east five hundred feet below, the slate-gray Hudson churned toward Manhattan and spilled into the oily ocean water at the foot of the island. Due north, Canada was submerging into its long winter. At the rate the Alfa was speeding it would hit the border in a couple of hours. An inky overcast night. A cloud as thick as Pointer's funk hung low over the road, threatening to open again. The macadam was slick from an earlier downpour but the Spider hugged it easily.

In spite of the storm threat, or because of it, the tan canvas top was down. The Alfa passed car after car, a blur of color and sudden glare, moving so swiftly it seemed to come out of nowhere. There was a blinding flash of headlights from the rear, a gust of wind, a blot of color in the left lane. A second later the taillights were red spots in the distance, then disappeared entirely.

Pointer's eyes were fixed on the road ahead. The radio

blared, trying to compete with the roar of the wind for his attention. Anything to blot out the reality. Anything to make him forget Matthias Conrad. In the booth he had left behind the telephone was ringing. The caller was persistent, allowing it to ring for several minutes.

Pointer tried to break it down. Throw away all the smells, the tastes, the touches—all the stuff that deliciously confused the issue. Boy meets girl. Boy is seduced by girl. Boy is set up by girl. He loiters—a misdemeanor—and almost pays for it with his life. Boy accuses girl. Girl protests her innocence.

Boy meets girl again. Girl seduces boy again. Boy is set up again—read marriage proposal. Boy accepts and... It was what came after the "and" that had Conrad worried.

Pointer pulled into the next rest area and dialed again. Conrad answered on the first ring as if there was nothing between them except an avuncular friendship, and nothing extraordinary about marrying Angelica. "Dear boy, I couldn't be happier for you both. I trust you'll invite me to the wedding."

"Okay, Matthias. What are you getting at?"

Conrad went on as if he hadn't heard him. "Has Mr. Merriman given his blessing?"

"The Merrimans couldn't be happier." Pointer's voice was tight. Conrad's sudden affability was unnerving. He felt like the fatted calf being led to the altar, Merriman on one side, Matthias on the other. "In fact," he went on defensively, "they're giving us a honeymoon trip on the new Orient Express from London to Venice."

"Back to the scene of such choice memories—exciting for you, though not necessarily relaxing."

"Don't say what you're thinking. I've seen the movie and read the book, too, and you can't believe everything—"

"To the contrary," Conrad interrupted, "I always believe everything I read, dear boy. And before I forget, don't worry about getting back to Livermore. As of today you're on an indefinite leave of absence...so you can concentrate entirely on your wedding plans."

"Don't you think—" Pointer tried to break in but Conrad began to cough so convulsively that the words were drowned out.

"I've also taken the liberty of changing your flight from San Francisco to D.C." The Dean's spasm sputtered to a wheeze. "I have an engagement present to give you—something with an historic perspective that should interest you."

The line clicked dead. Pointer stood gripping the receiver, wondering whom he should fear most.

*   *   *   *

"'Cast thy bread upon the waters: for thou shalt find it after many days.' Ecclesiastes."

"And I should feel flattered to be the bread...or more aptly, the bait in some half-cocked fishing expedition you've dreamed up." Pointer made no attempt to soften his anger out of deference to Conrad's age or experience. It had been building from the first call, gathering steam on the flight from Albany, and reaching a boiling point in the car that picked him up at Dulles and drove him on a crazy, roundabout route to the Rock Creek Park Zoo, where Conrad was waiting by the monkey cage eating popcorn.

A huge black baboon with Chaplinesque timing was urinating into a bucket and washing himself with the warm water. Conrad watched, vastly amused, ignoring Pointer's obvious pique.

"Metaphorically, I suppose you have a point. But practically, I'm not at all sure that you won't crumble before many days have passed."

"What in hell do you want?"

"What any father would want for his son, what presumably you want for yourself—a happy and fruitful marriage."

The more conciliatory Conrad sounded, the deeper Pointer's mistrust went. He wanted to have it out—all the facts on the table once and for all, with no reading between the lines or footnotes printed in agate allowed. "Let me get this straight. You *want* me to marry Angelica Merriman?"

"*I* want you to marry Angelica Merriman?" Conrad placed the question between them and began to circle it. "I'm not at all sure that's possible. You'll understand better, I think, once you've opened your engagement present."

Taking an envelope out of his pocket, he handed it to Pointer. It looked innocuous enough, a plain white envelope with probably a note or card inside . . . except Pointer wasn't at all sure he wanted to open it.

"I think I'll look at this later—with Angelica." He started to slip it into his pocket.

"No. I can't wait to see what you think, and it's not for Angelica. Only you." Conrad's tone was too insistent to refuse.

"Since you brought me all this way to give it to me . . ." He slit the envelope and took out a folded sheet of white stationery. Between the folds was a photograph of a grave-marker. He shook his head—the Dean had a macabre humor—then read the name engraved on the stone. "What the hell is this? One of your sick jokes?" He balled the photograph in his fist.

"Not at all. I thought you'd be interested in knowing the girl you claim to be marrying—or at least knowing what became of August Merriman's only granddaughter. Unless you've been keeping more from me than I imagined, the Angelica you plan to marry is more than two-years-old."

"You know damn well how old she is—"

"Precisely my point. I only wish I knew *who* she is. But don't think for a moment that I'm trying to talk you out of marrying her. I just want you to go into this with your eyes open."

Pointer didn't know whether he was more angry or incredulous or confused—or just scared shitless. He didn't even know whose side he was on—Conrad's or Merriman's or Angelica's—or if any of the sides were parallel. Should he trust Conrad... defend Angelica... confront Merriman? He smoothed out the photograph and stared at the marker, shaking his head.

"Do you really expect me to believe that Merriman—a man clever enough to have made billions, a friend of everybody in the world who's anybody—went to the trouble of adopting a KGB imposter and passing her off as his granddaughter so that she could trick me into marriage? And then what? What do you think we talk about when I'm climbing on her—particle physics?"

"Not being a scientist, I would have to say the Big Bang theory."

"Goddamnit, Conrad, this is my life you're pissing on. I love her—*whoever* the fuck she is."

"I only hope she returns the affection... for all our sakes, because I did some homework while you were in Maine to refresh my memory. Ludicrous though my theory sounds to you, it is consistent with history. Since the H-bomb the Soviets have invested a major effort in stealing scientific secrets instead of acquiring them through the traditional methods of research and development. You've heard of Klaus Fuchs and the Rosenbergs, the most notorious cases. But there's one little-known incident that parallels your own—the case of the naturalized British citizen and brilliant scientist, Peter Kapitsa, who was persuaded to become head of the Soviet Academy of Sciences. A very interesting case, particularly for you. Let's stroll over toward the zebra cages, since we're talking about stripes, and I'll tell you all about Kapitsa."

By the time Conrad was finished, Pointer had experienced his first taste of schizophrenia.

"I debated with myself about telling you the truth," Conrad admitted.

"You mean you were prepared to let me go ahead with this

marriage—or sham, as you make it out to be—without saying a word to dissuade me?"

"The last thing in the world I want to do is dissuade you. I
was just debating with myself whether to let you go ahead
blindly or with open eyes."

"You son of a bitch. You think I can marry Angelica now
... as if nothing at all had happened?"

"Certainly. I'm counting on you to do just that. In fact, I've
already sent my best suit out to be pressed."

"Well, you'll have to find yourself another patsy, because
I'm not going to let you play anymore of your sick games
with my head. I'm giving it all up—you and the Merrimans,
science, Livermore, everything—and taking Angelica Whoever away. We'll get a little berry farm in Maine, or something, work it ourselves, make love and babies, and forget we
ever got tangled in this craziness. If she'll come with me,
that's all the answer I need."

"Strawberry fields forever—blueberry fields in Maine. It
sounds idyllic, dear boy, if there were no Venice to remember. And that was only a part of it."

"What's your game now?"

"No game. I didn't want to frighten you, but your utopia
leaves me no choice. Two other people have already been
killed in this fantasy you believe I've constructed out of bore-
dom and senility. Nora Hewitt, an agent who went to Germany and took that picture of the grave, was murdered with
nerve gas before she could get the film developed."

"Jesus." Pointer swallowed and tasted his own fear. He
wasn't cut out to be a hero. "You said there were two."

Conrad's voice hardened. It was a damp day. The paths in
the zoo were littered with leaves that skittered on the cement when the wind blew. And there was the chill of fall in
his voice. He tossed the last of his popcorn to the zebras.
They reminded him of Cole Porter or Noel Coward. Who
else could be haughty in striped pajamas and get away with
it.

"The second was a case of mistaken identity. I was supposed to be the target, but my daughter Beth was wearing
my jacket. She was home alone . . ."

"In Little Compton?"

Conrad nodded.

That explained the missing light bulbs, Pointer thought.
He wished he'd been born a dumb shit like three-quarters of
his class at Roxy High. He'd be peddling insurance now,
driving a truck, clerking in a bank, selling shoes in Filene's
Basement. There was no point saying he was sorry. Death
might be part of the spy game . . . but your own kid taking
the shot for you . . . tough even for the Dean to take.

"What do you want me to do, Matthias?"

Conrad wasn't ready just to blow the case out of the water.
He preferred to cut a deal. At the wedding he would be able
to confront Merriman face-to-face with the evidence, and
take care of Angelica in his own way. Someone had to pay for
Beth and Nora, *and* for Pointer's busted heart.

"Marry the girl. Go ahead with your plans. Just be sure
I'm on the guest list."

"But if you're right—?"

"What the KGB has brought together, a divorce court can
put asunder. Don't worry, it will all be over before the honeymoon begins. Go back to Durandana. Keep an eye on your
girl and Merriman, Joseph, the whole lot of them until the
wedding. You know how to reach me if you need me. Throw
yourself into the plans. As long as you act like the happy
groom you're safe."

"A spy at my own wedding? Do you actually expect me to
go along with all this?"

Conrad shrugged, the subject closed. He never used to
hesitate, but this time he was unsure. He had the uncomfortable feeling that the evidence was a little too neatly stacked
against Merriman. What if the old man believed in his granddaughter as blindly as Pointer did? Or had. Conrad was
working outside the law himself. He had to be certain before

he made his move. *If* he was wrong, Merriman's power went deeper than money. It reached all through the government, accrued over decades of doing favors, buying friends, cutting deals, building up bonus points.

"I don't see that you have a choice. Love clouds the best of brains, so let me spell it out for you. I'm sure the KGB wants this wedding as much as I do, but for different reasons. As the husband of one of their own, there's only one place you'll be allowed to continue your research—and it ain't Livermore."

"Is that why I'm on leave . . . because you think I'm compromised?"

"I'm trying to help you. Otherwise I'd blow the whole damn case out of the water—and you with it." His voice had dropped below the freezing point. "If you refuse to go along, the Soviets can expose you. Once Angelica's identity is revealed, you'll never work again. You may be able to teach someplace small and undistinguished, if you're not charged with treason, but you'll never do research. It will be the Red Hunt of the fifties all over again. You're already compromised—guilt by association. You've got to play ball with them or me. It's up to you, dear boy."

CHAPTER
THIRTY

Pointer had finally agreed, thinking of Matthias' dead daughter, nodding yes to everything, nodding away the rest of his life because he felt so guilty. If Conrad had cried or blamed him—any hint of emotion instead of that implacable control. And then there was Angelica, a time bomb waiting to blow him up. Delete the last word—God, he was getting as bad as raunchy old Conrad.

There was only the trip back to Durandana to make the impossible choice—marry Angelica and sacrifice her to the Dean or warn her and risk delivering himself into the hands of the KGB. He couldn't dismiss Conrad's suspicions any more than he could erase two murders and a near-miss, and yet on the deepest level he could not believe that Angelica was a KBG puppet making love to him on orders. There was more to her than that—more to them—if he could only convince her in time. They didn't have to be on opposite sides. They didn't have to be on *any* sides. If he could get her away, out of reach of either side . . .

"Give me the soap and I'll do your back." He pulled open the shower curtain, squinting against the warm spray that hit him.

Angelica's head was thrown back, letting the hot needles of water sting her breasts and her stomach.

She turned with a sharp cry. She hadn't heard him come in. "What are you doing here, David?" Her eyes were wide with surprise, and with the love she hadn't had a chance to hide. Or was he imagining again? He'd caught her off-guard, thinking about him, he hoped, remembering how he drove along the river, one hand on the wheel, the other on her thigh, caressing it and moving up inside her . . . Her hair was plastered to her head and drops of water clung to her lashes, making her eyes shine brighter. Pointer had been telling himself that his memory was playing tricks on him. No woman could be as lovely as he pictured her. He was wrong.

"How did you get in here?"

"Joseph told me where to find you." He reached over to take the soap from her hand.

Reaching up, she turned the nozzle at him. He grabbed for it, and they wrestled, his hands sliding all over her wet slippery body.

"Jesus, I love you." The words sounded as if they were wrenched from his gut.

Angelica stopped. The shower beat over them. "What did you say?"

"I said, 'I love you,' goddamnit."

She handed him the bar of soap and waited. She couldn't think of anything or remember anything she was supposed to do, and right then she didn't care. "I've done the back already . . . you can start on the front." She smiled a slow, expectant smile.

Pointer couldn't keep his hand from shaking. She's magnificent, he thought, and dangerous? As dangerous as Conrad had warned. Stop thinking. He dried his face with a towel, pushing the wet hair back out of his eyes, and began to lather her throat and shoulders, rubbing the soap in slow, circular motions around her breasts, then moved down. "Listen, Angelica, listen very carefully, because we don't have much time." He took a deep breath, forced himself to go on. "It's over. CIA agents know who you are and they're coming here. For all I know they may be on their way already."

"What? Why? What do they want?" Her surprise sounded genuine, but...

"To arrest you for being a Soviet agent," he said bluntly.

Angelica stepped back under the water and closed her eyes against the stinging spray, and his searching eyes. She saw the accusation in his face, even though he was trying to protect her. His words struck her as hard and cold as the muzzle of a gun. All she felt was the sharp spray of hot water beating on her face and breasts.

Pointer grabbed a bath sheet off the heated rack and held it open for her. "There's no time to explain now. Hurry, I've got to get you out of here."

"They've got a strong case against you, but if we get away we'll at least buy a little time to decide what to do..."

Angelica turned off the shower and stepped out into the warm towel. Wrapping it around her, he enclosed her in his arms and held her.

"Show me you love me," she whispered.

He shook his head. "There isn't time." Taking her by the wrist, he dragged her into the bedroom. Angelica went along, letting him think and act for her. It didn't matter what she did now. She began to dress automatically, opening drawers and closets, putting on the first things her hand touched. She was zipping up a pair of jeans when a sound rang out.

They stood frozen.

"What was that?"

Pointer's voice was hollow, an echo.

"A gunshot... from downstairs."

They stared at each other for an instant, then Pointer was out the door. "Stay here," he called back.

"No." She followed him, pulling on her boots as she went.

At the library door Pointer stopped cold. Joseph was sitting at a leather-tooled table, composed except for a thin trickle of blood that ran out of the corner of his mouth. A revolver with one empty chamber lay on the table in front of him. A neat job. He had opened his mouth, placed the muzzle inside and squeezed the trigger.

"Jesus," Pointer gasped. "Why would he kill himself?"

Angelica turned away without a word, and found herself staring directly into black, sardonic eyes belonging to a man all too familiar to her. *Dostankov.*

"His timing was perfect. I can say that much for the man," Prudence said as she sailed into the library. "He's been replaced and I suppose he was insulted. Ridiculously proud, his sort. Considerate, though, not to make a mess. Well, I'm sorry, but he *was* terribly dour. I already have a much warmer feeling for our new Joseph." She smiled frostily at the newcomer. "We always call August's secretary 'Joseph.' That way we don't have to remember a new name. There's quite a turnover, in servants, even though we get ours through the UN employment service. You'd think new immigrants would feel some sense of gratitude but they become Americanized so fast. Just when you've trained them they pack their bags and desert you."

"Not old Joseph. He didn't bother packing."

"As I said, David, he knew he was being replaced today—insubordination. Of the worst sort." She shook her head.

"Joseph . . . insubordinate?" Pointer couldn't believe she was serious.

Prudence ignored his remark. "August is in New York for the day . . . one of his board meetings. We can have all this tidied up before he gets home. Joseph, call the local police chief. Rafferty, his name is. Just say Mr. Merriman needs a favor. He'll take care of the rest." The new man went off, but not before giving Angelica a searching look. A familiar look?

"Rafferty is very good, especially in a difficult situation," Prudence was saying. "By tomorrow the whole thing will be forgotten as if it never happened. Don't worry, Angelica. It won't spoil your wedding, I assure you."

Angelica was so pale... Pointer was sure she had never seen a dead man before. So much for Conrad's KGB scenario?

"Take her out for a walk," Prudence was saying. "There's no medicine like fresh air. By the way, David, what are you doing here?" She stopped abruptly and looked at him. "You're supposed to be at Livermore, aren't you... until the wedding?"

Pointer felt his face redden. He hadn't thought of a cover story for the Merrimans. "Yes... that was my original plan, but when the director heard I was getting married he gave me a leave until after the honeymoon."

"How nice of him. Be sure to put that man on the guest list. We can talk about the others you want to invite tomorrow, and set the date."

Outside the only signs of fall were the leaves raked into neat piles for burning. The grass was picked clean, as if an army of gardeners was kept on duty to attack any fluttering leaf that dared follow the course of nature over the dictate of August Merriman. The wind nipped, tossing Angelica's hair across her cheeks, forming a natural shield against him.

"Are you all right?" He reached for her hand and found it too cold.

She nodded, unresponsive to his touch. The distance between them seemed abruptly large and growing. Out of view of the house, he took her in his arms and kissed her. The sky was a pale gray-blue, undecided as they were. Should it drop a thunderbolt or lay back and let the sun break through.

Pointer was losing her—he could feel it. He should have kept his mouth shut, at least played along as Conrad said for a while longer until he was sure of her. But he *had* been sure. Upstairs Angelica had seemed ready to follow him, to go anywhere with him, do anything for him. Now she was inching away, wary, furtive even. When he touched her there was no response.

"Is it Joseph, or what I said before?"

She shook her head to one, both. "It was a lie to trick me, what you told me upstairs."

"How do you know?"

"Because no CIA has come."

"That much was a lie—but not to trick you. To save you—"

"From you?"

"From yourself. I have to know who you really are . . . what you really want before I marry you."

"I don't know who *you* are . . ." She kept looking back toward the house as if she expected the ghost of Joseph to come after them.

"Just a guy who loves you—that's all I want to be."

She smiled for the first time. "I think I like that . . . David, I want to think, to be alone for awhile. Why don't you go for a ride or something. When you come back I'll tell you everything."

"Is that a promise?"

"Trust me this once." She smiled again, or tried to.

She looked so tired, exhausted . . . and he should call Conrad anyway, tell him about the two Josephs.

A police car was parked in the circular drive when Angelica got back to the main house. Inside the murmur of voices drifted from the library, Prudence's commanding tone clear above the others. Angelica went directly to her room. She had pulled on the first clothes she laid her hands on, now she wanted to change before she faced the new Joseph.

A report must have reached Moscow from the dead Joseph

or her control: Unsatisfactory Performance. How could she
be faulted? She was obeying orders, marrying David, carrying out the charade of love—except it wasn't a charade any
longer... She tried to remember clearly his exact words
when he burst in on her. He must know the truth because he
wanted to save her from his own people. He was ready to
risk being called a traitor for her. He knew who she was and
he wanted her anyway. She should be singing with happi-
ness. Instead she was deathly afraid... for both of them.

With Dostankov here there was no hope of escape. She
began to undress—four buttons of her blouse and working
on the fifth when the door opened. The new "Joseph" came
in without knocking.

Anatol Dostankov had grown nervous waiting in Moscow.
Natasha's sex was nightly more chilling, and Angelica's control was making a habit of bypassing him and going directly
to Chebrikov. Once could be forgiven under the circumstances, but not routinely. The control didn't trust Joseph
any longer after Venice. He had to be replaced, and the
Operation had come to the critical point. The scientist would
soon be on his way to Moscow. The General Secretary was
anticipating his arrival. And lurking over all like an unde-
fined shadow was Dostankov's worry that Leon had been
right and the control wrong—David Pointer really was an
enemy agent.

Faced with that nagging fear and with Angelica Merriman's half-naked body, Dostankov did not regret his decision
to see Operation Counterpoint through personally. There
was no chance of being recognized. He had never been to
the U.S. before, and Chebrikov never allowed his deputies'
photos in the press.

Angelica pulled the blouse around herself.

"No need to be modest in front of me—unless you've forgotten your training, comrade. Go ahead. We can talk while you change."

"What are you doing here?" She still held the blouse to cover her breasts.

"Joseph was persuaded to take his own life. It was less painful than being returned. *Glasnost*, notwithstanding. Besides, I wouldn't miss your wedding for the world." He sat down on the bed. "Everything is still going ahead as planned. Of course, there have been complications—Joseph . . . Leon in Venice—"

Dostankov smiled. "Evidently, your new fiancé is more of a man than he looks. You can tell me all about that."

"No—" The word slipped out before Angelica realized what she had done. If she had any chance of saving David or herself, she had to go along with Dostankov, convince him she was still, the loyal agent he had known before. Otherwise, they didn't have a chance.

"The rest of the operation should go smoothly. I have made all the arrangements. Your honeymoon will not stop in Venice. There will be a special plane waiting to fly you and your husband home. I'm sure you're anxious to get back."

Angelica nodded. "Of course."

"You don't sound altogether convincing. I think it is time I re-tested your skills. So long away . . . perhaps a little re-education is in order."

Angelica backed away. A few months before she would have obeyed without a thought. Now she recoiled against the mechanical act. "I've followed orders—"

"You were *ordered* to use your body, not give away your heart." Dostankov was standing up, stripping off his clothes. She remembered his body as lean and hard, like his voice, and not without skill. "I doubt you'll pass with such high grades this time." He grabbed the waistband of her jeans, pulling her against him. "The American has made you forget everything you were taught."

"No—"

"His CIA training must be superior to yours ... or he is more loyal."

"No—"

"Then show me how skilled and loyal you still are." His breath was cool in her face. Pushing aside her blouse, he took her breasts. "You know Pointer is an agent. I haven't decided yet whether to eliminate him or go ahead with the wedding as planned and still try to use him."

Angelica forced herself to stand perfectly still before him. She couldn't be sure whether he was serious or testing her, but she could not take a chance. She steeled herself. "David will do anything I want."

He opened her jeans and pushed her back on the bed, raised her hips so he could pull them off. He was between her legs, moving up the length of her body with his tongue ...

"Angelica ..." *David's* voice at the door, his knock, soft so as not to disturb her if she were sleeping.

"*No*. Not now, David ..." She answered too late.

The door opened, and closed, and she was alone with Dostankov, forcing herself to remember every trick that she had not needed to use for so long ...

CHAPTER
THIRTY-ONE

On the surface little changed at Durandana, but there were differences. Instead of jetting around the world, often visiting several cities in a day, the Merrimans stayed at home, which meant a workout for Pointer. Every morning after breakfast the two men went to the gym to exercise— body and mind. Merriman's interest was apparently as keen as the first day they had met, but his knowledge of quantum physics was elementary, and Pointer began to take chances. It was a game he played out of the bitterness of betrayal. He wanted to protect the secrets of SDI and at the same time to give back some of what he'd got, make somebody else the fool for a change, so long as he was on the other side.

Instead of describing his own research, and in the process feeding it directly to the Soviets, he began to recite pure fiction, borrowing passages and ideas from the books he devoured. It was out of sci-fi, not Livermore, but Merriman didn't seem to notice anything, didn't question a word, and afterward Angelica would be waiting for him, the predictable pattern unchanged as if nothing had happened. Except that now they never made love and barely touched except casually in passing . . .

It was a sloppy fall day, pale light. The autumnal colors of the leaves seemed layered, super-imposed one over the other, a deep sienna over burnt orange over gold, and standing out apart from the others was the pale lemon yellow of the beeches like sunlight. Shafts of silver angled through the turning leaves, and Angelica had given him the royal shaft. Still, she was there when he came out of the gym as he knew she would be—suspicious and incommunicative when they were together, a happy soon-to-be-married couple in front of the Merrimans.

"I'm going for a walk," he announced to no one in particular.

Angelica fell in step beside him, keeping pace as he trudged beyond the manicured gardens into the woodland that surrounded them on three sides, the river the fourth border. They passed the miniature castle that was Prudence Merriman's private hideaway, Pointer thinking that he might just keep on going, never turn back except to look over his shoulder—a habit he'd picked up in Venice along with the sewage.

They walked in silence, shoulder to shoulder, over meadow and farm, and not the two of them but three, the image of Joseph going with them every step of the way— humping, screwing, banging, copulating, goddamn fucking Joseph. He remembered the first Joseph always hovering outside the door like some damn voyeur, and this new one doing a lot more than peeping. He hadn't been in the house twenty-four hours and Angelica was putting out for him. A new man—she couldn't wait.

Pointer only spoke to her once, and that was a question. "Do you still want to go ahead with this wedding?"

"I can explain—"

"A simple yes or no will do."

"Yes," she said, and she was crying. He was so remote. Even in Venice, after the attack, he hadn't closed her out.

Dostankov said that David was using her, just as she was using him. He was an operative. There was no difference between them except the initials of their organizations and the direction of their loyalties. Angelica tried to believe him, it would make it easier if she could, and sometimes she managed it . . . if she didn't think of the way they had been, if she didn't let herself remember the lighthouse in Maine, the hansom ride in Central Park . . .

No more cassettes came from her control. Dostankov, the new "Joseph," gave her orders. He was her control now, until the honeymoon ended in Moscow, *and then*—two words she tried not to think about, for herself or for David.

Believe Dostankov or her own heart? David had been using her, while it was supposed to have been the other way around? Could any man be that convincing if he were just doing a job?

"A consumate actor," Dostankov called him, "not just a scientist."

Actor, scientist, *spy?* Whatever, whichever, there was no doubt he was an unforgettable lover. Could any man be so many things?

The woods thickened the farther they walked, poplars, maples, oaks, pines, tulip trees, towering ash and beech, the branches fanning over them, shutting out the sky. The sadness in Angelica's eyes made Pointer turn away, steeling himself to go through with the scenario directed by Conrad. A whippoorwill cried somewhere overhead, the plaintive song echoing his mood . . .

Matthias had sounded more than sympathetic when Pointer tried to describe the picture that blotted out every other one, as though he cared, cared like a father. He didn't even say I told you so. Maybe he was remembering Prudence Merriman in pink at nineteen . . . remembering all-good-things-have-to-come-to-an-end-and-it-was-fun-while-it-lasted. No storybook ending for either of them.

"Love is like any other addiction," he'd said, realizing he must sound pompous. "There's no painless way to kick the habit. But it's just as well that you got it out of your system now so that you can go into the marriage with open eyes."

"You expect me to go through with this wedding now?"

"It's up to you, dear boy. But I'd say it's your only chance to save your career, and maybe your life. The Russians won't let you just walk away, never mind how we try to protect you or how much the climate is supposed to have changed between our two nations. The surface changes, the competition goes on, and it's still a very rough game. I'm not sure which they would do, eliminate or expose you. Simple, I'm afraid, to do in either case. Angelica goes back to Moscow, and Merriman calls a press conference to confess a public scandal. The girl has duped him, passing herself off as his granddaughter, and compromised you. He comes out like Nathan Hale smelling of roses and you look like Benedict Arnold. Appearances matter more than truth. Your real hope is to carry on with your plans, and give me a chance to force Merriman's hand at the wedding."

The ground was thick with leaves, soft with dampness. All around them were dark flat gray trunks like pillars, and the gray of the occasional stoney outcrop, glacial mementoes, and the paler, silverlike gray of the underbrush stripped bare, the light giving a violet cast to it so that from a distance it looked like heather. And there was the shiny red poison ivy curling around the trunks, clumps of moss blanketing them, and the toadstools squatting between the gnarled roots. A breeze swept through the trees, creating a cascade of leaves, a calendar picture, thousands of colors tumbling down.

A shower of leaves and wedding gifts. As many as fifteen and twenty presents arrived at a time from all over the world. Merriman opened each one himself, commenting on

the donor and the appropriateness, which Pointer trans-
lated as costliness, of the gift. The Saudis sent gold gob-
lets, the Emirates rugs, the Irish ambassador Waterford
crystal, the French Limoges china, the Russians an antique
emerald brooch. They could have sent the Tsarina's jewels,
on loan, Pointer thought. He was too angry to see anything
clearly, least of all his future bride and prospects for a long
and happy marriage. Announcements had been sent out to
a cast of thousands, but invitations were limited to fifty
guests.

The wedding presents tended to be either fanciful or extravagant, inappropriate, in either case, for a blueberry farm
in Maine... now a ridiculous dream.

Given his talent for self-promotion, which rivalled his
skill at self-aggrandizement, one would expect the wedding
of August Merriman's only granddaughter to be a public
relations extravaganza, the guest list a veritable Who's Who
as international as a UN General Assembly meeting, with
heads of state and corporate chairmen tripping over each
other to be first in the receiving line. On that question,
though, Pointer refused to give an inch. The sham of the
wedding was bad enough without inviting half the world to
bear witness to it. To his surprise, Angelica was equally
insistent.

"Just family, here at Durandana."

"And a few friends, since I have no family, a dozen or so."
Pointed thought about inviting Louise, decided against it.
Alongside Angelica she'd look like a Good Housekeeping
dress pattern next to a Balenciaga gown—and what was he
trying to prove anyway. He ran through the names he
wanted... "My friends at Livermore, Colonel Hancock and
Matthias Conrad—"

"Why would you invite him?" Prudence Merriman's voice
was a challenge.

"Because he's the closest thing to family I've got." It was

the way the Dean and he had planned it. He wasn't to
pledge any troth unless Conrad was right there to get it an-
nulled.

In the end Prudence overrode her husband's objections
and agreed to keep the guest list small.

The tensions at Durandana were electric. One felt that a
step in the wrong direction could set off a storm. Only August Merriman seemed oblivious to the voltage crackling
around him. When he wasn't opening wedding gifts he was
on any one of half a dozen phones conducting business as
usual around the globe. He was restless, though, confined to
the northeast corridor, flying a couple of times a week to
Washington or New York for meetings. Prudence did not ac-
company him on these short hops. The wedding was demanding all her attention, she said, yet Pointer thought she
preoccupied.

She had been tight as a bowstring since the old Joseph
took it in the mouth, even more caustic than usual, snapping
at the servants, her husband, Angelica—everyone, it
seemed, except the new Joseph. With him she was always
correct and almost excessively formal, even deferring to his
opinion on occasion. He was, formidable, no question.

Although he could not remain in a room with the man for
more than a few minutes, Pointer was acutely aware of the
new Joseph, and of his effect on the household. Joseph was
deferential and sometimes obsequious to August Merriman;
presumptuous, even arrogant to the Merriman women; toler-
ant and slightly disdainful toward Pointer. He would have
loved to alter the guy's superior face with a fist. That indul-
gence being self-defeating at this point, he tried to avoid the
man as much as possible. And avoid, remembering, the
image of him and Angelica . . .

Cutting a wide arc now through the woods, crossing a
stream, balancing on the small slippery stones, Pointer never

slackened his pace. Angelica kept right on his heels. By the
time they were headed back toward the house, toward the
unreal real world, it had begun to drizzle. The rain was a flat
ping-ping sound on the leaves. Mists gathered over the river
and rested on the embankments, the fog closing in the very
woodlands that had hid the Indian fighters from the British
in the War for Independence.

Pointer concentrated on putting one foot in front of the
other. It was too painful to look back, too frightening to look
forward.

CHAPTER
THIRTY-TWO

Acres of Peruvian lily fields were levelled to fill the glass
conservatory of Durandana. The organist from St. Paul's in
London was flown in to play Wagner's "Bridal Chorus."

It looked like a storybook wedding. But in fairytales, even
Grimm's, the groom doesn't fear the sight of the altar and the
bride doesn't turn into a KGB tool.

Actually, there was no altar, just five thousand stems of
delicate pink lilies that made Pointer worry about coming
down with an attack of hay fever and sneezing convulsively in
the middle of the ceremony, with a minister framed in the
center of them. At least the man was dressed like a minister
in black cassock, white surplice and an expression of sublime
certitude. For all Pointer knew, he was the KGB chairman.

The temptation to bolt was becoming irresistible. "What
the Kremlin has joined together, a divorce court can put
asunder," Conrad had assured him. Glancing nervously over
his shoulder, Pointer glimpsed the Dean in the second row,
pitching forward on a gilt chair as if poised to bestow his
personal benediction. Not for the first time, Pointer wished
he had never met Matthias Conrad, or the Merrimans,
never, for that matter, given up music for science in the first
place. He could have been the organist, blissfully ignorant,
playing the Wedding March while some other chump whose
only fault was that he fooled around with laser beams and fell

for a knockout of a girl, would be sweating in a monkey suit in front of the altar that wasn't there.

Pointer fidgeted with his cravat. For someone who felt over-dressed in a navy blazer and jeans, a morning coat was as bad as a toga. What am I doing here? He posed the question to himself with the incredulity of a man who has just been shocked out of insanity with a jolt of electricity to the brains and the balls, the two anatomical points that had gotten him into the predicament in the first place. He had been going along like a brain-washed victim, obeying orders from every side because he had no choice.

As Conrad had put it, it was a question of marriage or "elimination." Angelica's side still had no compunctions about creating dead ends... Nora Hewitt, Beth Conrad, the ubiquitous Joseph. Pointer almost missed the guy now. Anyone would be better than his replacement. And then there was Venice and that never-to-be-forgotten trip down the Grand Canal without a gondola.

Damn it, he wasn't an actor or a spy. Yet here he was in an espionage drama with too many acts and not knowing where he was headed but feeling for all the world as if he were stage center in a superpower snuff-flick.

The first chords of "The Bridal Chorus" sounded, drowning out his thoughts, and he turned to see Angelica, a vision of white satin and pearls. She was smiling directly at him as if there were no guests—no Conrad, no Merrimans, no new Joseph. He could not turn away. She was closer without seeming to move.

And now she was beside him. The minister was descending from the lilies to join together in unholy matrimony a KGB agent and a damn fool—or a man and a woman in love. Or both.

August Merriman kissed the bride and gave her away with a twinge of jealousy. He had never expected Angelica's cooperation to go so far, but he took a philosophical view. He wasn't losing a granddaughter, he was gaining continuous access to the most critical defense information, which he would use, as his crowning achievement, to bring world peace into reality. Officially, he would retire at the end of the year, but he would be able to keep his hand in with Pointer in the family. He would know what both sides were doing, keep the score even. He was uniquely qualified to do it. It had been his way, his special talent for many years.

Angelica and David were exchanging vows, her voice clear and sure, his too low to hear. Merriman reached for his wife's hand—Prudence in dove gray and emeralds, his bride of forty-eight years. She had planned the wedding as carefully as if it were her own, to make it an unforgettable occasion. Old betrayals forgotten and forgiven at last, he thought. There were tears in August Merriman's eyes, his wife's were dry.

Prudence looked across the aisle to the second row where Matthias Conrad sat, as if she expected him to stand up when the minister said, "If there is any reason why this man and woman . . ." Conrad actually winked, making her break into a long-remembered smile. The exchange did not escape Merriman, who questioned her with a look. She patted his hand and turned back to the ceremony.

Pointer was also waiting for Conrad to stand up and denounce Merriman, accuse Angelica, stop the music . . . the ceremony . . . the whole show. It would be dramatic, and Matthias had a definite flair for that sort of thing.

The minister's smile spoke a formality, nothing more. The ceremony was proceeding. He asked David for the ring, prepared to make the pronouncement. The Pointers were kissing, Mr. and Mrs. David Pointer. Their first kiss as man and wife was full of longing. Merriman wiped his eyes.

The music welled, and they were turning to proceed down the aisle. The receiving line formed outside the conservatory, with champagne waiting at the end of it. Conrad followed the other guests, shaking hands along the line, murmuring congratulations, his grin as unchanging as the Cheshire Cat's.

When he reached Angelica, he kissed the bride. "David didn't exaggerate. I only hope you're as loving as you are beautiful." Before she could answer he was pumping Pointer's arm. "Once again into the breach, dear boy," he murmured, moving on quickly to the next in line. The great August Merriman himself.

"Glad you could come. Have some champagne." Merriman greeted each of Pointer's guests with a smile, a handshake and the same seven words. He was looking right through Conrad, not, it seemed, recognizing him.

Conrad did not hang around to hear any more. Prudence was stepping out of the line before he could reach her. Helping himself to a glass of Cristal, he followed her through French doors out to the terrace.

"Hello, Matt." She spoke before she looked up from the arrangement of flowers that had toppled over in the wind.

"You knew I'd follow you."

"I had a hunch you might.

"Why did you walk out on me?" Just like that, a forty-year-old question out of context and with no prologue.

"You've been waiting all these years to ask me that?"

"In a way, maybe so. Was it something I did?"

It was a bright blue day full of bluster. A trail of lilies led from the conservatory to the ballroom where a band was already playing. Round tables covered with pink cloths were set up in the adjoining room with a buffet table at one end. Waiters circulated among the guests with silver trays of champagne and hors d'oeuvres. Other tables spilled onto the terrace, each cloth anchored by a centerpiece of lilies.

"It wasn't anything terribly profound, Matt. I couldn't see myself as a faculty wife, married to a professor whose nose was buried in medieval history while the world was blowing up around him. Do you ever look back, Matt?"

He wouldn't give her the satisfaction she wanted. Even

after so many years, he wanted her to suffer a little too.

"I only look back to admire a round firm ass. I've never seen one that matched yours, though."

"You should have come to our Georgetown parties. I invited you often enough over the years."

"I wondered why."

"And now you know?"

"I suspect your husband put you up to it." Conrad was probing carefully, as if her memory was a minefield.

"August?" Prudence's laughter was disturbing. "I never thought my leaving you would make you so suspicious. You never trusted anyone again, did you? A lifetime of suspicion —what a gift to give a man." She sighed, a touch of drama. Almost staged. He was getting uncomfortable.

"You flatter yourself, Pru."

She smiled at the easy intimacy, wondering how it would have been to be married to Matthias Conrad instead of August Merriman, but she didn't dwell on it. She had made her choice, against her desires but in behalf of furthering her convictions, and lived with it these many years. There was nothing gained by looking back. Regrets were unproductive, a waste. "Pru," he had called her just now. Nobody had taken such a liberty in years, and she had called him Matt. But the years did not fall away, as Conrad had hoped they would.

"You have a beautiful granddaughter. She reminds me of the way you used to be."

"She's not mine, as you well know."

"But you found her, I understand."

Her eyes were like jade, hard and gleaming. He remembered them differently, the soft green of spring, like new leaves. "Some details are insignificant."

"Are they?"

A sharp breeze slapped at the hems of the tablecloths, swept the dry leaves around the chair legs in small cyclones, snapped the tip off Conrad's cigarette and went after Prudence's hat so that she had to hold it to keep it from flying off.

"You must have changed, Pru."

"What do you mean?"

"You used to be a fireball. Remember the time you went home for the weekend and I took your roommate to the movies?" A Sunday matinee in the age of innocence, because it was a long afternoon and they were lonely with nothing better to do . . . Only Prudence had been waiting when they got back. He remembered the blaze of jealousy as green as her eyes. "I was thrilled. I was never sure you really cared until that day. I can't imagine you opening your arms to another woman's grandchild—a girl who only exists because your husband cheated on you."

"August and I weren't married at the time." She brushed it aside.

"But you were together, and I can't believe it was all platonic. I know you too well for that."

Prudence was beyond blushing, but she could still savor what seemed a compliment. "It's different with August . . . not at all the way you think. There are unique terms to our marriage. I don't waste my passion on men anymore, incidentals like fidelity, love . . ."

"What do you waste it on?"

"Changing the world, Matt. Still at it. Remember the way we used to talk, all night sometimes. August Merriman has never been just a man to me. He's an opportunity to turn all that talk into action—to make a difference."

Conrad drained his champagne. "An admirable sentiment, but I still can't believe you've changed that much, Pru . . . unless, of course, Angelica is not whom she claims to be."

She looked at him intently. "You've turned into quite a cynic. The Italians have a saying—leave it to them: 'The mother is always certain, the father never.' And it doesn't really matter now, because August adores the girl."

"Are they the insignificant details you were referring to? I understand you investigated her claim yourself."

"August is so busy. I handle as many of the personal details as I can for him."

"You give your husband's money away for him, too—through the ASF."

"You've been doing your homework." She smoothed a tablecloth although there were no wrinkles. "I wonder why?"

Conrad went through the diversionary process of lighting a cigarette. "I understand you found Angelica in East Germany. I think she told David she's from Mollenz."

"As a matter of fact, an excellent lawyer was recommended to me in Berlin who specializes in reuniting families on both sides of the Wall. Charming, and very helpful . . . his name slips my mind."

He considered her over his glasses, fixing her with an intensity that would have forced anyone except Prudence Merriman to turn away. "Perhaps I can help. Peter Braun, wasn't it? He's an old and trusted friend . . . but, of course, he told you all that, just as he told you that David and I are friends."

"You *have* done your homework, Matt. And I thought you were supposed to be retired. You know August plans to retire, too, at the end of the year."

"And you . . . ?"

"Me?" What in the world do I have to retire from?"

Someone was reflected through the French doors, coming to summon her to the first wedding dance.

"Who's that?" Conrad nodded toward the house.

"My husband's secretary, Joseph."

The new Joseph. Conrad smiled. "I've heard quite a bit about him."

"What is that supposed to mean?"

"Whatever you want it to, Pru." There was something vaguely familiar about the man, a face glimpsed before but one he couldn't quite place.

The French doors opened. Dostankov looked from one to the other, remembering the suggestion of a smile on Chebrikov's dour face at the mention of Matthias Conrad and his unsettling words: "I wish you luck, comrade." Two efforts, and the Dean had slipped through both traps. Now here he was with Prudence Merriman as a guest at the wedding. The man's audacity was arrogant, insulting... did he believe all Soviets were amateurs in espionage since Andropov?

Dostankov saw his future dissolving before his eyes... If Matthias Conrad was Pointer's control, Chebrikov would almost certainly abandon Operation Counterpoint, and with it would go Dostankov's career. Instead of leading the Soviets into the twenty-first century of science, Pointer would be eliminated as soon as he reached Moscow. Chebrikov would never risk taking Conrad head on...

Inclining his head in a grudging bow, Dostankov looked directly at Prudence. "Mr. Merriman would like you to join him in the ballroom."

"Thank you, Joseph."

He didn't budge.

"I can find my way to the ballroom unescorted. *Thank* you, Joseph."

He turned to go, but not without a challenge: "Mr. Merriman doesn't like to be kept waiting."

"After all these years I think I know my husband, thank you."

Her anger dissipated as soon as Joseph retreated. She suspected she would never meet Matt Conrad again. She didn't want to just walk away from him. Once in a lifetime was enough for that.

"We were good together, Matt." She took both his hands. "Damn good."

"Pru in pink at nineteen"—he held on tight—"and ready to break every rule. There's never been another like you, but I suspect you know that."

She smiled. "You're an old sentimentalist, Matt. Who would have thought? It was wonderful but it was puppy love—"

"Then why do we both remember so well?"

"Because we're both old fools." She laughed, breaking the spell that held them.

"That's what I'm so afraid of, Pru."

He looked beyond her through the French doors at the party swirling inside, and when he spoke again his voice was soft and only a little gravelly. "Did you know I had a daughter? I didn't know I loved her until she died... a case of mistaken identity, she was wearing my foul-weather jacket..."

"I didn't know." Prudence let go of his hands.

"They still haven't come up with suspect, or even a clue."

"I'm sorry."

"So am I."

CHAPTER
THIRTY-THREE

Slipping her arm through her husband's, Prudence walked out to the dance floor. The band began to play "Beautiful Dreamer"...what she had been in another life that only Matthias Conrad remembered now. She was straight and uncompromising in her slim dove-gray silk suit, the matching hat a cloche that dipped on one side, accentuating her profile. Angelica was a blur of sudden light, created by the whiteness of the swirling satin, her fair hair gleaming through the veil of Brussels lace and by her eyes, which were as bright as the day. After a few bars they changed partners, Angelica and her grandfather, Prudence and David. Then other couples moved onto the floor.

Conrad hijacked a glass of champagne from a passing waiter and sank back to watch the party unfold, and certain parties in particular. He wedged himself between the door frame and an enormous vase of lilies set on a marble pedestal so that he could see everyone entering or leaving the room but was himself half-hidden—tapping his foot to the music, sipping the wine, content to watch, and wait.

The Dean wasn't the only one. "Joseph" was watching, too, circling the edge of the dance floor, slowly moving in until he was close enough to brush against Angelica. With a bow to Merriman, he cut in and began to talk to her. The color drained from Pointer's face, but Prudence held him tight and kept on dancing.

Oblivious to the scene being played out on the floor, Merriman was working his way around the room toward the door, stopping to shake a hand, clap a shoulder, exchange a few words. A one-man band, welcoming, warm, he appreciated the value of the personal touch. Conrad followed him out, right on his heels.

"Matthias Conrad, CIA." His words were spoken in Merriman's ear.

"CIA, retired," Merriman corrected without stopping or turning.

Conrad made an amused sound. The old man was as sharp as Pointer had said. "I'm out of mothballs for the day. Where can we talk privately?"

"You'll have to wait until after the party."

"No. It's about your granddaughter and David Pointer . . . and there's not going to be any honeymoon for them, or for you, unless you cooperate."

Merriman was angry now. He wasn't accustomed to being threatened, but he led the way past the conservatory, empty now except for the lilies, crossed the main hall and opened the door to the library, which looked like a movie set for an exclusive British club: cherry bookcases floor to ceiling filled with leather-bound volumes, shuttered windows, two long reading tables and a pair of leather wingchairs set on either side of a tiled fireplace—a room Conrad thought he could stay in with perfect contentment so long as he was kept supplied with Camels and Dewar's.

Merriman sat down in a wingchair and crossed his legs. Conrad took the other.

Recovering his affable manner, Merriman said, "It's a helluva party, don't you think—though rather too subdued. I wanted to invite a thousand guests. I've only got one granddaughter to show off, after all."

"She's worth the price of admission. I grant you."

Merriman actually beamed. "Your friend Pointer's made quite a catch."

". . . That's what I'm afraid of."

"What is *that* supposed to mean?"

"I thought perhaps you would be able to tell me."

"Get to the point, Conrad." Affability went just so far.

On the surface, at least, they were absolute opposites— night and day, north and south, although other extremes, most notably saint and sinner, were not so clearly applicable. Merriman was dapper, well appointed, orderly. Conrad, wheezy, out-of-shape, doused with champagne and wishing it were something harder; also erudite, cynical. Merriman was proud, tending to smug—a man with an open manner and seemingly no axes to grind, while Conrad had personal scores to settle, old and new. In common were age, experience, and Prudence Merriman.

"I have a confession to make," Conrad began. "I was in love with your wife once. Puppy love, it's been called," he added quickly. "It was long before Pru met you."

"Pru." Merriman couldn't believe what he was hearing. In the forty-eight years of their marriage he had never heard anyone call her "Pru"—only "Prudence."

"She was very young." Conrad felt the need to explain the intimacy. "Nineteen, and I was twenty-one."

"Is this confession your urgent business?" Merriman's annoyance was clear.

"Call it an ice breaker. One confession tends to elicit another."

Conrad peered over his glasses. He was marshalling the facts in his mind, separating them from the conjectures, coincidences, suspicions and flights of fancy. When all was said and done, there were only four concrete facts—two about August Merriman and two about Angelica:

Fact Number One: August Merriman had passed atomic secrets to the Soviets during the war and continued to provide strategic information through the years.

Fact Number Two: He wanted classified information on the Strategic Defense Initiative, and he was using David Pointer to get it.

Fact Number Three: Angelica Merriman was an imposter. The only grandchild of August Merriman and Lynneth Carrington died in Mollenz, East Germany, in 1964 at the age of two.

Fact Number Four: Anyone who raised a question about the girl died. Insufficient evidence to convict in a court of law, but enough, Conrad hoped, to entrap.

"I'm interested in your Soviet connections, Merriman. You know the Germans have an expression... 'If at twenty you aren't a Communist, you have no heart. If at thirty you're still a Communist, you have no brain.' Daring social theories to pull down the privileged and lift up the rest of us go back at least as far as the Enlightenment. Marx and the social thinkers of the nineteenth century were responding to the dark side of the Industrial Revolution—the sweatshops, dangerous working conditions, child abuse, to the satanic mills, the individual chained to the machine, the artisan reduced to factory hand all for the profit of a few."

"What does any of this—"

"Please bear with me." Conrad cut him off and went on. "The Russian Revolution overthrew the last great autocracy, then came World War I, the greatest horror ever inflicted on modern man until Hiroshima, and rightly labeled an imperialist war. If anyone needed proof of the weaknesses of capitalism, the economic depression of the thirties provided it. Young romantics, idealists, flocked to the Red banner that ennobled the proletarian, urban industrial worker. He was even provided his own dictatorship, by God—the blasphemy of this overlooked for the greater good of the many. Also overlooked were brutality and murder, everything excused as the growing pains of the new society, and long after the nationalistic ambitions of the U.S.S.R. could no longer be disguised."

Conrad lit a fresh cigarette and dragged deeply. "To this day, there are those among us—old enough to know better —who call themselves Leninists, Marxists. But when their arguments are stripped away they stand out as merely apologists of their youth. Cowards, too, because they can't or won't admit that they were wrong so many years ago. Instead they go on adding insult to injury, compounding their mistakes . . . and hurting their countries."

"If you're by any chance referring to me, Conrad, you're *dead wrong*. Do you know how many times I've been accused of being soft on Communism? It's a tired old story and certainly not worth interrupting my granddaughter's wedding to repeat. I've devoted a lifetime to reducing tensions between the superpowers. If that makes me soft on Communism, then I welcome the charge. Men with vision and willing to take risk can make a difference. I think in my way I've performed a service by being an *international* patriot, a citizen not of one country but of many countries. I've led a full life, and I'm damn proud of it . . . I'm sure you know, Conrad, I was the one who persuaded the Kremlin to swap Gary Powers. I gave the State Department the names of double-agents operating in Europe—one of them in Willy Brandt's private office. I blew the whistle when the Soviets were beginning to muscle into the Middle East. I warned Carter . . ."

Merriman had been at it so long, Conrad was thinking, it had become a way of life. He genuinely believed he was performing a service not just for himself or for Russia but for the loftiest purposes—for "global stability," "world peace," "the future of mankind." How could he accept any lesser motives, a man of his stature?

"It's the other side of the coin I'm interested in, Merriman, the U.S. intelligence secrets you've sold to the Soviets for your special trading status. In the forties when you served on the Top Policy Group you turned over vital information on the A-bomb—"

Merriman tried to interrupt but Conrad overrode him.

"Don't bother denying it. I've got enough evidence now at least to charge you with treason. Now we're at an even more critical point. Instead of the atomic secret we hold the theory and much of the technology of Star Wars. Never mind your grand motives, you've been using David Pointer to get classified information—"

"Conrad, I won't submit to threats or distortions." His voice was calm. August Merriman was not a man easily intimidated. "My relationship with David Pointer is completely innocent. As you may or may not know, I've invested millions in scientific research since the Sputnik embarrassment through the American Science Foundation. But I'm also not a man to throw good money after bad. I want to find out just how viable this SDI project really is. If it *is* a sound idea, well, it could change history. Give the younger generation another New World, a world of guaranteed peace. And without the threat of war, I think that more than justifies my actions. But there's been so much talk going both ways, from the Pentagon on down the line. So I went to the one fellow who understands it better than anybody else. That's the way I've always operated, whatever the issue is. I look for the top authority and go right to him."

"Very moving, very noble, but I've got a file on you a foot deep. Keep on pissing into the wind and I'll let it all fly. Or start talking, beginning with the ASF, and *maybe* you'll be able to save your ass."

Merriman didn't flinch. "I see now why you were eased out of the CIA, Conrad. You've lost it, as my granddaughter would say. It's a shame, but I understand it happens to the best of you people . . . paranoia, an occupational hazard. Not that I need to explain myself to the likes of you, but there's nothing at all mysterious about the ASF. It's an *endowment* —one of the many that I fund—to encourage promising young scientists and experimental research programs. If you're really interested in the foundation, though, you should talk to my wife. It's hard to remember now whose idea it was, hers or mine. Not that it matters, because it's her baby now. She's chairman of the board. I put up the money, Prudence does the work."

"I don't think you want to drag Pru into this." He relished using the intimate name. "The ASF is under investigation as a Soviet front—and so are you for passing information elicited from David Pointer to the Kremlin."

Two counts of lying, but the Dean wasn't above stretching the truth when it suited *his* higher purpose.

"Preposterous," Merriman said, shedding his practiced air of insouciance. "Nobody would believe that, especially coming from you. You've been seeing Reds under beds for years. Everybody knows that... and just to make sure your benighted statements are dismissed as they deserve to be, I'll call on some old friends in high places who—"

"Pointer is prepared to testify that you coerced him into revealing classified information and that you used Angelica to entrap him."

"You're talking about my grandson-in-law now, and you expect me to believe that he would marry Angelica one day and condemn her the next? I'll be frank with you, Conrad. I did ask Angelica to come to the first luncheon meeting with Pointer. A young man is always more agreeable when he has a pretty girl to look at. Prudence assured me of that and she was one hundred percent right. My wife is wiser about that sort of thing than I am."

"You discussed it with her in advance—using Pointer and Angelica?"

"I don't accept your sinister implication. But yes, I discuss everything with my wife. She's my partner, the only one I've ever had or ever wanted—better than a dozen men, I assure you. She supported me, she always has. That's the key to a long happy marriage. But once David and Angelica met nature took over. They fell in love and... well, you know the rest."

"A romantic story... but as I understand it, the girl proposed to Pointer. Role reversal, I guess you'd call it today. I'm old-fashioned, though. I call it a set-up. A damned peculiar one. If you really didn't put her up to it for your purposes, and she sure as hell wasn't working for our side..."

Merriman stood. He had put up with Matthias Conrad out of curiosity, and because he didn't want to disrupt the wedding. But now he was going to have him thrown out. No one could insult his Angelica, and get away with it... "Are you implying that my granddaughter—"

"I'm not implying anything about *your* granddaughter. The real Angelica is buried in a cemetery in Mollenz, East Germany. She died at age two." Conrad took a copy of Nora's photograph out of his pocket and tossed it on the library table. It was creased where David had crushed it, but still clear. "Two people have already been killed because they possessed—or were believed to possess—that information."

Merriman took up the snapshot, studied it, sat down again. "It's a lie—a cheap trick—"

"You love the girl, don't you?" Conrad was thinking about Beth.

"She's the joy of my life, my heart's delight... everything you'll say is a grandfather's cliché. I always wanted children, then long after I'd given up hope of having any, we found Angelica."

Slumping down in the chair, he held the picture in both hands, staring at it as though everything had ceased to exist except the stone in the graveyard, and the doubt in his heart.

"How did you *find* her?"

Merriman now seemed anxious to talk, as though somehow the "facts" as he'd known and accepted them all these years would refute Conrad's terrible story, and its more terrible implications. "I got a letter one day from a German lawyer—Peter Braun, his name was—saying he'd come across a girl who appeared to be my granddaughter. After a lot of inconclusive correspondence between my attorneys and the German, Prudence flew to Berlin to investigate the claim personally. When she came home, she brought Angelica with her. I'm not naïve. Neither is Prudence, and at first we were worried that the girl's was too fortuitous, that maybe she and Braun were perpetrating hoax to get money. It's no secret how much I wanted an heir. But Angelica quickly persuaded us otherwise by her loving behavior. And now, with this evidence...."

The more Merriman talked, the clearer it became... For all his vaunted power and status as international power-broker, he was only a pawn. Pru, in dove gray, at any age was the *eminence grise,* purveyor of a fraudulent grandchild, se-cret opener of doors to her masters in the Kremlin. She had manipulated in ways he'd never imagined. August Merriman wasn't an international patriot, as a blind man, a husband-of-convenience.

"The girl is worse." Conrad got up to get an ashtray, and to allow the old man time alone with his shock and grief. "My hunch is KGB—a sexual operative by the look of her and by her behavior."

Merriman waved him away, trying to exorcise the words, then covered his face. Still not ready to accept the worst, he said in a subdued monotone, "I told you my wife investigated the claim personally, she's a stickler for detail... why should the Kremlin plant an agent in my house after all these years? I've been a good friend..." And if Angelica is... is what you say, she wouldn't marry Pointer. They'd never permit it..." He was shaking his head determined to discredit the charges. Anything to hold onto the girl.

Tapping a Camel out of the pack, Conrad leaned against the deep, polished sill and smoked in silence. He was think-ing about Peter Braun, Pru in Berlin, Pru in Venice, Pru in pink at nineteen, and how different it might have been. He looked out the window. A mist seemed to have gathered, or was it only in his eyes... A picture was framed in the leaded-glass square like an impressionist painting, a carefully ordered pastoral, an autumnal landscape. Saturday in the

Park with Pru. In the background beneath a startling sky, a huge silver bird hovered six feet from the ground, preparing to alight on the grass. In the forefront a party crowd was trooping across the lawn, following the lead of a slender dowager in gray silk.

"There's one person who can answer all that, and she's out there in the garden now. Your wife, Mr. Merriman, is no ordinary helpmate."

Merriman came up behind him as he spoke. "First you malign my granddaughter, then you insinuate things against my wife . . ."

If asked, Conrad probably could not have said just when it was that he began to suspect who Pru was or what she had become. It was not a sudden discovery, more a gradual dawning, remembered passions and fresh details combining in a bone-chilling awareness.

"You said it yourself. Pru brought the girl here. The ASF is her baby. She encouraged you to use David, she put Angelica in his bed—Jesus," he broke off, "why isn't David stalling for time, *he can't get on that chopper—*"

Outside, the picture was animated, one frame speeding after another like a video run in double-time. The helicopter had landed, the door opened. A shrinking span of grass separated it from the bridal party. The two men watched from the library window, the figures looking like dolls from such a distance. Now Prudence was standing by the door of the chopper, one hand planted on her hat against the rush from the propellers. Joseph was beside her. The pilot was loading the baggage, then the bridal couple climbed aboard, David stumbling, only Angelica remembering to turn and wave to the guests who had followed them over the lawn, some of them tossing confetti and rice.

"Are you going to let them take off?" Merriman's tone was guarded. He wasn't accustomed to holding an empty hand.

Conrad wheezed, winded even before he had begun. "How are you at the hundred-yard dash?"

Merriman did not seem to hear. He was staring out the window so intently his nose grazed the glass.

"Where does that guy think he's going? Look at him... *Why doesn't Prudence stop him?*"

Conrad was watching, too. Joseph had started to close the chopper door, but at the last second as the silver bird began to lift, he jumped in.

"Where did you find Joseph?"

"My wife hires all the servants, including my secretary."

"The obvious answer."

"You mean to say—"

"Let's just *say* I think his references would be enlightening. He doesn't strike me as a typical secretary... too self-assured, even arrogant. But we'll find out soon enough. Call the airport, have them hold the flight to London."

Merriman went over to the desk and picked up the receiver, but his index finger was pressed on the depress button.

"*No*. It's *my* goddamn plane. I decide." At a very late date, Conrad thought. "And I'm going to let her go... whoever she is. His voice broke.

Conrad had to feel sorry for the man. He had loved three women in his life, his mother, his wife and Angelica and two had betrayed him. He seemed to be trying to escape the awful realization, shaking his head, trying to deny the undeniable.

"I need time to satisfy myself that your accusations are true... just until Angelica and David come back from their honeymoon..."

Merriman couldn't break the habit of a lifetime, Conrad thought. Down at the count of nine, and still trying to cut a deal with the referee. Still, he couldn't help admiring the old man's guts. He'd play even a losing hand to win.

"What if they don't come back from their honeymoon? Have you thought of that?" It was clear from Merriman's face that he didn't know anything about the death in Venice.

"Someone tried to kill Pointer on the Ponte dell'Accademia. I'm still not sure why, although it's pretty clear that Angelica set him up. Didn't Pru tell you? She hushed up the whole unpleasant affair."

"What's that?" He seemed to have retreated into himself. "As I said before, my wife has always been a stickler for detail, she believes that as long as appearances are correct, no one wonders what may be underneath . . ."

He spoke as if she no longer existed, and she did not, in any way she ever had been for him.

"Are you going to make that call?" Conrad's tone was almost gentle.

"I'll phone the airport . . . to have one of my planes standing by for you. You can bring Pointer home yourself."

"And Angelica, whoever she is, will be safely out of the country. Is that your price?"

The two men considered each other uncertainly, neither sure the other was as good as his word.

"As I said, Conrad, I have lived a long life . . . but it seems it has been winding down. I was ready to retire on my own terms. I didn't want to go out with the balance of power tipping dangerously, even if the tilt was toward the West. I've devoted a lifetime to it. Balance, yes. Tip the scales and you upset the world . . ." "Do I sound too portentous? I suppose I do. I'm no philosopher, I know . . . I always left that sort of thing to my wife. I'm a businessman, with no apologies, but I can read the writing on the wall, and this Star Wars business seemed to be a threat to everything I've accomplished. The Soviets have their own program, but it's nowhere near as sophisticated as ours. That's why they've been so worried . . .

"There was no chance for an arms control treaty, nuclear parity, a reduction in warheads, no chance for *any* of it unless something changed. Why do you think the Kremlin suddenly softened? Because of me . . . yes, because of what I've done. For the first time in a dozen years there's a *real* chance to reduce the threat of a nuclear holocaust. I believe that's what makes a true patriot, knowing how to best serve all countries, not just saluting your flag."

"That's also what makes a traitor, Merriman."

The old man's eyes were lost in the maze of wrinkles, making it impossible for Conrad to gauge his reaction. "You want my price?" he said. "Give me your whole damn file and let the girl go. I'm still not saying I believe you—but I don't want to face an ugly scandal. Not now, not at my age. I think I deserve better."

"*Nolo contendere.*" Conrad said. "And Pru?"

Merriman's facade slipped at the stark question, erasing pretense and equivocation, he seemed to become a very small, very wrinkled old man.

"Prudence is my wife," he answered with bitterness. "I'll take care of her..."

The Dean did not stop to argue further or to see Merriman make the call. Moving faster than he had in years, he headed out of the library, back across the hallway and past the conservatory, following the lily trail to the terrace where he had parried with Pru and lost. The irony of the flowers, and their fragrance, as overpowering now. The lily, symbol of innocence and purity, neither of which had a place in the Merrimans' lives. On impulse he plucked one, stuffing it into his buttonhole as he crossed the gardens that stretched between the terrace and the drive where he had left Charlotte's Fiesta. Instead of unloading it and himself at the castle door, Conrad had parked the car personally just in case he had to make a quick exit.

CHAPTER
THIRTY-FOUR

Leaning out the door of the chopper, the wind from the take-off whipping her hair against her face, Angelica tossed out the bouquet and watched the wind carrying it toward the crowd of upturned faces. Prudence didn't wait to see who caught it. August would be occupied with their guests, and she didn't want to face Matthias Conrad again. It was uncomfortable to be around someone who knew you so well. Too well.

Slipping away, she walked along the garden paths toward her woodland hideaway, breathing in the smells of fall. It was the first time since Dostankov's arrival that she could breathe freely, and now he was gone, too. The wedding marked the end of an era. When August retired, her work would be over. She walked briskly along the paths, her steps silent, the fallen leaves too damp to crackle beneath her feet, exhilarated by the day, congratulating herself on a job well done.

But seeing Matt again forced her to look back, to ask herself the question she'd always managed to avoid, too caught up in the work at hand for reflection. Had it all been worth it? The price she had paid in solitude—without friends, children, love?

For all her dedication, the philosophy she had embraced in her youth had lost credibility. Now, it seemed, only the poorest, the most ignorant, the most desperate of the world flocked to the Red banner. There were a few stalwarts like herself, but by and large the many who had supported the cause in the thirties and forties had fallen by the wayside. Post-war history, the Stalin purges, the partitioning of Eastern Europe making cynics of them, and nothing the Kremlin had done in the last thirty years—Hungary, 1956, Czechoslovakia, 1968, Poland, 1980—had served to restore their faith. Still, she believed . . . she *had* to believe. And, she told herself, remembering the early self-justifying faith . . . capitalism continued to exploit all but the few, the rich got richer, the poor got color TV and welfare . . . And so she embraced its antithesis, the way a priest, disgusted by the material wealth of the Church, prays for an anti-Christ.

From the terrace of his baronial castle August Merriman watched the silver chopper until it looked like a bird banking against the sky. Then slowly he followed the winding trail that led to his wife's private hideaway. Anchored on a cliff overlooking the river, it was made of the same stones as Durandana, with the same eccentric turrets, but it was the size of a child's playhouse, the door padlocked and a single key, exclusive property of Prudence Schaeffer Merriman. August had built if for her when he built Durandana. It was the only thing she had ever asked him for. And she had never let him visit.

"The rest of my time is yours, but when I'm there I want my privacy respected. Even wives need a place of their own, a space and time that can't be infringed," she'd said. And he had agreed to the trade-off. His life had been a series of trade-offs, after all . . .

The leaves were beginning to show their true colors in the silent woodland where Algonquin braves had slithered, tracking the forests for food and furs to trade to the palefaces. In the valley below, through the range of Adirondacks like a long tunnel, the Hudson snaked, principal artery in the founding of the nation. The Indians called it "the river that flows both ways" because the current moves in two directions, down from the mountains where the water rises, up from the ocean where it empties, salt and clear water swirling sixty, eighty miles up from Manhattan, brine as far north as Albany.

A sailboat was passing on the water below, only its main jib unfurled. Dutch patroons plied the same waters, Iroquois canoes, explorers searching for a roadway into the New World's interior, settlers moving into the Mohawk Valley, and Robert Fulton's baby puffing up from New York City to Albany, the maiden voyage of the steamship *Claremont*.

Merriman truly loved every inch of the place—the Indian forests, the tunnelled valley, the wall of Adirondack rock dividing the coast and the heartland, the solemn, solitary river running south in a beeline, straight as an arrow, in perfect harmony with the mountains. He thought of Benedict Arnold and Major André meeting on the bank below the redoubt of West Point, stronghold of the Continental Army, and Arnold fleeing down river to the enemy.

For Prudence Merriman, there could be escape from treason.

She was unlocking the door of her small castle when he reached her. As it swung open he could see over her shoulder a bank of shortwave radio transmitters.

"What are you doing, here, August?" Her voice was as sharp as the wind that cut in from the river. "How could you leave our guests?"

"The question is, what have *you* been doing here all these years?"

"Taking a few minutes away to compose myself. I'm not the glad-hander you are, after all. Go back now, and I'll follow in a few minutes."

She seemed to stand even straighter than usual—a straight arrow, Boston brahmin, all the right schools and connections, aristocratic, refined—and a liar. Prudence Merriman would never stoop to fib. She propounded grand lies to suit her grand ideas. A lifetime of deceit made her perform with equanimity. She gave nothing away. He had never realized it before—never even stopped to *think* about it.

For the first time he felt the weight of almost nine decades. "We were a perfect team. You were more than a wife, more than a partner. You were my conscience.

"Matt..." She mouthed the syllable barely audibly, but the wind carried it to her husband. "To think that he would come between us after all these years."

"He accused me of being a traitor to my country. Me, August Merriman, a *traitor*. And when I challenged him, he told me...everything. The girl I gave away so proudly today was a sexual operative for the KGB, and my wife..."

Prudence stood as though rooted to the spot, then with a shrug faced her husband.

"And, my husband, *you* acted like a baying ass over her— an old man like you. Your beloved granddaughter who was doing exactly what I told her. After all, I found her—"

Merriman could hardly speak.

"*You* were Angelica's control?"

"She never knew, of course, no more than you did. I was just a voice on a cassette relaying orders, but she obeyed to the letter. Very professional, I admired her for that. Why do you think she let you cloud your binoculars over her naked body? It was quite entertaining. And you never suspected, not a thing. Your ego, August, is so monumental you can't see anything except your own glorious reflection."

He was shaking his head, back and forth, back and forth. "Why, Prudence? Why did you do it?"

In the beginning I did it for Georgie, so that he would live on through his ideas and never be forgotten. And then I just went on."

George Aloysius Schaeffer, dead in Spain in '37, her brother he had never met, only knew from the photograph on her dresser.

"Big Brother is watching you." It was a cheap shot, petty revenge itself, but he wanted to punish her.

Prudence was unfazed, seemingly as hard as the Adirondack rock beneath her feet. "...And I don't believe you helped the Russians or anyone else for laudable motives. You saw a way to help yourself and make it seem noble. I never believed your talk about one world and global unity. To me it was just another way of saying, blessed are the capitalists for they shall take over the world. I believed, and believe, there has to be a better way to live..."

Conrad's words came back to him like a portent: *When their arguments are stripped away, they stand out clearly and pathetically as merely apologists of their youth. Cowards, too, because they cannot or will not admit that they were wrong so many years ago. Instead, they go on adding insult to injury, compounding their mistakes—and hurting their countries.* And those who love them...still love them.

"Why did you let Angelica marry Pointer?"

"I didn't let her—I ordered her, arranged every detail. After a beautiful wedding and a glorious honeymoon— locked on a train so there's *no* chance of escape or outside interference—David will be 'persuaded' to go home with his bride to Moscow. On an impulse they'll get off the train in Innsbruck—on Angelica's impulse. A car will be waiting to drive them to East Germany, and from there, an Aeroflot jet—"

"Pointer's going to defect?"

"Abdicate, I prefer to say, for the woman he loves. It's a grander, more romantic word, don't you think, for a bridal couple? Edward VIII did it for Wally Simpson, and she was a bitch on wheels...Oh, I know what you're thinking, the disgrace and humiliation of it all. Angelica is supposed to be your grandchild. A ticklish detail, darling, but it couldn't be helped. And you're retiring anyway. It can't really hurt you, August, your usefulness is over."

"You've made a mockery of me, of my life...everything I've done."

"Our marriage was no different from any other. Years of give and take...I have no regrets."

Her eyes were bright with a passion he had once mistakenly thought was for him.

"You gave me more than any other man could—the opportunity to make a difference in the world. And I took it, August. I took it."

He shook his head, still not able to absorb it.

"You look like a girl again, Prudence, the girl I fell in love with. Remember when we met...London, 1937, I was just back from Russia and you were trying to get to Spain. I always thought our marriage was my greatest success, a true partnership—"

"I guarded your delusions, darling. I was careful to do that, not to take away your pride, your confidence, your illusions of power. You were president, premier and prince all in one—I saw to that. And you must admit, you gloried in it."

"*Stop* it, Prudence." He was in his eighty-eighth year of life, forty-eighth year of marriage. Her words were too stunning to bear.

"You like to say you did it all for world peace, international stability. They were bonus points. You did it for August Merriman because you wanted more—more money, more power, more prestige than any other man. I married you for your boundless greed, August."

Three hundred feet below the Hudson snaked, revolutionary path in the making of a nation, the unmasking of a myth.

"You always had all the answers. You never needed me— you never needed any man."

"If I had, I would be as much a fool as you. You say I never loved you, darling. How could I? You would not see the world through my eyes."

"And now it's too late." Merriman's voice was strangely calm as he walked toward her.

"Too late for what?" She stepped back as he came closer, wearing a triumphant smile.

"To love me."

"I have no regrets, August."

"And I have a lifetime of them."

"You never understood, that was your trouble. Money was just a means for me, a way to reshape the world. For you it was an end. The end. You never knew me. As long as I fed your vanities, you never bothered to take a closer look. My wife is my only partner, you liked to say, with a smile for the little woman."

She laughed. She had wanted to laugh at him for so long that once she began she couldn't stop. And still he kept coming toward her, and she kept moving back.

"You made me sell out my country. And called it a higher good than patriotism. All the time you were using me. Spied on by my own wife, manipulated, controlled."

"Well, it's all over now, darling. I'm retiring, too... remember?"

He kept moving toward her. The hideaway was set on the highest crest of a cliff, perpendicular to the river that flowed from Algonquin forests to the imperial city. A single sapling clung to the stoney face, its roots having somehow worked their way into the solid rock, and beyond were the smokey green highlands, and the sun slipping toward the hills.

"I could forgive you all of it... except Angelica. You kept me childless, and then you gave me a fraud to love."

"No, August. You made your own bed. I just made it more interesting."

Her smile broke into laughter, as though quite pleased with her wit. And the laughter made her careless. Or perhaps she merely stepped back instinctively as he seemed to stumble forward, the uneven ground making him unsteady.

It was a three-hundred-foot drop of sheer rock to the river below. August Merriman clung to the sapling branch. He thought he could still hear her laughter, but it was only a remembered sound now. In the river below the water splashed, like sturgeon jumping, then smoothed. When Durandana was new and they were young, he and Prudence used to fish in the Hudson for sturgeon and trout. He remembered her wearing a wide-brimmed straw hat to keep her nose from burning.

Now the water was too polluted. And there was nothing to fish for . . . except a dove-gray cloche floating south toward Manhattan and the open sea.

CHAPTER
THIRTY-FIVE

Newburgh had few of the amenities of the major international airports like O'Hare, Kennedy, Orly or Heathrow, its arrivals and departures being limited for the most part to local traffic. But it did house Merriman's fleet of Lears—twelve in all, ten in the hangar, one on the runaway, the blue-and-gold *AM* emblazoned on the wing. The silver chopper idled beside it.

Ignoring the signs warning against it, Conrad drove right out to the runway, never braking until he was inches from the jet.

"Hey, mister, where do you think you're going?" A mechanic yelled as he got out of the car.

"I'm going to throw rice at the bride."

The man took off his earmuffs to hear better, but he didn't look as though he was buying Conrad's story. "Nobody's allowed on the runway except authorized personnel. Can't you read?"

"Did you see the bride?"

"Sorry, Mac, you missed her by five minutes. You her father or something?"

Conrad took out his wallet and flashed his license. As mug shots go, it was a pretty good picture, flattering, Charlotte had said.

"Matthias Conrad. One of August Merriman's planes is standing by for me."

At the mention of the name August Merriman, the mechanic became instantly respectful and apologetic. "Not standing by, exactly. It'll be a couple of hours before the pilot gets here and the plane is ready to make a transatlantic flight. It takes time—"

Conrad got back in the car to wait. Time was the one thing he wasn't sure he had. He closed his eyes and tried not to think about Pointer going back to Venice—and never getting back, maybe even ending up like Nora and Beth. It didn't really make any sense to terminate him . . . David was giving the Russians what they wanted. But as far as he could figure it, the first try hadn't made sense either.

Senseless deaths. Especially Beth's. Children were supposed to bury their parents, not the other way around.

And Sam Daniels' investigation wasn't going anywhere. The morning before the storm there had been a stranger in the general store asking directions—a nondescript man, late thirties, no distinguishing features, driving a white Ventura. A check with every rental service in New England turned up one questionable entry: An overnight rental was made at Greene Airport in Warwick, Rhode Island, and paid for in cash. Both the name and address given proved false. At that point the investigation into the murder of Beth Conrad came to a full stop, as her father knew it would. The KGB didn't bother with amateurs.

As it turned out, the two-hour wait stretched into three, almost four. Conrad watched the day slip away, as he often did in Little Compton. In summer the change was languid like the weather, the sun fading gradually, the evening drifting in, a gentle tide. Now the night dropped suddenly, wiping out the afternoon before it knew what hit it, like a dum-dum bullet to the brain.

Conrad tried not to look back. Turning on the ignition and

lights, he coasted across the runway to the airport and placed a long-distance call to a friend in Britain's MI5. During the interminable wait, he stocked up on cigarettes from a vending machine.

* * * *

At 9:13 A.M. Sunday morning the second Merriman jet in twenty-four hours taxied into London's Heathrow Airport. At 11 A.M. sharp, the southbound Venice-Simplon Orient Express was scheduled to depart from Victoria Station.

Looking as though he had slept in his suit, although, in fact, he had slept in a paisley silk dressing gown with the ubiquitous AM monogran on the cuff, Conrad shuffled off the plane into the waiting arms of a certain Mr. Timothy Wrightson who doffed his bowler and introduced himself. Circumspect and proper enough to play Jeeves to somebody's Bertie Wooster, Conrad thought, following the bowler through customs to a waiting black Austin coupe.

The morning was barely visible through the curtain of drizzle and fog that formed the usual backdrop for London in the cooler months. On the drive into the city and Buckingham Palace Road, the two men talked about the seasonably gray weather, then Conrad reviewed the subject of Peter Braun.

Braun was responsible for two deaths. He was the only one who could have fingered Nora, and the only one who knew about the Dean's connection. Then there was the matter of the false Angelica. Braun had been instrumental in placing the girl in Merriman's house. Although Conrad would have liked to take on the German personally—for Beth and Nora —MI5 had more resources at its disposal.

Buckingham Palace Road was an undistinguished street in spite of its name, and dingier than Conrad remembered, as if permeated with a feeling of transience from the ceaseless flow of air, bus and rail traffic that rushed along it.

Conrad got out at Victoria Station, one hundred English pounds now in his pocket and looking passably respectable with the addition of a beige canvas overnight bag. In a zippered pocket were a passport, French visa and reservations for a single compartment on the London-Venice Orient Express, departing in twenty minutes. The famous clock was gone, but otherwise Victoria Station, gateway to the continent for generations of Britons, was just as he remembered it. Flocks of pigeons to rival the doyens of Piazza San Marco crowded his footsteps as he walked through the glass-roofed concourse, but there was no sign of either the Pointers or their traveling companion picking their way through the feathers and crumbs. He hurried on, not wanting to bump into them but at the same time worried that the honeymoon trip had just been a ruse to get Pointer out of the country.

At the turn of the century the Venice Simplon-Orient Express was a moveable feast for peers and pretenders traveling to the continent. The luxurious accommodations were taken for granted then, the individual appointments in each compartment, the formal dining, the leisurely mode of travel. The war changed more than the map of Europe. It changed perceptions and values. Air travel and a disposable society made the Orient Express obsolete. Elegance was time-consuming, and the world was in a hurry.

Conrad's shuffle slowed to a crawl. On the platform, no more than thirty feet away, Joseph was handing over the baggage to a porter: a woman's set of matching green leather luggage with navy monograms; a black-and-red parachute-cloth suit-bag and tote, looking like poor relations beside the others and obviously belonging to David; and a single black calfskin roll that by the process of elimination had to be Joseph's.

Expensive for a secretary's bank account, Conrad thought, no matter how generous an employer August Merriman is. He peered closer like a lepidopterist examining rare speci-

mens. Off to the side, as if disassociated from the keen anticipation that affects most travelers and honeymooners,
Angelica waited, a picture of patience—or just a picture,
plain and simple. A knockout by any standard. She was
wearing a brown tweed walking suit flecked with orange and
royal blue. Her hair was pulled back in a ponytail, and a
brown felt boater, flat-brimmed and veiled, sat above it. Her
gloved hands rested lightly on the handles of a wheelchair in
which a man appeared to sleep. A watchplaid mohair throw
blanket covered his knees, and an Irish slouch hat hid most
of his face.

Down the tracks, the gleaming brown-and-cream carriages
of the British Pullman gushed steamy vapors—the original
cars resurrected from forgotten railyards. Refusing his offer
of help, Angelica followed the porter to the last carriage,
Joseph hurrying them both along as if afraid the train would
leave without them.

Pushing his glasses up on his nose, Conrad looked over the
other passengers crowding around the reception area reserved for travelers on the deluxe train. Some of the women
were dressed in styles he hadn't seen since he was a boy,
long-waisted flapper dresses with short flouncing skirts.
Many of them wore extravagant hats, and a few of the men
doffed broad-brimmed fedoras, all in the spirit of elegant
fun, which was the specialty of the new Orient Express.

One by one the passengers were escorted to the waiting
carriages, until Conrad was left alone on the platform. He
lingered, refusing to be hurried. The chief steward approached him, resplendent in liveried uniform and possess-
ing a diplomat's tact. The Venice-Simplon Orient Express
prided itself on steaming out of Victoria Station at eleven
o'clock sharp, twice weekly, Thursday and Sunday mornings,
without fail. Rain, snow, sleet or ice.

He should never have let them get away. Now Joseph and
Angelica were the honeymooners, and Pointer . . . the possi-

bilities were boundless, and Conrad knew better than to discount any of them, even the most outlandish.

Conrad's seat was in the first carriage, a sufficient distance from the Pointer party so that he could relax and take in the first lap of the trip at least, from London to the Channel. Passing up the complimentary champagne, he ordered a double Scotch on the rocks and surveyed his surroundings.

An open Pullman, infinitely more elaborate than the old parlor cars he remembered. On either side of the aisle was a single row of plush armchairs upholstered in a reddish floral design against a black background. Between the chairs intimate tables were set for lunch with fine silver and crystal.

Millions had been sunk into the antique cars. Each detail of the restoration, down to the crocheted antimacassars on the back of each seat, was exact—the polished brass fixtures, the panelled walls, the ornate marquetry. Even Rene Lalique's original glass panels had been brought back and framed in mahogany.

For all its authenticity, though, the new Orient Express could not duplicate the original's opulence that reflected a way of life. This was an ostentatious display, an opportunity for the newly rich to flaunt their gross assets.

The Venice-Simplon Orient Express from London to Venice took two days and a night and followed the Alpine route, traveling southwesterly from Paris and crossing the border at Basel, then cutting across Switzerland from Zurich to Innsbruck, and down through the Dolomites, affording some of the most breathtaking views in Europe. There were three legs to the trip—the British, "naval", and continental—and nothing to do before Paris in any event, Conrad thought, except keep to himself and make sure the Russians didn't find out he was aboard.

The British Pullman traveled from London through the Kentish countryside with its charming calendar-picture landscape to Folkestone, where the passengers boarded a waiting ferry for the Channel crossing. Conrad waited in his seat, nursing the last drops of Scotch until he saw Angelica and Joseph pushing the chair to the ferry. He followed at a safe distance.

The crossing was rough. The drizzle that dampened London had matured into a full-fledged storm. By the time the ferry pulled away from the dock the day was as dark as his mood. Retching weather, Conrad called it. From the lower deck where he retreated to avoid the first-class lounge reserved for Orient Express passengers, the white cliffs of Dover looked like streaks of chalk on a blackboard.

Gale winds swept down from the north, whipping the Channel water into giant swells that crashed against the ferry's prow, showering even the highest deck. The blue-and-gold coaches of the Continental Train waited warm and inviting at the dock in Boulogne, but the Channel crossing had drowned the most intrepid spirits. The gala atmosphere of the trip had been lost, along with many of the four-star lunches. Conrad, alone among the passengers, felt considerably better than he had in London. He was a seasoned sailor who had ridden out many a storm, and the glimpse of a green-faced Joseph weaving uncertainly across the gangplank to the welcome firmness of Gallic soil buoyed his spirits.

Again he waited until Joseph and company were safely on the train, noting the number of the car they entered, before boarding himself. If anything, the Continental outdid the British Pullman in lavishness, offering both the privacy of individual compartments and the camaraderie of the elegant bar and dining cars.

Like the rest of the train, Conrad's compartment was richly appointed and panelled in two shades of polished wood, the squares alternating in a chessboard design. The subtle fragrance of freesia tinged the air. The flowers were set on one side of a solid brass reading lamp covered with a rose silk shade, pleated and fringed. On the other side of the lamp was a bowl of red grapes.

Fresh flowers, fresh fruit, and most refreshing of all, his compartment was one carriage down from the dining car. The Pointers would have to pass by. Leaving the door ajar so he could observe the passing parade, Conrad settled in for the evening by ordering a fifth of Scotch, three packs of Camels, and an early dinner to be served in his cabin. Strictly speaking, dinner was served exclusively in the dining car, but a generous tip to the steward bent the rule.

There were two seatings, and midway between Boulogne and Paris the early diners began to drift by, like models in a fashion show. Although black tie was optional, almost everyone made the choice. Understatement was unheard of. The gowns were true couture creations that made the fashions at a New York charity ball look shabby by comparison. The Dean grew bug-eyed, but there was no sign of the one woman he was waiting to see.

By the time the late diners began sauntering by, the Continental was drawing close to Paris, and Conrad was so well fortified with whiskey and a four-course dinner of steamed turbot and fillet of beef, he appeared to be nodding off. A flash of black and white—black velvet that bared more white flawless skin than it covered—brought him up to attention.

Angelica's dress could arouse a dead man. Except for the long sleeves and long skirt there wasn't much material to it at all. Both bodice and back were cut into V's of such a dangerous depth they looked like arrows leading directly into temptation. Her hair was swept up, adding to the amount of naked flesh on display. Joseph was a step behind her and obviously taking in the view. Although he wasn't in formal dress, his dark suit looked as though it had cost more than Conrad had spent on his entire wardrobe in the last fifteen years. There was no sign of Pointer.

Conrad waited until he was sure they were seated in the dining room studying the evening's menu before he started working his way back, Scotch in hand, to admire the rest of the train, if anybody questioned him, and car twenty-three in particular. The carriage was silent. He started down the aisle tapping on each door. His first knock was answered by a middle-aged woman. Excusing himself, he went to the next compartment. When no one answered he tried the door. The compartments only locked from the inside. There were no keys, and the door opened easily. The room was empty. So were the next two. At the fifth door, he knocked and waited. When no one answered, he tried the door.

The conversion from sitting room to sleeper had already been made, and a man was stretched across the bed. Conrad stepped inside and locked the door behind him. In the glow of the brass reading lamp the face of David Pointer looked like a death mask. Letting fly every obscenity he had collected through seven decades, he started slapping Pointer across the face, saying his name, wanting to shout it but afraid to take the risk. Although he began to mumble incoherently, Pointer was too deeply drugged to respond.

The Orient Express shuddered to a stop. *Gare d'Est.* Somewhere between Boulogne and Paris the storm had quieted. A noisy rush of passengers trooped on at the Paris station in a gust of cold air. Conrad could hear them outside in the aisle, their voices both muffled and high. Someone fumbled with the door, bumped the wall, trying to get into the wrong compartment, he thought. There were enough stewards to straighten out the confused newcomer.

If he could find what the Russians were giving David. . . .

Taking a swallow of whiskey he went into the bathroom to search. As he did, he saw the door begin to open and heard Angelica's voice.

"I guess my husband woke up and locked it while I was at dinner. It's the only explanation, although he certainly looks sound asleep now."

Quickly, Conrad shut himself in the bathroom and slipped the lock. Either she had forgotten something or she had come back to check on Pointer. Whichever the case, it shouldn't take more than a minute or two, then she'd go back.

He waited, leaning against the marble washbasin, admiring the expensive fixtures, when the knob began to turn. Conrad swore under his breath. He couldn't let Angelica call the steward again. But elegant though it was, the bathroom was no bigger than a coat closet. He had no room to hide, and no weapon.

Matthias Conrad did not make a habit of wasting good whiskey—exactly the contrary—but this time he made an exception. He cracked the glass against the hard edge of the marble sink, sending glass and ice flying. The Scotch splattered all over him, making him smell like a taproom as he slid back the lock.

Angelica tried the door again, unprepared for what awaited her. She gasped and shrank back into the bedroom. The Dean leered like a gargoyle and advanced on her, brandishing a wedge of French crystal, sharp enough to slit the fairest throat with a single slash.

"What are you doing—?"

"Visiting an old friend . . . and I might ask you the same."

"You know Dostankov will kill you if he finds you here." The broken glass was too close for caution. With the bed opened there was only space to take three steps back, and she had used the last one.

Dostankov . . . Anatol Dostankov, the new and youngest counter-intelligence chief in KGB history. Conrad repeated the name to himself. No wonder the face was vaguely familiar. Although photographs of the KGB were not distributed, even in Moscow, the CIA had managed to get mug shots of the ranking members.

"He will kill you, believe me," Angelica said again.

"Not before I kill you, pretty lady."

She inhaled whiskey fumes and felt the cold edge of glass

against her throat, just at the windpipe. "... What do you want?"

"David... and some information. What are you giving him?"

The crystal nicked her skin, causing a bubble of blood to surface.

"I don't know what Dostankov put in his champagne at the wedding, but now we're giving him morphine every four hours—"

"And it's medicine time—that's why you came back, a veritable Florence Nightingale. I doubt if it will touch his pain."

Angelica winced, wanting to explain, his words cutting deeper than the glass ever could. The Dean took note. Maybe Pointer had been right, after all. Maybe she did feel something for him—not rose-covered-cottage-and-white-picket-fence love, but at least something more personal than an agent's job well done. Conrad weighed his options. Finish her, then face Dostankov and the messy consequences of murder, or take a chance on the girl as Pointer had in Maine, but look where it had gotten him...

He pressed the glass against her throat, angled just enough to keep the jagged edge from cutting. "Where's the morphine?"

Angelica looked toward the wheelchair, afraid if she moved a fraction more she would feel the glass jab into her neck again.

"The handles are hollow under the rubber grips—"

"Turn and back over toward the door."

They moved together like awkward dancers in some bizarre tango. If Conrad dipped unexpectedly...

"What are you going to do?" She didn't beg.

He opened the door just wide enough to push her out. "Your dinner's getting cold... and I'm sure your friend's getting anxious."

* * *

"I was about to come after you. What took you so long?"

Angelica slid into her chair, breathless and flushed. "The aisles were crowded with passengers getting on in Paris. Then I took care of David, freshened my make-up...you know, the little vanities that eat up so much time in the West. Did you finish your dinner already?"

"No, I waited for you."

Although he was watching her closely Dostankov seemed satisfied with her answer. He wasn't worried about leaving Pointer alone, even though the door didn't lock. The stewards had been told that Mr. Pointer was seriously ill—his wife and personal physician were taking him to Innsbruck for treatment—and the morphine was necessary sedation until they arrived.

Dostankov signalled the waiter to begin serving the *prix-fixe* four-course dinner that came with the price of a ticket. Steamed turbot with saffron-flavored sauce, fillet of beef with asparagus tips, fresh baby carrots, baked tomatoes and Duchesse potatoes, followed by a selection of cheeses and a dark chocolate mousse with coffee sauce. Dostankov felt at ease ...Matthias Conrad was the only threat to Operation Counterpoint, and they had left him far behind at Durandana. If he were going to stop them, agents would have been waiting at Victoria Station. Dostankov tasted the fish, savoring the bite.

Angelica couldn't eat any of it. She kept seeing the gargoyle face of Matthias Conrad and the lethal crystal in his hand. A part of her, by far the most important part, wanted David to escape. But it was impossible. The train didn't stop again until it reached the Swiss border at dawn, and the stewards would never allow Conrad to take David off... unless she went with them. The loving bride...Even more impossible.

She feared Dostankov, and despaired of David. There was no hope of forgiveness, no matter what she did or said. Without the morphine, he would begin to wake up, to remember, and when he saw her with "Joseph" . . . As for Dostankov, he was the second most powerful man in the KGB. If he even suspected her loyalty she might as well throw herself off the speeding train as return to Moscow.

"You seem preoccupied tonight." He leaned across the table so that he would not have to talk above the clatter of the dining car, and so that he could look down her dress at the V cut at her cleavage, revealing the curve of her breasts on either side.

"Just thinking about what it will be like going back to Moscow, and with a husband. I've been away so long . . ."

"We should drink to our last evening in the West."

He raised his glass to hers and listened to the fine crystal chime.

Dostankov was in a mood to celebrate, and the waiter had kept his glass filled with champagne all evening. He had drunk too much waiting for Angelica to return—but why not? A few more hours and they would be crossing the border into the German Democratic Republic—the final step in Operation Counterpoint. Once Pointer saw what the Soviets were offering, he would be more agreeable to his new life, to the inevitable, in any case. He was theirs. That idiot Leon had nearly ruined everything—jumping to the conclusion that Angelica had been compromised by Pointer —that Pointer was more dangerous alive as an agent than valuable as a scientist. Personal feelings didn't belong in this business, except in the case of someone who knew how to handle them . . . someone like himself . . . Soon the papers would grind out copy about the romance of the brilliant Star Warrior who gave up his country for his beautiful wife.

Dostankov would deal with the putative CIA connection once they were safely back in Moscow and he had been commended personally by the General Secretary and selected to replace the intransigent KGB Chairman . . . For now, though, he had more pressing matters on his mind—the very tangible matter that Angelica's plunging black velvet was offering.

He thought of Natasha's childish body, the breasts little more then pebbles, and Angelica . . .

Walking back to their carriage, she felt his eyes on her, following the lines of the V down her back to the point of her lowest verterbra where they met. She stopped at her compartment, one hand on the door. He slid his fingers down the velvet back and touched the crack of her ass.

The door was locked again. Either Conrad was still there, or the morphine had worn off. In either case . . .

She turned in the narrow passage into Dostankov's arms.

"I'll go in with you to check on Pointer," he said.

"I was thinking I'd go in with *you* and Pointer could wait." Her breath was warm and quick against his cheek.

"I want you in this dress—and then out of it."

Dostankov's compartment was next to hers and David's. The room had been made up for the night while they were at dinner, the bed opened, the covers turned down. In the space that remained, it was impossible not to touch.

Angelica, undressed him, letting the velvet of her dress brush his naked body. The first time, Dostankov spoiled her gown before he could raise it up over her. His apologies were effusive.

"I'm going to recommend you to Chebrikov—to the General Secretary himself—for your service —"

"So they can test me personally, too?"

His desire was too absorbing for her sarcasm to register. The sheets were damask, a tablecloth, and when she stepped out of the soiled dress he spread her on them—a royal spread. She undulated with the motion of the Continental as it rolled through champagne country, rolled through the night, train and body one erotic machine driven by Comrade Dostankov, self-appointed successor to the head of the KGB.

The first morning light was breaking over the Zurich Sea when he finally slept. Wrapping her dress around her like a sari, Angelica went back to her own compartment. This time the door was open, and Conrad was waiting for her. Although he didn't gasp or shrink back, it was his turn to be surprised.

"Where have you been all night?"

A superfluous question, but Angelica answered anyway, glancing around the room for the broken crystal. It was on the table beside the freesia.

"As usual, doing my job." She bit off the words. "In this case, distracting Dostankov." She dropped her dress without apology or ceremony. "You can't be here when he gets up, you know."

"I was hoping to get David off in Zurich, but he's still too drugged to move."

"You've only one more chance. At Buchs, when we stop to change engines. We take him off at Innsbruck, the arrangements have all been made."

The Dean was stunned. "What about Venice?"

"We're not going that far." She shrugged and went into the bathroom, leaving him with nothing to look at except the verdant Swiss valleys dotted with chalets and picturesque villages, the snow-peaked Alps looming in the distance.

On the bed beneath the sheets Pointer began to stir unnoticed. He was dreaming of Angelica, but the picture was so vivid he thought it had to be true. She was standing in front of him, naked, almost close enough to touch. After ten morphine-free hours, he opened his eyes and tried to reach for her. She was coming out of the bathroom in a pink silk kimono with matching mules, and her hair was brushed to a sheen, reminding him of his mother, in the perverse quirks memory takes, one hundred strokes each night of her life, and it didn't make the difference. She died anyway.

"What are you going to do?" Conrad asked Angelica. His voice seemed to come out of the sunlight that was so bright Pointer had to close his eyes again.

"I'm going to bed, and when I wake up again I'm going to

be as shocked as Dostankov to find David gone—or to find you here."

*   *   *   *

Dostankov reached out for Angelica and embraced an empty bed. His head was empty, too, of everything except a monumental hangover, though at least champagne was not as lethal as vodka. He was struggling into a sitting position when the door eased open and Angelica tiptoed in.

"You won't disturb me, I'm awake already."

Forcing a smile, she went over to the side of the bed and kissed him as though they were lovers.

"Good morning, darling. Look out the window, the view is spectacular."

The Orient Express was climbing steadily, creating the illusion that the mountains, distant just a short while before, were moving closer, surrounding the antique train on all sides. "And I have a passion for you as towering as those Alps."

"You're insatiable," he said, wanting to be the man who could satisfy her, but afraid of failing.

"Only with you." Her voice was soft and coaxing. "I learned to use my body in a thousand different ways, but never my heart until you touched it."

He moved away from her, tightening the sheet around his waist. Angelica had used the same words the first time they made love—the very words. She had forgotten, but he remembered.

"I'm not awake enough yet. After breakfast..."

"But there's so little time before Innsbruck."

"Give me twenty minutes, then come back."

He needed time to sort out her game.

She pulled at the sheets: "Breakfast can wait."

"No." He held the damask close and pushed her hands away. "Twenty minutes, Angelica, then we will melt the snow on the Alps."

She backed off and blew a kiss from the door. "Twenty minutes..."

The Orient Express was approaching the Swiss frontier. Ten or fifteen minutes and it would pull into Buchs to change engines, picking up a pair of fire-engine red ones, powerful enough to pull the antique train up the steep ascent to the Arlberg Tunnel.

Matthias Conrad was watching the clock like someone waiting to catch a train, not lose one. He had gotten Pointer dressed and propped him against one wall, stationing himself four or five feet away.

Angelica watched, counting the minutes until she would have to return to Dostankov. It was the last time she would see her husband. But if her heart was breaking her face did not show it. It was a beautiful cast on which she painted whichever emotions suited her immediate needs. And right now those were to camouflage the only real emotion she had felt toward a man until she met David Pointer. "Come on, dear boy, it's now or never." Conrad was urging Pointer to walk.

The Dean's plan was simple. While the engines were being changed he and David would get off the train to stretch their legs, then wander away. By the time Angelica and Dostankov finished their exercises for the morning the Orient Express would be crossing the ten-mile width of Liechtenstein, heading towards the Austrian Tyrol. A reprieve for David, and an alibi for her. Basic, uncomplicated. Such were often the best plans, he'd found.

"You can do it, David. Put one foot in front of the other."

Pointer took his first step.

The door to the compartment burst open, slammed shut.

Angelica's face turned as white as the snow on the Alpine peaks.

"You should never use the same lie twice—at least not to
the same man." Dostankov covered the three of them with a
revolver equipped with a silencer.

"I surprised them trying to escape. I was afraid to leave
them, even to get you—"

He cut her off and turned to Conrad, aiming the revolver
at his temple. The girl would obey now because it was her
last hope, and Pointer was too weak to be a threat. There was
only Matthias Conrad . . . Dostankov remembered Chebrikov's jeering words. "You've managed to get away twice, Mr.
Conrad. Not this time."

The old spymaster looked at Dostankov like a wayward
child, affecting a mix of bemusement and tolerance.

"Beth, and the radishes?"

"She was an honest mistake. We all make them. Even
you."

"She was your mistake, but she was my daughter. And for
the record, if you ever to live to make one, I loathe radishes
and Brussels sprouts. I'd never have either in my garden."

"That will be what I believe you call trivia very shortly.
The KGB has at best a passing interest in a dead man's pref-
erences in vegetables."

"Now, it's your turn." He turned to Angelica. "Your turn to
show me which side you're really on. When we get to the
tunnel you will open the window and help me push out the
old man's body. It will never be found. Matthias Conrad will
disappear without a trace from the Venice-Simplon Orient
Express. Do you like Agatha Christie, Mr. Conrad?"

"Not particularly. But apparently you do. Too bad M.
Poirot isn't here to—"

With a flick of the wrist Dostankov spun the revolver and
stepped up close to the Dean. Conrad saw the blow coming
and tried to evade it. If he could reach his shard of glass . . .
on the table beside David . . . He started to rush for it, then
stopped as his eyes met Pointer's. The barrel of Dostankov's

revolver smashed into the back of his skull where his hair
had thinned. He crumbled to the floor.

The train had started up again without Dostankov notic-
ing, the pair of engines climbing straight up through the
Swiss Alps into the ten-mile-wide principality of Liechtenstein. The immense snowy mountains closed in on them so
that the lofty peaks seemed about to come through.

Slowly Pointer came fully awake. He had reached for the
table to steady himself as the engines started to climb, and
felt cold, hard glass beneath his hand. His fingers closed
around the crystal wedge. The jagged edge cut into his palm.
Blood oozed between his fingers but the residue of morphine
numbed the pain.

The blur of figures came into focus, though their talk
swirled around him too quickly to follow. Trying to understand was like trying to keep his balance after twirling in
circles until he was dizzy. A child's game, and he was as
helpless as a child. All he knew was Joseph—the hated Joseph he had seen in bed with Angelica—was in the room.
Angelica was there, too, although he'd lost her for the moment, and Conrad . . .

Dostankov had stuffed the revolver in his belt and was
crouched over the Dean, reaching under his arms to drag
him to the window. For a moment Pointer watched in confusion. Matthias Conrad had been almost a father to him, and a
son of a bitch. And now . . . His grip tightened on the glass as
he lunged for Joseph.

Dostankov felt more than saw him come. He looked up
just as Pointer struck out. The broken crystal slashed his eye,
cutting across the surface of the pupil. A scream froze in his
throat. If he called out it would bring the stewards to the
door. The socket filled with blood. He swatted Pointer back
and covered the bloody eye. The pain felt like stiletto points.

Too weak to fight, too weak even to stand unsupported,

Pointer threw himself back at Dostankov and held on tight, the way a boxer wraps himself around his opponent's body when he can't take another punch. Only there was no referee to pull them apart. Still protecting his bloody eye with one hand, Dostankov struggled to free himself and reach the revolver in his belt...

There was scarcely room to move in the compartment with the bed still open, Conrad's body crumpled on the floor, Dostankov and Pointer in a deadlock beside it. Frightened for herself, for David, for all of them, sickened by Dostankov's eye, Angelica flattened herself against the wall. Now she saw the glint of the silver nozzle, saw Dostankov trying to aim the revolver, saw David all over him... The bedside table was directly opposite her. She began to edge around the walls toward it.

Pointer was still clinging, Dostankov, who was still trying to shake him off. In the struggle Pointer stumbled back and tripped over Conrad's body. The old man groaned. Pointer went sprawling on his back, crashing into the far wall head-first. Dazed, he tried to pull himself up on his knees. If he could dive for the Russian's ankles, tackle him...

Angelica reached the table just as the Orient Express roared into the Arlberg Tunnel. Dostankov had leveled the gun at Pointer, trying to see well enough to fire. She yanked the reading lamp off the table, pulling the wires out of the wall, plunging the carriage into darkness.

The Arlberg Tunnel is an extraordinary feat of skill and daring, carved one hundred years ago through six-and-a-half miles of solid Alpine stone. The Orient Express, train of mystery and romance, coursed through its stoney darkness, and when it came out into the Austrian Tyrol only three people remained in the Pointers' compartment.

Anatol Dostankov had disappeared without a trace. Matthias Conrad, nursing a nasty bump on the back of his head and numerous contusions on his upper body, discovered the only evidence of foul play—a few hairs stuck to the base of the solid brass reading lamp. He wiped the base clean.

By the time they reached Innsbruck, the blood stains had been washed away, the broken glass flushed down the toilet, soiled clothes changed, and the compartment restored to its elegant state, except for the lamp wire that dangled behind the table.

CHAPTER
THIRTY-SIX

Overhead a ragtag sky, autumnal blue patched with paper-white clouds. The ocean was a chilling gray-green streaked with red, the seaweed carried onto the beach marking the tide line as far as the eye could see.

Angelica and David raced down the bluff, stripped naked on the desolate beach and plunged into the surf. The shock of the water took their breath away. They surfaced, teeth chattering, swam a few more strokes, then surfaced again. A ritual cleansing, as if the sea alone could purge their hearts, could wipe away the betrayal and calumny they had committed, leaving them free and clean to start over.

Scooping her up in his arms, he carried her, shivering, back to shore and set her down beside two sandpipers, courtly and correct, engaged in an elaborate mating game. The imprints of the birds' claws like fine hieroglyphics and the two sets of fresh footprints were the only marks in the sand. They did not stop to pick up their clothes, but hand-in-hand ran back up the bluff to the cottage. Still speaking only with their eyes and hands, they climbed the creaking stairs.

The bedroom was a typical New England summer cottage room, cut into a triangular shape by low-hanging eaves—a wrought-iron bedstead painted white, white wicker rocker chipped and dulled, rough pine bureau. There was a pink-

and-white-woven throw rug on the bare floor, faded by the salt air and too many washings, and outside the curtainless window was the widow's walk that girded the eaves.

David lifted her onto the bed, and she pulled him down with her, his wet body slithering over hers. Bits of seaweed clung to her breasts, stuck in her hair. He picked it out, kissing her hair, her eyes, tracing the line of her lips with the tip of his tongue, licking the salt from the corners of her mouth.

"I think I can explain it all," she whispered, "if you'll let me . . ."

"Later." He moved down to taste her dark nipples. "We have a whole weekend."

"More than a weekend, I hope." Her breath was cool in his ear, making him shiver.

"What are you saying?"

"Nothing important. Only that I made a wedding vow—and I meant every word of it. I want you, David, Pointer. If you'll still have me?"

He didn't answer immediately, and the only sound in the house was their breathing, the comfortless silence making it seem as loud as the wind that veered in from the ocean and lashed at the house, making the loose shutters knock, whistling through the locked windows, intensifying the sense of isolation that still kept them apart.

"I'm sorry," she whispered.

"Tell me about Leon."

"There's nothing much to tell. Anyway, he's dead now. Dead to me."

"I met a man named Leon once. You remember. It was on the Ponte dell'Accademia. I thought I was with a girl, a knockout of a girl who turned out to be something else."

She sighed . . . the futility of explanations, excuses contained in a single expiration of air. "You always come back to Venice."

"No, that's Rome—'Three Coins in The Fountain,' Deborah Kerr and Clifton Webb. But Venice is tough to forget when you've been treated to a ride in the Grand Canal without a gondola." He didn't like the sound of that. Too self-righteous. Still . . .

"There were special times, too . . . our first and last nights in Venice."

"I remember, and I also remember the fairytales—"

"They were true . . . "

"As far as they went, which was just far enough for someone else's purposes. And you did set me up on that bridge with Leon, with never a backward glance, a by-your-leave or—"

"*That's not true.* I brought you there, yes, but then I couldn't go through with it. I tried to get you to come away. I begged you, even though I knew I'd be sent back and punished for disobeying orders. Leon didn't trust me anymore . . . "

David listened wanting to believe her but unsure. . . . Angelica's breathing was quick and shallow beside him, and outside in the gathering dusk a nasty squall was gaining force.

"The new Joseph certainly seemed to."

"That's not fair, David. I had to make him believe in me— for *both* our sakes."

"Did you have to be that convincing?" He knew she did, but it still didn't make it any easier to take.

The house, set high on the bluff, was unprotected. It trembled in the storm, shaken by the sudden, furious gusts —a house that had weathered generations of hurricanes, family gatherings and children streaking sand, becoming slightly worn over the years but never losing its charm or graciousness. David loved the place and the memories it held, but even they couldn't erase the other picture.

"Anatol Dostankov was the second most powerful man in the KGB. He was testing me, and he was already suspicious. I was trained to use my body as a weapon . . . "

"You must have been an A student." He was angry still.

She closed her eyes against the futility of explanations. Jealousy was a poison—lethal against reason, candor, love. Especially love.

David watched her drift away. Her face was cast in shadows. Night blackened the windows, shrouded the room. As a boy, lying alone in the too-big bed in the high corner room that seemed to move with every wind, he used to pretend that he was the captain of a clipper ship and the white curtains beating against the open windows were a cloud of sails. He was afraid that he was still pretending, dreaming— and that he would wake up too soon.

He wished they could just lie together and make love, all questions of politics, intrigue, treason and trust, decisions and responsibilities suspended indefinitely.

"And now," he murmured, "what's really left?"

Angelica opened her eyes, and turning toward him threaded her fingers through the hair of his chest.

"Only you and me—if you love me, or want me enough to forgive, and maybe even try to understand."

He searched in her wide eyes for the answer he wanted. He thought he was beginning to detect it, and said almost lightly, "How can I be sure that you'll love me in December when May has been such a goddamn pluperfect disaster?"

"Try me." Her sudden smile lightened the shadows. "Maybe the calendars are wrong . . . our Decembers are over, there's nothing left for us now except Mays, springs, summertimes."

"Then I'll fall for you all over again." He would have done his lousy Groucho Marx imitation except that he was laughing and almost crying at the same time. And all at once it just didn't matter anymore whether she was teasing him or warning him or promising him, because she was reaching for his lips. Fears were lost, caution forgotten in their kiss. Their hands and mouths were everywhere, trying to make up for lost time.

"I wish—" he began, but she stopped him with another kiss that touched his lips like a sea breeze, and he saw the salty drops gathering in her eyes and held her against the storm, picturing the ghostly women, full black skirts whipping their ankles, watching from the widow's walk through countless storms, narrowed eyes fixed on the horizon, praying for their whaling men to come home.

Angelica's eyes were half-closed, and her damp lashes moved against his cheek like wings. He thought about angels, guardian angels, archangels, all the heavenly choirs. And there were avenging angels, fallen angels, Lucifer, and the most beautiful of God's angels . . .

And there was Angelica.

EPILOGUE

August Merriman and Matthias Conrad met again at Durandana two weeks after the wedding. The occasion of their last
meeting was the funeral of Prudence Merriman. After
dredging the Hudson for four days her body was recovered
and cremated. Following a funeral service in the conservatory by invitation only, (none were sent out) the ashes were
returned to the river.

Coincidentally, the funeral of Peter Braun was held in
Berlin that same day. Braun was shot while crossing the
border between East and West in what was being called a
"tragic accident." Each side blamed the other for the incident.

The day was nasty on both continents, a raw cold that even
Merriman's Russian mink coat couldn't shield him from.
After the service, such as it was, he and Conrad returned to
the library for brandy. They sat in the wingchairs flanking the
fireplace and watched the flames. Few words passed between them. Once or twice, Merriman's new secretary interrupted to refill their snifters and stir the fire. Joseph Lister,
deferential, discreet—and watchful. Otherwise, the two
men watched the flames curl around Nora Hewitt's volumi-
nous file, which was thick and slow to burn.